LIGHT
OF
DAY

LIGHT OF DAY

WEBB HUBBELL

BEAUFORT
BOOKS

LIGHT OF DAY

For inquiries, please contact:
Beaufort Books
27 West 20th Street, 11th Floor
New York, NY 10011

Published in the United States by Beaufort Books,
www.beaufortbooks.com

Distributed by Midpoint Trade Books, a division of Independent Publishers Group
www.midpointtrade.com, www.ipgbook.com

Printed in the United States of America

paperback: 9780825309403
eBook: 9780825308222

Cover Design by Michael Short

To:
Suzy, my sister Patti Sharp, and George

PROLOGUE

THE DIRECTOR OF NATIONAL INTELLIGENCE watched closely as the men and women he summoned to the West Wing read the one-page document placed in front of each person. He knew them all and respected most: the heads of the FBI and CIA, the Deputy Attorney General, the Secretary of Homeland Defense, the Deputy Secretary of Treasury and, of course, the President's Chief of Staff. At his nod, an aide walked around the table, picking up each document; there would be no leaks if he could help it.

He scanned the room one more time before he spoke, using silence to convey the seriousness of what he was about to say.

"This software must never see the light of day. Its development would cause immediate and serious harm to our nation's security and no telling how badly it would affect the economy."

A similar meeting was taking place in the large conference room at the Dooley Law Firm in Silicon Valley. Despite antitrust concerns, the participants were the CEOs of a group of influential technology companies. Jim Dooley, founder of the firm and respected advisor to many of these companies, had called the meeting. He was unaware of the White House gathering when he spoke. "This code must be destroyed; it must never see the light of day. The mere possibility of its existence is concern enough: this one product could wipe out your market valuations in a single day and thrust the entire world into a depression."

The result of both meetings was the same. The attendees were to do whatever was necessary to make sure the software in question simply disappeared. The word "whatever" was the telling directive.

1

I WAS IN A BAD MOOD. My lanky body didn't fit in the narrow second-row seat of the plane, but it had been my only choice. Fortunately, my seatmate was a small, stylishly dressed woman who had returned my smile with a glare and buried her head in a paperback for the flight. I stared glumly at the city emerging from the clouds as the smallish commuter jet began its approach into New Orleans. Clovis Jones had called yesterday to tell me I'd been summoned to lunch with the men who controlled organized crime in the state of Louisiana. I'd known this day would come—it was an invitation I couldn't refuse.

The meeting was to take place at Charlie's Steak House in Uptown. I'd heard the radio ads for Charlie's: "There's nothing fancy about Charlie's, just a great steak, a cold drink, and a good time." A good time was the last thing I anticipated.

As I stepped onto the jetway the blast of intense, muggy heat reminded me why I seldom came to New Orleans in the summer. I was a Washington, DC anti-trust attorney. I'd paid my dues, working first for the Department of Justice and then for a multi-national law firm before establishing my own offices in an old, unassuming building near the White House. I now split my time between my anti-trust clients and Red Shaw, a successful defense contractor and owner of the NFL's San Antonio Lobos.

Why had I dropped everything to meet with the heads of Louisiana's organized crime? The answer was simple—I owed them. Years earlier, during a highly charged lawsuit, the opposition had hired an assassin to kill my daughter Beth, who then lived in New

Orleans. I learned of the plot through an unlikely acquaintance who convinced me to hire a New Orleans "family" to provide her protection. The syndicate dealt with the issue quickly and efficiently, and I had continued to employ their services to ensure Beth's safety when she and her fiancé moved to St. Louis. They were very discreet—neither Beth or Jeff had any idea she could be in danger, and I slept much better knowing my daughter was safe. I knew that one day the true cost of my daughter's safety would be exacted. Someday my phone would ring, and the syndicate would ask for a favor. Today was that day.

Why would a respected lawyer get in bed with a crime syndicate? The answer is both simple and complicated. The simple answer is that I would do anything to protect my daughter. Beth is my only child and, since the death of my wife more than five years ago, she is my only family.

The more complicated answer dealt with the nature of the practice of law. A well-trained lawyer has been taught that everyone is entitled to a defense and zealous advocacy on his or her behalf. That training, coupled with experience, gives most lawyers the ability to see beyond their client's faults and alleged crimes.

The only person in my circle of friends who knew about this arrangement with the 'family' was Clovis Jones, my good friend and occasional bodyguard, who was waiting at the taxi stand on Level One. A former All-American linebacker at Middle Tennessee State, Clovis manages a security business in Little Rock and has saved my life more than once. He'd volunteered to be the contact between me and the syndicate and didn't hesitate when I asked him to join me in New Orleans.

As the cab carried us uptown, I couldn't help but worry. Most lawyers have a line they won't cross. My friend and Arkansas co-counsel Micki Lawrence drew the line at representing rapists and sex traffickers. My clients are usually big-business types who've run afoul of the government, accused of misdoings based on what I thought of as food for the ego—money, power, and greed. So far, I haven't refused to represent anyone. What if the syndicate asked me for something I couldn't give? Could I refuse?

The cab pulled to the curb with a jolt, and I woke from my

musings. A small white neon sign flashed—Charlie's Steak House. When I told Beth I was going to New Orleans to meet an old college buddy, she'd asked if I'd remembered to make reservations for lunch—a necessity I frequently forgot.

"Well, I thought we'd meet for lunch at Charlie's, sort of break the ice. I haven't seen him in a long time," I lied.

"Charlie's is great," she said. "Be sure to get the blue cheese salad. But Dad, I'm pretty sure it's not open for lunch. You'd better check."

I had checked and was told the meeting would be a private gathering. No other customers.

I suppressed a smile as Clovis frowned at the shiny suits leaning against the late model SUVs that lined the narrow street. They looked like caricatures of the types portrayed in old gangster movies, as did the two younger guys lounging near the front entrance. Their function was obvious: no one would enter the restaurant without permission. They followed us through the front door, guiding us to what was the coat room during normal business hours. The search was perfunctory, but efficient.

*****

Clovis gave them a little lip as they opened the door, but the smaller of the two just grinned and pointed toward a man waiting near the host desk. He flashed an easy smile and introduced himself as Royce Peters. I recognized the name as Clovis' contact with the syndicate whenever we had reason to worry about Beth's well-being. I always hoped we would never need him again, but I was always wrong.

Royce looked like an aging golf pro. His dark hair was flecked with gray, and a Peter Millar polo highlighted a deep tan. The lines on his face showed the effects of the sun, and one hand absently twirled a pair of sunglasses. His face was marred by the white line of an old scar running from the corner of one eye back toward his ear. He raised a casual hand to my shoulder and said, "Jack, Mr. Thibodeaux has asked that you sit in the open seat next to him. Clovis, you and I will take the table right behind. Okay?"

2

"ROYCE WILL PROVIDE YOU THE DETAILS, but my grandson has run into trouble in your city. A group of major technology companies have sued him in Federal Court. The government has arrested him, taken possession of his computers and cellphone, and seized his bank account. They haven't allowed anyone from his family to speak with him or have any contact at all. He needs a lawyer, a very good lawyer."

Not much information, none of it good, but given the scenarios I'd imagined, I was relieved. I rose and said I would be honored to help in any way I could. Thibodeaux stood as well, grasped my outstretched hand, and led me around the table. Each man stood, quietly introduced himself, and extended his hand. I felt as if I were joining a fraternity. Clovis and Royce followed us as we walked toward the front door. Thibodeaux put a hand on my shoulder and said,

"I hope you'll call me Tom. I'm sorry to have to cut our first meeting short, but as I said, we use these occasional lunches to discuss business. Royce can tell you everything we know about my grandson's situation. None of us will forget your friendship."

Without another word he turned back to the table, and Royce again took my elbow, guiding us through the door to a waiting taxi. "I know you must have lots of questions. I've booked a suite for you at the Hotel Bienville in the Quarter. It's not a tourist hotel—we can talk. Wherever you want to eat tonight, let me know. I'll make the arrangements. But I need to go back to this meeting for another hour or so. Get comfortable, and I'll be along as soon as I can."

Before either of us could say a word, he vanished into the restaurant, carefully closing the door behind him. Clovis turned to face me.

"Well, Jack, what have you gotten us into this time?"

Clovis and I had packed to stay overnight, figuring we could get a room in an airport hotel and catch an early morning flight back to DC. I'd assumed that dinner at one of New Orleans's classic eateries was out of the question, so we'd planned to eat at the nearest Theo's. You don't think of New Orleans and pizza, but neither New York nor Chicago can claim pizza as good as Theo's. Now we had rooms at the Bienville, and our dinner options seemed to have broadened.

When we'd settled into the cab, Clovis asked, "Have you read or heard anything about the grandson in the press? You'd think a group of tech companies suing a single individual whose computer equipment has been physically seized by the Feds would have made *The Post*."

"Not a word, but these days I try to limit my newspaper reading to the sports and the comics. The news is too depressing."

It wasn't long before we stood in the small but elegant lobby of the Hotel Bienville. From a quick Google search, I had learned that the building began life as a rice mill in 1835. Both its identity and purpose had changed many times since then. Over the years it had served as a firehouse, an apartment complex, and a boarding house, just a few of its incarnations. The property was acquired in 1972 by the Monteleone family, who had transformed it into the refined space I saw as I approached the front desk. I reached into my pocket, but the receptionist shook a playful finger at me and said, "No, no, Mr. Patterson. Mr. Peters has taken care of everything. Your rooms are on the fourth floor. Here are your key cards." I wondered how she had recognized me, but decided not to ask.

The bellman escorted us to a spacious suite with two bedrooms separated by a large sitting area. Two small plates, silverware and napkins lay next to a large tray of fruit and cheese on the table, and I noticed that the bar was well-stocked. I saw Clovis give the bar a wistful glance, but he pulled his bag into his bedroom, muttering something about phone calls.

I unpacked, washed my face, and kicked off my shoes—it felt good to relax. I'd been on edge since Clovis's call the day before, but hopefully my anxiety had been for nothing. I had no idea what kind of trouble the grandson had gotten himself into, but Tom's request wasn't unreasonable. The young man needed a DC lawyer, and that's exactly what I am.

I set up shop with my laptop at the conference table and was quickly engrossed in my work. Red Shaw, the owner of the San Antonio Lobos, was completing a deal with the city of San Antonio to build a state-of-the-art, multi-purpose stadium. Every contract, every letter or email, seemingly every handshake, required my review and approval. I dove into the details, happy to earn my keep.

I was roused from my work by a knock at the door and looked up to see Clovis opening it for Royce and a short, dark-haired woman who carried a box of what appeared to be files. She introduced herself as Lula Gonzalez and dropped the heavy box on the table next to me.

Royce frowned at the untouched bar in the corner and turned to me.

"Hey, where's your drink? Is there something wrong with the bar?"

I couldn't help but notice the sharp look he directed toward Lula.

"No, not at all. The bar is perfect. We've both been dealing with work." I saw visible relief in Lula's face.

"Lula, you know what I like," Royce barked as he plopped down on the sofa.

"Here, Lula, let me help," I said, meeting her at the bar before Royce could protest. Lula poured bourbon over ice for Royce and handed Clovis the beer he asked for. I opened the bottle of Merlot and poured two glasses.

"Is this okay, Lula, or would you rather have something else?"

She nodded her thanks and took the chair Clovis held for her. Royce frowned, clearly annoyed. Too bad—my hotel room, my rules. Lula gave me a cautious smile as I handed her the glass.

I closed my computer and said, "Okay, Royce, what have you got for me?"

Royce took a healthy swallow of bourbon and began, "First, thank you again. One of the lawyers on our payroll would usually handle any charges brought against a family member, but this matter is anything but usual. Your commitment to help solves a big problem."

"How is this matter different? What exactly is the problem?" I asked.

"First, let me give you some background." He swirled the bourbon in his glass, taking his time before continuing.

"This young man is a favorite of Mr. Thibodeaux, a grandson who has caused no one trouble—not his mother, not his grandparents, and not the syndicate. He's a computer genius; his curiosity is boundless. He's respectful of his elders and has plenty of friends—even a girlfriend, although I haven't met her. But he spends most of his time in front of a computer screen."

"Sounds like a thousand other kids in Silicon Valley," I responded easily.

"Oh, I think you'll find he's much smarter than the average computer nerd, which brings me to why this case is out of the ordinary. This young man..."

"Does the young man have a name?" I interrupted.

"Yes, of course he has a name," he snapped, but recovered quickly. "Please forgive me—I'm not used to... Well, his name is David, David Ruple. He grew up in New Orleans, went to high school at Country Day, and got a degree in both computer science and math at Santa Clara in California. After he graduated, he moved to DC and started a software design and consulting company with two college friends."

"Sounds innocent enough." I commented, wondering why David had left the West Coast.

"Yes. And as far as we know, it is. David has never been involved in the family businesses. He made spending money in high school repairing computers and teaching his friends' parents how to use them. He went to college on a scholarship, again earning money on the side consulting."

"What about the company David started? Is it still doing business? Did Mr. Thibodeaux invest in it or provide any seed money?" I asked.

"Why do you ask? Surely David's troubles couldn't get Mr. Thibodeaux in danger or in trouble with the Feds." A slight stammer in his voice betrayed a new anxiety.

"It's a stretch," I said with a shrug. "But I wonder if David's troubles might be an indirect way to go after Mr. Thibodeaux and even his associates. It's a well-known government strategy to go after a weak family link with threats of prosecution to get him to talk. Spouses, siblings, even mothers, have been held as ransom by the Feds for cooperation or a plea."

"We are aware of these tactics," he said, his manner again confident. "That's why all the heads of the families were at today's meeting. David's problems must remain David's alone. Your presence helped calm the waters. You, Mr. Patterson, are the perfect solution." He smiled and raised his glass to me. "His grandson will be well represented, and you have no known ties to the syndicate."

"Did any family member invest in David's business?" I asked, choosing to ignore his gesture.

"Mr. Thibodeaux would have, but David never asked. I know this is hard to believe, but David hasn't asked for money from anyone, not even his mother, since he graduated from high school."

I raised a doubtful eyebrow and he responded, "No, really— David and his friends started the company and ran it on their own. As far as I know, even his mother has no interest in it. Sure, she cooked for him sometimes and bought him clothes, but that was about it. Family members are constantly asking Mr. Thibodeaux for money or a job, but not David."

"You've mentioned David's mother several times. Does David's father work for either the syndicate or Mr. Thibodeaux?"

Royce glanced at Lula, who had yet to say a word. "David's father suffered an untimely death some years ago. I prefer not to discuss what happened or why." He went to the bar to fill his empty glass.

3

LULA HAD GATHERED AND ORGANIZED David's high school records, his college transcripts, and the names and addresses of former teachers who could be character witnesses. She had obtained a copy of the civil suit filed against David. It alleged copyright infringement, antitrust violations, unfair competition, and violation of the racketeering statutes. The named plaintiffs were a laundry list of the top technology companies in the country. I recognized many of the lawyers on the pleading—top-flight corporate litigators from DC, the Silicon Valley, and NY. Lead counsel was the prestigious Romatowski Law Firm. My small office of one lawyer and two paralegals would face an army of the nation's best attorneys.

Neither Royce nor Lula said a word while I skimmed the seventy-five-page complaint. At issue was software that David had developed, but for the life of me I couldn't tell what the software did or why the plaintiffs found it so offensive. As for the criminal indictment, either there wasn't one, or it was under seal.

"These appear to be significant charges—sort of David versus Goliath stuff. Why hasn't there been any press coverage?"

"We have no idea," Royce responded. "They filed the civil complaint in the late afternoon, and the FBI arrested David at his girlfriend's house that night. Scared the poor girl to death. David barely had time to tell her to call his grandfather and reassure her that everything would be all right."

It sounded as if someone had coordinated the civil suit and the arrest, but usually the Feds use this sort of tactic to maximize publicity, not prevent it.

"How did you get a copy of the civil suit?" I asked. The pleading indicated it had been filed under seal.

"Lula has her ways." Royce answered with a shrug. I looked at Lula, who flashed an innocent grin.

I raised my wine glass to her and said, "Thank you—too bad you can't work on the case full time. Looks like we may need all the help we can get."

"Lula will be ready to help if you need her." Royce responded a bit stiffly.

"I thought one of our purposes was to distance the family from David as much as possible," I commented.

"You're right, but there are things we can do, people who can help. Lula is one."

"I'll keep your offer in mind. Besides putting together his background information, what else have you done for David?"

"Nothing more than we would do for any family member behind bars. For instance, no one will harm him while he's incarcerated."

"Well, sometimes that kind of message becomes a challenge in prison," I pointed out. "The last thing I want is for David to be attacked."

A few years ago, a client had died in jail before she had even been charged. The guards tried to convince me it was suicide, but I knew it wasn't. I remain dubious that anyone can commit suicide with a bed sheet in a jail cell. No matter how miserable the circumstance or how depressed the prisoner, almost no one turns to hanging, nor do they know how to do it. Using a worn and tattered bed sheet as a rope isn't as easy as it sounds, and the staff doesn't teach the procedure during prison orientation. The number of people who die in jail for any reason is a national disgrace: prison suicide should never occur, and in reality, seldom does. From credible reports I've read, and from my own experience, alleged suicides usually entail some measure of assistance from either a guard or fellow prisoner who has been adequately reimbursed for his efforts.

Royce interrupted my thoughts. "I'm telling you—David will be okay. Mr. Thibodeaux will make it clear. No one will so much as touch him."

His attitude had become slightly belligerent, so I let it go.

"What about his business partners? Do they know? Has anyone spoken with them? Any further communication with the girlfriend?" I asked.

"David and his partners split up about a year ago—they returned to California. Lula has their contact information. I bet the girlfriend has told them about David's arrest. She knows how to reach me if she needs anything. I'll let her know you'll call. That reminds me: you should go through me when you want to talk to Mrs. Ruple. She's staying at the Willard."

"Why?' I asked.

"Mrs. Ruple has some, well—emotional issues and is prone to self-medicate, if you get my drift." He reached for his own glass, looking slightly uncomfortable. "There are certain times of day when she's not at her best. I won't interfere, but I think I can help, maybe run interference."

"Okay, thanks. Good to know," I said, wondering if the woman had issues other than the obvious implication. Royce gave a little sigh and continued.

"Look, Jack, David appears to be in deep shit, and we don't have any idea what he's done. Mr. Thibodeaux knows the situation is difficult. We'll do whatever we can to help you help David."

He paused for another swig of bourbon, then continued, switching to a lighter tone. "So—like most lawyers, you probably want to know how you get paid. Right?"

He smiled broadly at the insult, but I had already decided not to take a fee—it would be a favor for a favor. My daughter's safety was more than worth it.

"The New Orleans families have done an excellent job of protecting my daughter..." I began.

Royce raised his hand to protest. "Sorry, but no. Your daughter's protection is an accommodation for which you paid the agreed sum. It would raise all kinds of flags if you represented David for free or at a reduced rate. Mr. Thibodeaux insists on paying your normal rates. A deposit will be wired into your firm's trust account tomorrow as a retainer. Send me a monthly statement; it will be paid promptly."

"I understand your rationale, Royce," I said slowly. "But it's a bit ticklish when someone else offers to pay a defendant's legal bills. I'll need to discuss your offer with David. He must be aware of and consent to the source of payment. For all I know, David may not want me to represent him. But if he does, he will be the client. It will be up to him whether I tell you anything about his defense or our strategy. I hope you and Tom understand this. The person who pays the bills rarely agrees to give up control."

"Mr. Thibodeaux is not a man who gives up control easily. That said, he's put his grandson's future in your hands and trusts in your abilities."

I couldn't help but wonder what would happen if I failed to live up to such high expectations. Would I find myself at the bottom of some backwoods bayou?

Royce continued, "Before Mr. Thibodeaux invited you to New Orleans, we did our homework. Your reputation as an advocate is impeccable. Given what David is up against, Mr. Thibodeaux believes you are David's best chance. Maybe it was luck that gave us the opportunity to protect your daughter, or maybe it was fate that brought you to us. Either way, you'll get no interference from us. Your challenges are daunting enough already."

"Thank you. I appreciate both your opinion and your trust," I said, ready to get beyond the oddly formal speeches. "Now—other than making sure David remains safe and sound in the D.C. jail, what other steps have you taken?"

"When the court sets bail, we will post bond," he answered.

"The bail amount could be substantial," I pointed out.

"There are several bondsmen in DC who will post bail as an accommodation. Don't worry—no one will connect David's bond with Mr. Thibodeaux. Call me when the judge sets bail. I'll take care of the rest."

"Sounds like you've thought of everything," I commented.

"We have some experience in these matters," he smiled.

"I must warn you: the Feds have no problem using the words 'national security' to get around the Constitution. My experience tells me to expect the unexpected for anything related to computer or privacy issues. You might also check for listening devices and be wary of hackers."

"We already pay someone to take care of internet and phone security."

"What about Mrs. Ruple?" I asked.

The confidence in his eyes wavered—his answer came a little more slowly.

"Gloria won't take a request to check her phone or computers well. She'll think I'm using David's situation as an excuse to invade her privacy."

Great. First, she self-medicates, and now she doesn't trust Royce.

"Why don't you let me ask Stella Rice to check her computer and phone. She is Clovis' wife as well as an expert in computer security. I can raise the idea in the context of the litigation."

"That might work." Royce responded, emphasizing the word "might."

"I take it that Mrs. Ruple can be difficult," I said, careful to keep my tone neutral.

"To be honest, Gloria can be a handful. She loves her son, but that love has its limits. David will have three adversaries: first the Feds, second the tech companies, and finally, his mother, who has learned over time that she needs to protect herself."

"Can't Mr. Thibodeaux talk sense into his daughter? Explain just how bad the situation is for David?"

"At one point, Gloria and her father were very close—she would have done anything he asked. But their relationship cooled after her husband died, and now they hardly speak."

I waited for Royce to explain, but he offered nothing more. Just as the silence became awkward, Lula stepped up with the work she had done. She produced contact information for David's clients, college friends, business partners, and former girlfriends. She knew where David banked, what credit cards he had—almost as much information as Google or Amazon has on any American. I got the impression that although David valued his independence, his family kept a very watchful eye on Thibodeaux's favorite grandson.

None of us had much more to say. Royce and Lula had answered my questions, but I felt sure they were holding back until I proved my worth. For my part, I was tired and ready to rehash the situation with Clovis.

The silence lifted when Lulu cleared her throat and began to gather her things. Royce asked where Clovis and I would like to have dinner.

"Well, we thought we might stand in line at Galatoire's and get a seat at the bar," I joked, knowing it would be impossible to get even close to this classic New Orleans restaurant given the convention. No matter who you are and how long you've been going to Galatoire's, you or your stand-in waits in line outside the restaurant until your table is ready. Unless you have a relationship with a specific waiter, reservations are impossible. I've heard they now take reservations for the upstairs dining room, but it books up months in advance.

"Ridiculous. With all the doctors in town you'd be standing outside all night." Royce scoffed, confirming what I already knew. "What time works for you?"

"I'm still full of lunch. How about eight o'clock?" I answered, willing to play along.

Royce laughed. "C'mon, Jack—have a little faith. Your driver, Frank Grant, will pick you up at 7:45. When you get to the restaurant tell the man at the door who you are and ask for Raymond. He'll take good care of you. Frank will be waiting for you outside after dinner."

"Thank you," I said, beginning to realize he was serious.

"It will please Mr. Thibodeaux that he could extend this small favor," answered Royce, once again in old movie tones.

4

Tiled floors, mirrored walls, and motionless fans of polished brass with bright, unshaded light bulbs, create half the atmosphere at Galatoire's. The rest is supplied by the jammed-in customers, all well-dressed and deeply engaged in sending a convivial energy back and forth, all to the accompaniment of enough noise that makes conversation impossible.

In my opinion, it's the best place to dine in New Orleans. Some restaurants serve more contemporary offerings, many have equally haughty waiters, and a few are just as opulent, but no other spot is as lavishly and unapologetically New Orleans. Birthdays and anniversaries are celebrated, engagements are announced, deaths and sorrows are mourned—the good times and the bad always validated by impeccable service and excellent food and drink. Sure, there are tiny restaurants tucked away in the Garden District or most any other spot in the city that serve excellent food, but none can compare to the overall dining experience at Galatoire's.

I wasn't particularly hungry after lunch at Charlie's, but I wasn't about to skip this meal. Clovis and I shared Oysters Rockefeller, and I ordered one of my favorites, Crabmeat Yvonne. Clovis wisely let the waiter order for him—soufflé potatoes, their house salad, and crawfish étouffée. We shared the Black Bottom pecan pie for dessert.

It was an unusually pleasant evening. We told our driver we would walk back to the Bienville. Frank wasn't at all happy, but we insisted. Between restaurants and the many shops that never seem to close, the Quarter is always bustling with tourists. With a major convention of doctors in town, the sidewalks were sometimes hard to navigate, but with Clovis leading interference we made it back to the hotel in no time.

Royce was waiting for us in the lobby. It was almost midnight, and I didn't think he was here to tuck me into bed. He gestured toward the bar, and we followed him to a quiet table, refusing his offer for a nightcap. A server delivered a bourbon on the rocks, and we waited while he took a healthy sip and paid the bill.

"I hope you enjoyed your dinner," he began. "But, Jack, you should take advantage of Frank while you're in New Orleans. He'll take you anywhere you like, so please, no more walking the Quarter."

I wanted to object out of general principles, but his tone made it clear he wasn't just suggesting. I remained silent, and he sighed.

"There have been developments."

"Developments?" I asked.

"It appears that the FBI is aware of your agreement with Mr. Thibodeaux. You could be in danger."

"How did that happen? And why would I be in danger?"

"We don't know yet."

"Come on Royce, I deserve better than that. How do you know the FBI knows?" I paused and lowered my voice. "Look, I know the syndicate operates in secrecy, but if I'm going to represent David, I need to know anything that could affect his case or involves me. The FBI doesn't much like me, but surely they're not a threat."

"I'll tell you what I can. You were followed to Galatoire's tonight. Frank called me as soon as he dropped you off. We figure the Feds staked out the lunch, saw you walk into Charlie's, and decided to tail you. Our sources have confirmed that the FBI knows you and Clovis were at the lunch at Charlie's. They also know you've agreed to represent David."

"Did they have the place bugged?"

"Possibly," Royce conceded. "There's more. You and Clovis were followed again when you left Galatoire's, but not by the FBI. And yes, Frank is sure. I've stationed guards at the hotel, and we're working to find out who they were and for whom they work."

I frowned. "Could there have been a fox in the henhouse today?"

"That's very unlikely. Such a person would be putting his life on the line as well as his organization's continued viability. And why? Your agreement to represent David won't be a secret much longer. You have enemies, as do we, but they aren't stupid enough to cross Mr. Thibodeaux and the other families. But the fact is—you were followed tonight, both to and from dinner. Please don't leave this hotel again without Frank."

He threw back the rest of his bourbon. The FBI had probably bugged today's meeting, there could be a mole in the syndicate, and Clovis and I had been followed tonight by an unknown party. His boss would surely be unhappy—no wonder he looked miserable. I felt bad for him, but sure didn't want to be part of a war within the syndicate or get crosswise with the FBI.

Royce perked up a bit when Clovis asked him where the guards would be stationed and how we could identify them. He assured us we would be perfectly safe both in the hotel and in New Orleans. "No one would be foolish enough to harm you in New Orleans. You are here under the personal protection of Mr. Thibodeaux; to cross him would be a life-ending decision."

I almost asked why we needed guards if we were so safe but thought better of it. I was tired and ready for bed.

"Listen, guys, I need some shut eye. You can stay and discuss logistics, but I'm going to bed. Why don't we meet for breakfast around eight?"

They agreed, and I left them talking about how the FBI could have bugged Charlie's. Too bad Stella wasn't here. She would have enlightened them in a New York minute.

I was asleep before my head hit the pillow. Galatoire's will have that effect.

I woke several hours later to the unexpected reality of the point of a knife at my throat, and as my eyes focused, I saw two men. One held the knife and the other waved a gun at my head.

"Don't make a sound."

5

⟨─────⟩

IT'S AMAZING HOW QUICKLY you can wake up when you feel a knife at your throat. So much for being "perfectly safe." I wondered vaguely what had happened to Clovis and Royce's guards.

The man holding the gun waved it about a bit, and I flinched. He leveled it again and said, "Easy does it, Jack. You know, I can read your mind. Your friend Jones is out cold in the other room, and the guards are sound asleep. Make even a whimper and Jones will be killed. His life depends on you doing exactly as you're told. Got it?"

"Yes, I understand." It was simple: he had a gun, I didn't.

"Get dressed and pack your things. And be quick about it. We're leaving the hotel, and you're coming with us. Don't try anything cute."

The man with the knife backed away so I could get out of bed. I noticed that it was long and pointed, more like a dagger than a kitchen knife. I quickly threw on my khakis and golf shirt from the night before, pulled clothes from the drawer, and grabbed my dop kit. I started for the closet but dropped everything when I felt the knife on my neck again. The man with the gun gestured toward the common area of the suite, where we met two other men. One raised his arm.

"I've got his laptop," he said. "What should we do with this box of files?"

"Get his bag, leave the box; he won't need it anymore. Give him his wallet and keys but leave the cellphone here. He's always losing his phone. We want it to look like he left on his own."

I wondered how he knew my cellphone habits.

He laughed and said, "If you're a good boy, I'll explain once we're in the car. Let me repeat: if anything goes wrong, anything at all, Jones won't live to see another day. Now out the door and to the elevator, Mr. Patterson. We're going for a ride."

I noticed that all four of the men were dressed exactly alike—short haircuts, dark suits, and shiny black shoes. If I didn't know better, I'd think they were Secret Service agents. In fact, one of the men even wore an earpiece. He remained behind as the rest of us left the room. I assumed he'd been told to kill Clovis should I not do exactly what they said.

As we headed toward the elevator one of them said, "We're going to walk straight through the lobby. The car will be at the front entrance. Keep your eyes straight ahead—no looks, no signals. Walk straight to the car."

I did as I was told. The hallway and lobby were empty, no one at either the front desk or valet station. Where were Royce's guards? It was pitch-dark outside, and I was shoved into the back seat of a large, black SUV. The man who had held the knife jumped in the front seat. The man with the gun eased in next to me in the back. He spoke into a cuff microphone after we pulled away.

"Clockwork, no problems at all. You can leave now. Meet us at the boat dock." He then turned to me. "Bet you'd like to know what's going on."

"I am curious," I said, staring at the gun still aimed in my direction.

"This SUV was rented in your name a few hours ago. When Peters shows up in the morning, he'll find a very groggy Jones and the guards sound asleep. They won't have any idea what happened, either to you or them. You, your bag, and your computer will have disappeared. Both the woman at the front desk and the front doorman will swear you waved and wished them well when you left the hotel around three a.m. The doorman noticed you were carrying your bag, but decided it was none of his business. You left your phone in your room, which won't surprise Jones one bit. Thibodeaux will be suspicious, but he won't have a clue where you went or why you disap-peared. It was easy for the woman at the desk and the doorman to disappear in all the confusion. What d'ya think—pretty good plan?"

"You may fool Thibodeaux, but you won't fool Clovis," I replied.

He smiled. "For the next several days your credit card will be used at hotels and restaurants all over southern Louisiana. People will see you checking in and out and eating in small town restaurants. You'll buy gas and rent fishing boats and equipment. You'll even get a fishing license and buy a handgun at a local Walmart."

"Don't you think someone will notice that I'm always accompanied by a gaggle of men in dark suits?" I asked.

"Aw, gee," he said with a smirk. "Guess I forgot to mention that someone matching your description will do all those things. You, on the other hand, are going to take a long ride into the swamps."

We'd gone over at least one bridge and were leaving the city, but that was about all I could be sure of. The nights never got this dark in DC. I tried to keep my cool, but my stomach was in knots. I'd been abducted once before, in Arkansas, and a wait and see strategy had saved my life. I could only hope it would work a second time.

"Why not kill me?" I asked.

"You still don't get it, do you? You came to Louisiana under the syndicate's protection. If you were killed in New Orleans, every crime family in Louisiana would turn over every rock and stone to discover who was responsible and take revenge. We were prepared to kill Jones if you didn't cooperate back at the hotel, and I'm more than ready to kill you if you try anything, but that's not the plan. You'll get a chance to live—for our sake, not yours. But don't get any ideas. If you even think about being uncooperative, you'll be found lying on the side of the road with your throat cut and your wallet stolen." He paused, and added with a leer, "Quicker than you can say Jack Robinson."

I didn't respond—couldn't think of anything to say. At least someone other than this jackass had a plan. If I didn't cooperate, they'd make it look like I'd left the hotel on my own, was carjacked and killed somewhere in southern Louisiana. Thibodeaux wouldn't believe it, but he wouldn't have any proof that his umbrella of protection had been violated. The good news was they hadn't killed Clovis. My job was simple: stay alive until he came to the rescue.

"How did you rent a car in my name using my credit card? You don't even have my driver's license," I asked.

"Piece of cake. Everything about anyone is on the Internet. We can rent a car, buy a meal, or get a hotel room in your name in a blink of an eye. Same for getting a hunting or fishing license. There are no secrets left in this country. Hell, we know more about you than you do yourself."

I had no doubt that what he said was true. But who was "we?" And why were they willing for this guy to give me so much information?

"Okay, but why get rid of me? I'm just a lawyer hired to represent a client. I'm not a threat to anyone."

"Your disappearance accomplishes two purposes. You have a reputation for pulling rabbits out of a hat in the courtroom. With you out of the picture that possibility is eliminated. Thibodeaux will be livid that you took a flyer, and his only option will be to hire someone else.

"Your disappearance will also be embarrassing to Thibodeaux and that asshole Peters. The big man is losing his touch—it's time for new leadership. Whether you chickened out or someone was able to snatch you goes a long way to proving that he shouldn't be the head of his family, much less the syndicate. Your disappearance will be the mistake that brings about his downfall.

"Old Tom didn't have an inkling that someone might be listening to yesterday's lunch or that someone might care who he'd hired to represent David. It never occurred to Thibodeaux that the moment young David told his girlfriend to call his grandfather, every step Peters took would be monitored. When we learned that you were being considered as David's lawyer, it was only a matter of time before we were told to make sure that didn't happen, no holds barred."

"How can you be so sure the next lawyer won't be better than me? I'm an antitrust lawyer, for God's sake."

"Come on, Patterson. You got the man who shot a U.S. Senator off with a ten-year sentence. And that football player, too. Why anyone wants to send the kid to prison is none of my business, but it's your bad luck that you agreed to help. The next attorney Thibodeaux hires will have a great reputation, but he'll take his directions from us."

"In other words, he'll talk a good game, but make sure David doesn't have a chance in Hell," I said.

"Exactly," he responded with a grin.

I leaned back and closed my eyes, hoping he'd quit talking. The adrenaline was wearing off, and I was exhausted. I'd learned a lot, but nothing I could use just now. The last time I'd even been near a swamp was in Little Rock, and I'd almost been lynched. My current situation didn't look much brighter.

6

WE DROVE FOR WHAT SEEMED FOREVER down a two-lane road. Civilization quickly disappeared. It was so dark I couldn't see much of anything but the vague blur of trees and the occasional glint of water. Just when I thought there couldn't be a more remote part of Louisiana, the driver pulled over at an old road-side garage. A single light dangling from the end of the building revealed a sign advertising "boats for rent," and I could make out a dock behind the building. He turned off the engine, and we sat in silence. Before long a second SUV pulled up and out popped the two guys we'd left at the hotel. Why the overkill, I wondered. One man with a gun was enough to keep me on good behavior.

One of the suits signaled to our driver, and the man with the gun told me to get out of the car and walk slowly toward the dock, where I could see a series of small boats rocking against each other. I didn't feel any wind, not even a breeze. The dark water seemed to be creating its own energy. My spirits rose when I noticed they were all marked as belonging to the local sheriff. Maybe any minute now a group of sheriff's deputies would jump out of the shadows and surround my captors.

Instead, the guy with the gun waved his gun and pointed me toward the bow of the one unmarked boat. It was powered by an old outboard motor which roared to life when our former driver pulled the rope. We were soon gliding into what looked to me like a swamp, followed by two of the sheriff's boats manned by the two other suits. So much for my imminent rescue. I wondered idly what kind of fish live in a swamp.

I thought about diving into the green slimy water, but the man with the gun never took his eyes off me. He seemed eager for me to make a wrong step.

If the circumstances had been different, I might have enjoyed the ride. The sun was rising, and the mist was beginning to lift, revealing cypress knees, trees laden with Spanish moss, and various birds taking flight. I didn't see any alligators, but I felt sure they were lurking just beneath the surface of the dark water, hoping for an easy breakfast.

As we went deeper and deeper into the swamp, thick clouds darkened the sun again; at least the noise of the outboard motors prevented any conversation. I tried to think about escape, but knew I needed to focus first on how to stay alive. These guys seemed to fear Thibodeaux's retribution. Maybe they'd just drop me off on some remote island. With no food or water, no defense against hungry critters, and no way out, I wouldn't last long. But at least I'd have a chance.

Who was I kidding? The more likely scenario was they were going to kill me deep in the swamp where no one would ever find me. Before long the boat began to slow, and my heart sunk when we pulled up to what looked like one of the islands I had imagined. The man at the motor hopped out and began to pull the boat to shore.

"Ride's over, Jack. Time to get out." My companion pointed his gun directly at my head, and I obeyed.

"Wait a minute, now," he said with a grin. "I've got a better idea. You just sit down—yes, right there in the water—'til I decide what to do with you. Don't worry—it's shallow enough, and I'll watch for gators."

I wondered which could be worse: sitting here in the murky water or him deciding my fate. The other boats finally pulled in, and he motioned me up onto the island. One man hauled the boats up onto the shore. The other grabbed the gas can out of my boat and emptied the remaining fuel into the swamp. He pulled the drain plug from the bottom of the boat, and for a second, I thought he was going to hand it to me. Instead, he laughed and chucked it into the swamp.

My guy sat down on a convenient stump and grinned. "You

didn't think we'd leave you a way out of the swamp, did you? When this boat is found, people will say, "Damn fool ran out of gas and didn't even bring a paddle.

"Anybody checking your credit card records will see that you spent a few days in cheap hotels, then rented this boat to go fishing."

"I thought you were going to give me a chance. What about not killing anyone protected by the syndicate?" I asked, trying to keep my voice steady.

"Oh, we're not going to kill you. You do have a chance. Not a good one, but still. You're supposed to be a real Boy Scout. Maybe what you know about surviving in the wilderness will finally come in handy."

We were now a circle of five men, not a good sign. One of the other three said, "Too bad you ran out of gas." Then his fist slammed into my stomach.

I bent over gasping for air and saw the guy with the knife approach. Another blow came to the back of my head, and I fell to the ground.

"Don't be a fool, Don!" My guy was clearly this mob's boss, thank heavens.

The man with the knife grumbled. "But if I slice his Achilles, he can't walk more'n just a few feet. No match for a hungry gator."

I cringed at the thought of a knife severing my Achilles tendon. A hungry gator was more than I could even imagine.

"Don't! Don't do it!" His gun wavered from me toward Don who quickly backed away. "We want it to look like some animal got him, or he drowned. A few bruises are okay, but no knife wounds."

The guy with the knife took out his frustration by sending me to the ground with a swift kick to my ankles.

I curled up in a ball as they started kicking my head and mid-section. The odd thing was that none of them said a word, just kicked for the pure pleasure of it. Finally, the leader shouted, "Enough! It's time to get out of here. There's a bad-ass storm heading this way, and the gators won't show until we leave."

They all laughed, and one of them passed around a bottle of booze. I didn't move, just listened and tried to remain conscious.

Finally, they all clambered onto the one boat and roared back into the swamp. I tried to stand but couldn't get any further than up on my knees. I couldn't help but think of that tired query about the tree falling in the woods. I managed to get myself to the same stump my captor had found and leaned against it, trying to get my breathing under control. Here I was alone in the middle of a swamp with a useless, half-sunk boat and a suitcase full of clothes. No use yelling, who would hear?

The sky was growing ever darker, and I wondered what time it was. I remembered that a tropical storm was on target to hit southern Louisiana sometime in the next couple of days. I hadn't given it much thought before but felt pretty sure it wouldn't bode well for me now.

7

I KNEW I NEEDED TO COME UP with some way to get off the island, but
the blows to my head had left my brain feeling mushy. Nothing
seemed to make much sense. I wasn't sure I could stand, much less
walk, so I decided I to just stay put for a while. I was wakened from
my stupor by the noise of strong, gusty winds blowing through the
trees, a sure sign of the approaching storm. The men had tossed my
laptop into the swamp, another source of amusement for all but me.
I thought maybe I could find something in my bag to use as a drain
plug and get a big stick that could act as a pole for the boat. It was
a long shot, but at least my brain was working again. First, I had to
find a way to stand. My whole body hurt, and I had trouble catching
my breath. I diagnosed maybe a couple of cracked ribs, hoping for
nothing worse.

I managed to wriggle my way to my bag and was rifling through
it when I heard the roar of a fast-approaching motorboat. My first
thought was "Oh God, they're coming back." Now I was wide awake.

I could only see one person sitting toward the rear, using the
outboard motor to guide the boat. He backed off the speed just a bit
before running it up onto the muddy bank of the island. He wore
camouflage pants and jacket, a Pelicans cap, and sunglasses. At least
he wasn't in a dark suit. I hoped he wasn't from the sheriff's office.

Leaving the engine idling, he hollered, "Get in, quickly now. We
need to beat the storm."

I got to my feet somehow, but halfway to the boat my knees
buckled.

"Oh, shit, that's just great." He hopped out of the boat, grabbed my bag, and threw it into the boat. Looking at me in disgust, he waited for about half a second before pulling me to my feet and half dragging me into it. He carefully edged the boat through the trees and stumps. Suddenly the air lifted, the water took on life and we sped out into what I figured must be a real bayou.

I sat on the middle plank facing forward with my rescuer to my back. If I hadn't been in so much pain and so relieved to be off the island, I would have been scared out of my pants. We flew across the bayou, the boat just skimming the water as we wove in and out of trees and cypress knees. I didn't think we were going back to the rental place, and I wasn't about to complain.

After about half an hour of the scariest boat ride I've ever had, the boat slowed as it approached a small dock. I could see a house on stilts a little distance behind it. I couldn't tell if we'd reached the mainland or had landed on another island.

"Just sit quiet 'til I get the boat out of the water." His voice was oddly low and rough.

I did as I was told, trying to get my heart rate under control, as he quickly positioned the boat, tied it down, and operated the lift that raised the boat from the water. With his assistance, I managed to walk into the house upright. He steered me toward a large sofa and shoved me onto it.

"Here, try to stay warm," he said, pulling a blanket off a nearby chair. "I'll get your bag in a minute. I need to make sure everything's locked down before the storm hits." He was gone before I could say a single word.

I wrapped the blanket around my shoulders and looked around as best I could. From the outside the house looked like a large shack on stilts, but the interior was nothing like a shack. I found myself in a comfortable room with a wood-burning fireplace, the sofa I had collapsed onto, a couple of armchairs, a big screen TV, and a surprising mix of Creole and contemporary art on the walls. The room opened to a small dining room and beyond that to a larger kitchen.

Peering around a corner into a hallway, I could also see what looked like a commercial lab: tables laden with microscopes, glass beakers, and all kinds of electronic equipment. I was just beginning to wonder if I'd landed in Wonderland, when the front door swung open and in walked my new best friend.

"It's getting ugly out there. Sorry to leave you alone, but we're in for a rough few days." He tossed my bag onto a nearby chair.

I was finally able to get a good look at my rescuer. He stood around five feet nine with a thin, wiry frame. He caught me staring, laughed, and pulled off the baseball cap and glasses, shaking out his short, almost blond hair. I felt like an idiot—my rescuer wasn't a man at all: he was she.

Her eyes were a deep grey, slightly slanted like a cat's eyes. She clearly spent a lot of time outdoors; her skin had tanned to a deep brown. I couldn't easily gauge her age, maybe a few years younger than me, maybe a lot younger. She looked oddly familiar, but how could I possibly have known her?

We both laughed at my confusion, and she said, "I don't know which of us has more questions. You might not feel up to it, but I'd love to know how Jack Patterson landed in my bayou."

She knew who I was? Had I fallen down a rabbit hole?

I gave a start and looked toward the ceiling as an almost feral howl of wind rushed through the trees outside. She smiled and reached out to put her hand on my arm.

"Don't worry. My house might look fragile, but it's built to withstand a Cat Four. There's no reason you should recognize me; we met at an environmental conference. When? A few years ago? My name is Abby Broussard."

My memory banks went into high gear trying to remember, but an environmental conference? Nothing came to mind, nothing at all.

I said, "I'm sorry—guess my brain's still a little foggy. I'm sure it will come to me."

"No reason for you to remember. Now let me get you something for the pain and make sure you're okay. We can't go anywhere for the next few days. Listen to that wind—and it's just getting started. We should have plenty of time to talk about what a bunch of black-suited fools were doing in the swamp and why you were with them."

Before I could respond she had jumped up and gone to the

kitchen. *Abby Broussard?* My brain was trying hard, but I still had no idea.

She returned and handed me a cup of something warm in an oversized coffee mug. Some kind of tea, maybe.

"Drink this slowly. It's better than any prescription drug."

I took a deep breath and then a sip. I gagged a bit and could feel my face reddening and my eyes tearing. She handed me a Kleenex and chuckled.

"It's potent alright, but I promise it will make you feel a lot better, so drink up. It's a family recipe. Do you feel like talking while you finish and before I treat your wounds?" She sunk into one of the armchairs, legs curled under her.

I nodded, and she asked, "Who were those guys, and what were they up to?"

I gave her an amended version, leaving out the part about my new client and my history with Thibodeaux.

"When I came along, they were doing a real number on you. I thought about interfering, but I saw the gun and decided to wait them out. No sense both of us getting killed. I'm just glad they didn't shoot you."

"Me, too. And you did more than enough by getting me out of there," I said.

We heard another angry howl from the storm and the hammer of rain that came down in sheets on her roof. It was so intense I could hardly hear her speak.

"You never would have survived this storm on that little island." Her voice was deep and oddly comforting.

"How on earth did you happen to be so close? You were a godsend."

"Oh, it wasn't luck. I have electronic monitors all over the bayou, even into the swamps. It's part of my work. Three boats from Earl's heading deep into that swamp couldn't be up to any good, especially with a storm coming, so I decided to check them out. When I saw the boats belonged to the sheriff, I knew something was amiss. Our sheriff's as crooked as they come. He's always hiring out his boats and equipment to people trying to skirt the law. I thought they were after gators or endangered birds, but when I saw they had you curled up on the ground at the point of a gun I knew this was no ordinary game hunt.

"I hated to sit back and watch them kicking you, but I really didn't see any other choice. We were lucky to get out of there—you looked pretty beat up, and I knew I couldn't carry you. That other boat tried to follow us, but not for long."

"Other boat? I asked.

"Two sheriff's deputies. I don't know if they were part of the group who held you or they were just keeping a look-out. They're why we went flying out of the swamp at full throttle. I sure hope they didn't recognize me."

"Sheriff's deputies watched those guys beat the hell out of me and didn't do anything about it?"

"Remember what I said about the sheriff?" she laughed. "Well, the same goes for his deputies—brothers Teddy and Mitch Cruz. They're lower than catfish and have about the IQ of a rock. Your kidnappers must have paid the sheriff to use his boats and make sure no one interfered. Once I got you off that island, I knew they couldn't follow me; my boat's faster, and they don't know this bayou like I do. But if they did recognize me, they'll be here as soon as the storm blows over, probably with your suited friends. The storm will buy us a few days, but that's it."

Great. She'd just saved my life. Now the bad guys would be after both of us. I said "I should leave. Those men won't hesitate to harm you to get at me. Where's my phone? I'll call Clovis—he'll figure a way to get us out of here."

I tried to stand but felt light-headed and sank back onto the sofa, trying to fight the rising nausea and sudden chills.

When I'd finally stopped shaking, she said, "They left your phone at the hotel, remember? And we won't have any cell service or internet during the storm. We'll be lucky not to lose power, although I do have a generator. We have at least three days before anybody even thinks about trying to get here. Besides, I've lived most of my life right here. They'll play hell if they come after me."

As if to emphasize her words, the winds howled even louder, and the rain beat against the windows fiercely, sounding almost alive, almost as if it were a living demon. She was right. I would never have made it through this storm on that island.

"Now," she said, "let's go check out the damage."

8

SHE REACHED OUT TO HELP ME out of the chair. The potion had done wonders for the pain, but once I started to move, my ribs woke up. I felt like an old man taking baby steps back to her bedroom and into the bathroom. She told me to sit on the tile landing surrounding her tub.

"I'm going to cut your undershirt off," she said as she helped me unbutton my shirt. "It would hurt too much to get it off the regular way."

She took a pair of scissors from a drawer and began to cut the back of my shirt. In a calm voice she said, "I was afraid of that. Let's get the rest of your clothes off and get you into the shower."

I stuttered, "What do you mean? Afraid of what?"

"Leeches. You've got leeches on your back," she said calmly. "From when you were sitting in the swamp water. Not too many, but you're better off without them. The best way to remove them is in a hot shower."

Leeches? I'd figured the itching was just mosquito bites. All I knew about leeches came from an old movie where Katherine Hepburn pulls leeches off Humphrey Bogart. I hesitated, and she said firmly, "Come on, Jack, don't be modest. I'm a doctor, and I know what I'm doing Now off with your clothes and into the shower while I get some containers for the leeches."

I slowly pulled off my jeans and underclothes and stepped into her shower. The strong stream of hot water felt like a gift. She returned with the plastic containers and what looked like a long butter knife. I stepped back quickly, and she laughed again.

"Don't look so scared! I'll use the flat edge to dislodge the little rascals. I could even use a credit card; anything thin and rigid works. Now turn around and raise your arms," she ordered, all business. I did as I was told and heard her step into the shower with me.

"Removing these suckers might sting a bit, so try to keep still."

This was not my idea of how to shower with an attractive woman, but she didn't seem to think anything of it as the warm water poured over us. She was right about the stinging—probably a good thing.

"All done," she said after removing the last critter. "I'm going to take these specimens to the lab and put on some clean clothes. Please use this bar of soap to clean up. You're rather ripe after sitting in that mucky water. The soap is another family secret. It will soothe any other bites, and get you clean, too. When you're finished wrap yourself in a towel and sit back down on the tub. I need to wrap your ribs and put ointment on your bruises."

Before I could say thank you, she was gone. The soap did smell funny, but she was right; the mosquito bites had stopped itching. Have I mentioned how much I dislike mosquitos, and how much they like me?

She returned just as I was trying to get situated on the cold tile again. She had changed into jeans and a plaid shirt and was drying her hair with a towel.

"I've brought supplies," she smiled, rooting around in an old-fashioned black doctor's bag. "Ah, here we are, the perfect thing. Turn around and raise your arms; this will only take a sec." She quickly wrapped my chest and ribcage with Ace bandages, chatting as she worked.

"I see this isn't the first time you've been in a fight. Hold still for a minute longer. I've got some ointment that will help."

"Well, most of them are from a long time ago, and one is from a bullet that went astray," I answered. None of the scars had been the result of a fight, I thought absently.

"Rumor has it you were shot by a spurned lover," she needled, as she worked her hands into the muscles around the old gunshot wound.

"Not exactly." I answered, remembering Brenda, wondering again how I could have been such a fool.

"It's a good thing they didn't throw your overnight bag in the swamp. I hope you don't mind, but I opened it and laid out some dry clothes on the bed. Come back to the living room when you're dressed.

She walked away, and I managed to get into my clothes. Who was she? Did she really live alone on the bayou? And how did she know who I was?

9

WHEN I RETURNED TO THE LIVING ROOM, I noticed a second cup of her pain potion waiting on the table beside the sofa. The rain was pounding, and the wind was so loud it sounded like a freight train. I wondered if tropical storms could produce tornados.

"Don't worry. This house can withstand just about anything," she said. "And I haven't been a very good host—you're bound to be starving. I've pulled some gumbo out of the freezer; it's warming on the stove now."

"Well, I think saving my life probably earns you a few hospitality points. And gumbo sounds terrific. Is there any way to get a message out to my friends? You know, tell them I'm safe?"

"I checked. Both cell service and the Internet are down. The other problem is there's only one way out of here, and that's by boat. Unless you know the bayou like the back of your hand, you'd never find this place. I could try to give them directions, but I've laid all kinds of traps for dirtbags like Mitch and Ted. I wouldn't want your friends to get caught in one trying to get here. A woman living out here all alone has to protect herself from men who've had too many beers and think I'm all alone and available."

She had a point, and she'd also triggered my thinking. The dirtbags, as she called them, probably had taken Clovis's cell phone and computer as well as mine, and surely had the technology to intercept any attempts to contact him. I needed to think long and hard before I called or emailed anyone.

"You're right. I wasn't thinking. I know we're stuck for now, but

I need to come up with a plan that gets me out of here and keeps you safe."

She looked amused "Jack, this isn't all about you. I knew what I was doing. And look at it this way—sooner or later those guys are going to have to report to their boss. I wouldn't want to be in their shoes."

"Okay, you're right. But look—I've been racking my brain trying to remember where we met. Please tell me what I've forgotten."

She smiled and her eyes brightened. "There's no reason why you should remember. About a year ago or so, I attended an environmental conference where I applied for funding from a foundation headed by your daughter. Anyone who was anyone in the world of environmental science was there. It was a great opportunity for me.

I didn't think I had much of a chance, but I presented my proposal to a panel, and, lo and behold, I received a grant. I never thought my research would get that level of recognition. Much of the equipment you see in my lab was purchased with funds from that award, and the grant has drawn a lot of attention to my work.

You came to the awards reception, and a colleague introduced us. We were still in the "do you know" phase, when one of the panelists barged in. He was rather rude, insisting he couldn't wait. You apologized, and he led you away."

Of course! I thought, as the events of that day flooded my brain. Many years ago, a friend I'd known in high school, a very good friend in fact, had created an environmental trust, naming Beth as its sole trustee. Several summers after she and Jeff graduated from Davidson, they decided to kick-start the work of the trust with a conference on climate change and sent out a request for grant proposals, winners to be announced at the conference. She didn't feel like she had the expertise to evaluate the applications, so she pulled together a panel of experts to review the requests.

The conference brought together some of the best environmental minds in the country. The panel that heard the grant proposals made its recommendations, and in all but one case Beth agreed with their decisions. That request had been submitted by a Dr. Abby Broussard, who had obtained both her environmental science and medical degrees from Louisiana State University. The work she had done and the proposal she had submitted were both unique in substance and exciting in scope. But without Ivy League credentials, the panel had suggested that her work lacked "academic integrity."

Beth had disagreed, overruling the panel and awarding Abby's proposal a fully funded grant. Abby and I met by chance at the reception, but a very insistent member of the panel pulled me away just as we'd begun to talk. The guy was determined to convince me of the value of Ivy League credentials, but I managed to escape before too long by turning him over to a hopeful UPenn grad. I tried to find Abby, but the reception had ended, and she wasn't among the few guests still lingering at the bar.

"I can't believe I didn't recognize you," I said, a little shaken by this lapse of memory.

"Why should you? It was only a chance encounter. Let me bring you a bowl of gumbo. Don't get up. The less you move, the less those ribs will, and the faster they'll heal."

I watched her walk to the kitchen, struck again by how much chance or maybe providence can influence our individual lives. By all rights I should be dead. I was alive only because a woman I'd totally forgotten had decided to intervene. Under different circumstances I would've liked to get to know her better, but the sooner I got out of her bayou, the better chance we both had to stay alive.

10

THE GUMBO WAS AS GOOD AS I'D EVER tasted. The dark mahogany roux, spicy andouille sausage and okra gave it a distinctive, pungent flavor. I wondered what else she had stashed away in her freezer for stormy days.

When I'd finished my second helping, she picked up my empty bowl and said, "If you hadn't left the reception, you would have found out the answer was yes."

"Yes?"

"Yes, to your dinner invitation. I could tell you were about to ask before that jerk Schwartz interrupted. Too bad. Might have been an interesting evening." She smiled and turned toward the kitchen, leaving me to think about what might have been.

She returned a few minutes later, all business again.

"Look, Jack, I have work to do. This storm is terrific for my latest project. I think you should try to get some rest. Will you be okay on the sofa?"

I nodded, more than willing to sink into my cushioned refuge again. I dozed for a while before falling into a deep sleep. No dreams, no nightmares, just sleep. I was wakened by a loud clash of thunder that shook me as well as the house. I waited for my heart to return to its normal rhythm, then went to look for Abby.

I found her in her lab and ventured in.

"Well good evening, sleepy head," she said with a smile.

"That potion you gave me just about knocked me out; what was in it? And if you don't mind me asking, what you are working on?"

"Mostly herbs, and, well… nothing that you'd recognize," she answered. "I'm studying the restorative nature of swamp and bayou life, especially after a major weather event. This storm is a godsend, at least for me. Normally a storm moves through the bayou in a matter of hours. But if the weather reports are right, this one is barely moving and will leave tons of water and wind damage in its wake. How these lowlands and their inhabitants recover could give us vital knowledge into how our planet might repair itself from the damage caused by climate change."

As we walked through the lab, she described what each instrument did and explained that once the Wi-Fi was restored she would be able to download data from at least a hundred sensors placed strategically throughout the swamp.

"The storm is predicted to get worse tonight—we're right in the middle of its path. Not much we can do but ride it out. At least it will keep the bad guys away. Do you feel up to a glass of wine? And are you hungry? You slept a long time."

"A glass of wine sounds great. And I'm hungry if you are. I can't believe I slept so long. Got any of that gumbo left?" I asked, following her toward the kitchen.

"Sorry, no more gumbo. But how about a pulled pork sandwich? My freezer is an amazing place," she said, laughing at my surprise. "Jack, please go relax on the sofa. I can handle the wine, and the more you rest, the better off you'll be."

I returned to my comfy sofa, still feeling unsettled by my surroundings. Last night Clovis and I had enjoyed a wonderful dinner at Galatoire's. This morning I'd been left to die on a tiny island in the middle of a swamp after a couple of thugs had kicked me half to death. Now I'd been rescued by a scientist whom I'd once met briefly and was riding out the storm with her, in her own home, in the middle of the bayou next door. It was a lot for my mushy brain to absorb.

But as I waited for her, I realized these hours were the calm before the real storm reared its ugly head again. As soon as the weather cleared, the bad guys, whoever they were, would descend to finish the job, the job they'd figured the swamp would do. Abby would be nothing but collateral damage. Not a nice thought.

I heard a door close and turned to see her bringing in a tray of cheese and a California cabernet. She poured two glasses of wine, and I raised mine in a toast.

"This is a very nice wine. How did you manage to get it down here?"

She raised hers in return and said, "I didn't. I was at Stanford lecturing last summer and took every opportunity I had to visit the wine country and learn about various vineyards. I spent almost my entire honorarium on wine and shipping it back to Louisiana, but it's been worth it. When I get lonely, a glass of wine cheers me up. I only bring out the good stuff for company, so not very often."

"Thank you," I said. "Definitely an unexpected treat. But why do you live here, alone? Why don't you live in Baton Rouge?"

"You know what they say. You can take the girl out of the swamp, but you can't take the swamp out of the girl." Her eyes sparkled as she settled easily onto the sofa, one leg tucked under the other.

I watched her as she cut a few slices of cheese. Her eyes were narrow, framed by dark thick eyebrows that curved all the way to the edge of her eyes. She'd told me that her nickname was Cat, and over the cabernet I coaxed her into telling me some of her life story.

She'd been raised in a small Louisiana town south of Lafayette. She had two older brothers who taught her about the swamps and their critters—egrets, alligators, plenty of fish, and especially snakes—which ones were harmless and which ones could kill her. Her family was descended from French Canadians and their lives reflected their Cajun heritage. Her father worked for an oil company and her mother taught school. They knew everyone in town and hosted crawfish boils, danced to the music of fiddles, harmonicas, and accordions and, of course, went to Mass every Sunday morning.

Most of her friends had married young, produced babies, and never ventured any farther from home than the next parish. Abby wanted to become a veterinarian, but her parents had insisted that she become a 'real doctor.' She earned a scholarship to LSU, and worked her way through grad school and finally med school, earning a Master's in environmental science along with her MD. She had offers from various research hospitals and universities, but her love of the swamps and bayous called her to independent research. She was able to fund her work through support and grants from individual donors and environmental organizations like Beth's. During the last fifteen years she had earned her PHD and been invited to lecture at some of the finest universities in America, despite her supposed lack of credentials.

She'd almost married her high school boyfriend at sixteen, but he didn't want her to go to college. He wanted someone who would "cook, keep house, and tend to the kids" while he worked on oil rigs. The breakup wasn't pretty, but her brothers made sure he didn't come around anymore. She shrugged off my casual questions about her future. "I haven't given up on marriage or a serious relationship, but right now it's not in the cards."

She was equally inquisitive about me, and I gave her a very short version of my life, my marriage to Angie and her untimely death. I told her I'd recently had a lot of first dates.

She laughed, aiming a gentle kick at my mid-section. "You are so full of it. DC is full of eligible women. The only men down here who can count to twenty are just like Mitch and Ted, sleazeballs whose only goal is to get in my pants, with or without permission. Besides, I've heard a few stories about you. Apparently, you tend to fall for women who would rather you were dead."

I didn't know what stories she'd heard, but I couldn't deny the allegation.

"Guilty as charged, but I hope maybe my luck has changed." The words spilled out of nowhere.

"Does that mean you've fallen for me?" Her tone was cool and edgy. "And in just these few hours?"

She was an intelligent, attractive woman. She'd also just saved my life. Sure, I was drawn to her, but jeez—now I was no better than Mitch or Ted. She waited until it became clear I had no credible answer, then rose awkwardly from the sofa, almost spilling my wine.

"Gosh," she said. "I can smell the pork—don't want it to get dry. Do you like slaw on your sandwich or just sauce? Now don't you move a muscle. I'll be back in a few."

She was through the kitchen door before I could say a word. I'd heard that tone before—why on earth had I spoken out like that? I couldn't very well blame it on a squishy brain.

11

SHE WAS GONE FOR LONGER THAN "a few." I was beginning to worry when I heard the swoosh of the door opening. She carried a large bamboo tray filled with the basic requirements for a barbecue—a platter of pulled pork, a bowl of coleslaw, buns, two squeeze bottles of sauce, and a jar of bread and butter pickles.

"Wow," I said, trying to take the tray from her. "How did you manage this? Don't tell me that roasting a pig is another of your talents."

She put the tray on the coffee table and handed me plates and napkins. "Nope, no pig killing around here. My grandmother taught me and my brothers how to cook. She used to say, 'anyone who can read can cook; it's not rocket science.' But my mother also taught me there's nothing wrong with take-out. Why should I try to fry a chicken or butcher a pig when other folks manage it so much better?"

"Well, my hat's off to both your mother and grandmother." I raised my wine glass toward her, but my words sounded slurred, even to me, and I felt dizzy, a little disoriented. I couldn't think of anything even vaguely intelligent to say.

We ate in silence. She had just picked up my empty plate when the winds suddenly picked up again. The howl of the rain beating against the storm shutters was truly frightening. I'd been in scary weather before; tornado sirens are a regular feature of spring in Arkansas. But these winds were different. They seemed to have intent, a purposeful, almost visceral intent to destroy. My face must have revealed the sudden panic I felt, because she quietly sat down next to me again.

"It's okay, Jack. It sounds worse than it is, and we're on the inside.

The house is strong, and I promise we're safe. The storm won't last forever; we just need to wait it out."

Her voice was calm, her words reassuring, and I took a deep breath, feeling like an idiot. What was the matter with me? Where was my normal male bravado?

She watched, looking slightly amused, as I wrestled with my ego. Giving up, I gave her a sheepish grin and tried to take the plate she was still holding.

She put it on the floor and turned to me. "Jack, you're exhausted, just running on fumes. Give your body a break, let it rest. I've got something to say, and we need to come up with a plan."

She was mostly right on all counts, but as I leaned back against the cushions, I heard her take a deep breath.

"Look, I know you wish you hadn't said what you did, and I'm sorry I let it get under my skin. Truth is, I think we both feel a mutual attraction. Who knows if it's real or a result of the stress of our current circumstance. Maybe we'll have the chance to pursue that attraction, but right now we need to figure out how to get out of here and back to what most people think is civilization. We need to stop flirting and concentrate on saving our necks. Maybe..."

She was right, and I told her so, relieved to hear my normal voice again. "You're absolutely right, Abby. But promise me this: dinner next week in New Orleans. Now that I've finally had the courage to ask, please say yes."

"It's a date, Mr. Patterson," she answered. "Now let's figure out how to get out of this mess."

We discussed the possibility of calling her brothers. But one or the other of them might say something to their friend the sheriff, or worse still, Mitch and Ted. Apparently, the deputies were always called 'Mitch and Ted,' like they were one person instead of two. Her brothers might end up cooperating with the sheriff in what they thought was an attempt to rescue Abby from the DC lawyer who was up to no good down here.

"I love my brothers, but they aren't the brightest bulbs in the parish. No matter how many times I tell them to keep quiet about something, in the end they always blab. They can't help themselves; it's just who they are. You'd think I'd learn," she said with a rueful smile.

"Let's leave your brothers out of this," I said. "We need some way to get word to Clovis without alerting the bad guys. We need Stella. She's a technology whiz, a professional who also happens to be married to Clovis. I think I can send her a message from you, something totally innocent, that she'll send to Clovis. If you can give me some idea of where and when we can pull your boat onto dry land, there's a good chance Clovis will be there to meet us."

"I can give you the where," she replied slowly. "But what if he's not there? What if your dark-suited friends beat him to it?"

"We can worry about that en route," I smiled. "No sense borrowing trouble."

She didn't look convinced.

I'd thought about contacting the FBI, but Royce had been pretty sure they were behind the wiretapping of the lunch meeting at Charlie's. In fact, other than Clovis, Stella, and Brian, my staff of one, and now Abby, I didn't know who I could trust.

We went over other possible options, but soon realized there were none. I had to assume the bad guys could listen to any conversation on Abby's cell phone and read any text or email she sent. I felt sure the guys in the boat weren't actual agents, but the FBI could easily have provided them with the technology. Of course, that would have been illegal without a court order, but in my experience the FBI preferred to ask for forgiveness rather than permission, and usually got it. What's the old question—who will watch the watchers?

Abby pulled a map from a kitchen drawer and showed me how she hoped to leave the swamp and where she intended to make landfall. It was a place called Cary's Landing on Lake Charles. She said Cary was a former Razorback football player and an old friend.

"He has no use for our crooked sheriff, and he's the toughest man I know. It's a longer boat ride, but if we make it, I know he'll help. I had a huge crush on Cary once upon a time, but his heart was always with another. He's as trustworthy as they come."

She handed me her iPad and watched as I drafted the following message to Stella:

"Dear Ms. Rice,

You may not remember, but Jack Patterson introduced us at an event hosted by the Cole Environmental Trust. He said you had formed a consulting business, and that I should call you if I ever had any problems with my computer system. I think I may have been hacked, that someone might be trying to steal my research. We're in the middle of a big storm down here, but when it finally winds down, I'll have to make a trip to Cary's Landing in Lake Charles to restock. Cell service in the swamp is spotty at best, so I'll call you when I get there. Just didn't want you to be surprised. Thanks in advance. Dr. Abby Broussard."

Stella hadn't attended the conference but knew all about the Cole trust. In fact, she had developed its website. Hopefully either she or Clovis would read between the lines of this unexpected message.

I handed the iPad back to Abby, and she quickly pushed send. Of course, the message wasn't sent. We were counting on the Wi-Fi to return, hopefully before Mitch and Ted did.

The email was clumsy, a long shot at best. I hoped that anyone who intercepted the message would read it as a legitimate request for computer help. I'd been tempted to tell Stella to bring an army but of course anything so obvious would result in a raid on Abby's home before the storm ended.

She was sure she could navigate the swamp better than anyone else. But getting to Cary's wouldn't solve the problem if there wasn't a friendly face there to greet us. We could only hope that Clovis would be waiting on the dock with plenty of back-up. We decided to leave as soon as the storm began to die down.

Speaking of the storm, it was still raining buckets, and the house was still shaking from the force of the wind. I felt another surge of gratitude for Abby's rescue. But for her bravery, I would surely have drowned or been dinner for a lucky gator by now.

She said, "I'm tempted to leave tonight, but no telling how this storm has affected my route. Trees will be down everywhere. My bet is we'll have one more day of storms and high winds before anyone can venture out. My sensors will detect anyone headed this way, but I'd rather we were long gone before they get here. We must be ready to leave quickly, whether you've reached Stella or not. Keep your bag packed."

We both laughed, and on cue, the power went out. The generator kicked in after a few minutes, but even then, the lamps in in the living room were dim. Abby had jumped up to rummage in a closet and returned carrying several small lanterns.

"The house is wired so the generator powers my lab and the freezers first. The rest of the house will remain a bit dark, but these lanterns should give us enough light. And the power usually comes back in a day or two."

"You seem to be prepared for every contingency," I said, as she handed me a lantern.

"Oh, I wouldn't say that. Mother Nature has a way of teaching us who's in control, and it's sure not us. Right now, I think she's out of patience with every one of us. Remember the snowstorm that covered Texas a couple of years ago? Or how about the fires in Canada that brought layers of toxic smoke to the states? Or the heavy rains that flooded Vermont and New York a few months ago? We used to think of those as once in a hundred-years events. Now we watch them on TV or the internet, mesmerized by the images for a couple of days before we move on, completely ignoring the fact that we humans are the cause, that it's our own fault. And we go right back to our wicked, wasteful ways. No wonder she's fed up. Why on earth can't…"

She was interrupted by another roar of wind from outside followed by a crash that made the house shudder and just about scared me to death.

"Well, time for me to get off my high horse," she laughed. "You know, as long as my boat doesn't break loose and float off down the bayou, we should be fine here." I tried to match her nonchalant attitude, but she wasn't buying.

"Jack, I've told you—this house is secure. We'll be okay. But we both need to get some real sleep before we can deal with tomorrow. I left something to help you sleep on the nightstand next to my bed. I need to make sure the lab is secure and the fridge and freezer are running properly before I can sleep."

My eyebrows arched sharply at her casual reference to her bed. "Look, Abby," I said. "I'm happy to sleep on the couch. Just tell me where to find a pillow."

"Don't be silly—my bed is plenty big for the both of us. Although I admit it may be the first time I will have slept with a man before our first date."

12

I FOUND SOME PAJAMAS in my battered suitcase which now lay open on a chair near the bed. I had no idea what was in the concoction she'd left on the nightstand, but it must have worked. I was asleep almost before my head hit the pillow. I was woken suddenly by another crash outside the house and was relieved to find her curled up beside me, sound asleep. It was still dark outside, and I tried not to move, but it wasn't long before she stirred and nuzzled a little closer.

Murmuring "This is nice," she pressed her backside against me and moved still closer. I was obviously aroused, and she rolled over to face me. We kissed and she wrapped her legs around my waist. Unfortunately, the grip of her legs resulted in excruciating pain to my bruised ribs. I couldn't help a little gasp, and still worse, I went limp.

I felt the creeping flush of embarrassment, but she shook her head and put two fingers over my mouth. Before I could say a word, she curled up next to me, and we were both soon fast asleep.

I woke slowly the next morning, stretching like a cat, reaching out for her, quickly aware of her absence. I threw some water on my face and rushed into the kitchen, immensely relieved to find her at the stove frying sausage.

I watched her from the doorway for a few seconds, but she heard me, turned, and smiled. "Why don't you take a shower and get dressed while I finish up here. Be sure to use the special soap I left out for you. Mosquitos tend to swarm after a storm; they've been known to carry off a polecat. I'll rewrap your ribs after breakfast."

The warm water streaming over my sore body felt terrific, but

I showered and dressed quickly, glad to find I'd managed to stuff jeans and a golf shirt in my suitcase.

The storm was still raging, its furor an ever-present reminder of the protection it provided. I almost wished it could last forever.

When I returned to the kitchen, she was sitting at the table sipping from a mug of coffee. She motioned me to sit down and said, "I feel like I owe you an explanation."

I pulled out the chair across from her and took a second mug from her outstretched hand.

"You don't owe me anything," I said. "I should be the one..."

"Please," she interrupted. "Let me explain."

I nodded. She was clearly bothered about something.

"After you went to bed, the eye of the storm came through. For a few minutes the Wi-Fi was up and running, and I could see that your message had been sent. I hope Stella gets it in time, but even if she does, I figure it's better than even odds that both you and I will be dead in the next day or so. They're after you, but they can't let me live. I'm a witness—collateral damage.

"I thought what the hell. I've been attracted to this man since the moment we met. If I was going to die in a matter of days, why wait? I mean, you can't take your regrets with you. I crawled into bed with every intention of having my way.

"But I forgot I'd given you an extra dose of medicine—you were sound asleep. I curled up beside you, hoping you'd wake up, but you didn't move a muscle. I could almost hear the Fates laughing. I have to say, even asleep you were an excellent bed partner. I slept like a baby.

"I hope you don't think less of me," she said without a hint of a smile. "Anyway, I felt I owed you an explanation. And if you still want to have dinner in New Orleans, the answer is still 'yes'."

She came around the table, gave me a quick kiss, then turned to pull a tray of biscuits out of the oven. She'd pushed the sausage to the edge of the pan, and I watched as she carefully dropped eggs into the middle of the sizzling skillet.

No mention of my ribs or anything else that had happened. Maybe I had dreamed it, but I didn't think so. Damn the Fates. I fumbled for a response but might as well have been talking to a wall. There wasn't much I could say, so I let it go.

Breakfast is my favorite meal, and this one did not disappoint—country sausage, fried eggs, and biscuits already slathered in butter, waiting for strawberry jam. We both ate quickly, and I volunteered to do the dishes while she checked on her lab again. About the time I had returned the last dish to the cabinet, the house began to shake, and I heard what I thought must be a train, or maybe an earthquake. I braced for whatever was coming, but it was over almost before I could move.

"That was close—not a direct hit, thank goodness! I've made the lab as secure as I can, so let me wrap your ribs one more time. We need to be ready to leave as soon as the storm lets up—your 'friends' will surely be on their way, and it wouldn't hurt for us to get a decent head start."

She was all business wrapping my rib cage, but when she began to massage the soothing cream into my bruises I couldn't resist, pulling her close with every intention of completing what I had failed to accomplish the night before. She didn't resist, and we fell back on the bed, mouths meeting and hands exploring. Her clothes slipped off easily, and I had just pulled her to me when the screech of a very loud alarm tore through the room.

I looked around wildly, but the noise stopped almost as quickly as it had begun. What now, I wondered—another tornado?

Abby was trying unsuccessfully not to laugh. She gave me a sweet kiss, then jumped up and grabbed her clothes. "Don't worry—it's just my alarm system. They're putting their boats in the water. The alarm is linked to the sensor closest to the sheriff's boathouse. Looks like they're going to brave the tail of the storm and try to get here before we slip away. I'll be right back."

She pulled her clothes on and was gone before I could say a word. I found my own clothes and dressed quickly, muttering a few choice words about timing and the ever-laughing Fates.

When she returned, she had pulled a poncho over her clothes and wore a pair of surgical gloves. She thrust a second set in my direction, and I threw the poncho over my head.

"I need you to sit on the front of the boat—watch for logs and keep us out of trouble. We need to be as quiet as possible until we hear them, so I'll keep us real slow. Make sure you wear the gloves, too. We can't go very fast anyway, too many trees down and lots of debris in the channels. I know the way to Cary's like the back of my hand, but nothing will look the same after this storm. At least it will be just as tough for Mitch and Ted."

She lowered the boat into the water, and we both climbed in. She handed me a long pole with a gaff on the end and motioned me toward the bow. The water was choppy, and the rain made it all but impossible to see. I found a rope tied to one of the cleats and wrapped it around my left hand a few times, determined not to fall, either inside the boat or into the water. She laughed and we slid out into the bayou. I wondered why I needed the gloves, but figured she knew what she was doing.

"Be careful," she hissed. "Gators are hungry after a storm."

"Great. Not only do I have to worry about running into a log, but I'm also supposed to watch for gators. Next thing, you'll tell me snakes will be crawling into the boat. I hate snakes."

"Oh, snakes are the least of your worries. After a hurricane, flesh eating bacteria multiply like wildfire. It's one of the phenomena I study. That's why we're wearing gloves. Try to keep your hands out of the water."

Here I was worried about a bunch of thugs coming to kill me, when I should be worrying about flesh-eating bacteria?

I managed to shove away the various stray logs and branches lying in our path as we crept forward. Once I shoved a form that wasn't a log. It quickly rolled over and swam under the boat toward shore. I took a deep breath, but said nothing, hoping we both would live to tell our tale. We were making slow but steady progress when we heard motorboats approaching the house. Abby quickly revved up the motor and shouted, "Hang on."

Suddenly a bright flash of light appeared, followed by a large boom. I could hear Abby's voice coming through a loudspeaker.

"You are trespassing on private property! Leave immediately or suffer the consequences!"

The sound of Abby's voice faded as we sped away from the house. I wished I could have seen and heard the reactions of the guys on the boats.

"I told you I set traps set for anybody who comes to my house without permission," she shouted. "If they're stupid enough to keep going toward the house, they'll learn I'm not joking. It won't be long before those boats are full of holes, and they'll be running from hungry gators." I could hear her giggle over the motor.

We didn't hear anything more coming from the house, but the steady hum of an engine, increasing to a dull roar, made it clear the motorboats were headed in our direction. Abby pushed the engine to its maximum. I could hardly see a thing—Abby clearly had better eyesight. The boat swerved every which way without warning. Only after we had passed an obstruction in the water did I see the danger.

The drone of the other boats was constant. They didn't seem to be getting closer or farther away. It was if they knew where we were going. Had they hacked the email Abby had sent Stella? If that were true, we were headed into a trap, a trap I had set.

How to protect Abby? Should I tell her to drop me off somewhere in the swamp and send her back to her house? That wouldn't work, and I knew it. My mind was racing, but it was going in circles, getting nowhere.

We continued to make progress toward our destination, the other boats following at a safe distance. Our only hope was to go aground and seek some form of shelter. Or maybe, just maybe, Clovis had seen the message.

Abby didn't look even vaguely worried as she guided her boat through the swamp. The sun was beginning to peek through the trees, but she remained concentrated on dodging debris and on what now appeared to be a dock in the distance.

It wasn't long before I could read the sign—Cary's Landing.

Abby made a beeline to the pier. Surely she was aware that our followers were closing the gap. I saw the figure of a lone man at the end of the pier. He was wearing army fatigues, and he certainly wasn't the size or shape of Clovis.

13

He was the same man who had aimed his gun at me a few days ago. I didn't see anyone else. He held the same gun, and he flashed the same sickening grin. Abby guided the boat straight into the dock, and he motioned for us to get out.

I looked back at her and was surprised that she didn't seem to be afraid or even nervous. I heard engines and turned to see the other boats approaching. We were surrounded.

The man spoke, "You're a hard man to kill, Jack Patterson. Too bad you had to involve Dr. Broussard. Nothing personal, but we can't afford witnesses. Now don't do anything stupid. Both of you—out of the boat." He waved the gun in my direction, and we obeyed. Abby slipped her hand into mine, and we began to walk slowly off the pier and up the ramp.

"You'll see a car waiting to take you... well, you'll know soon enough." The bastard was clearly enjoying his moment.

"Your email to Stella Rice was a bit obvious, don't you think? Once the deputies told me who rescued you and where you were, it wasn't rocket science to intercept any messages or emails from Dr. Broussard. I bet you that right now Clovis is cooling his heels at Terry's boat landing, about, oh, I'd say an hour away. It wasn't hard to substitute it for this place."

My email hadn't fooled them one bit. I'd been too cute and blown it.

"I knew we shouldn't have taken you to the swamp. It made much more sense to kill you in the hotel room, make it look like a robbery gone bad, but I was overruled. We also couldn't anticipate Dr. Broussard saving your ass. Now she'll suffer your fate—after the boys get their payback."

I didn't want to think about what he meant by payback. By now, the other boats had docked, and a bunch of grinning thugs came ashore. The two smirking deputies, Ted and Mitch from their badges, walked directly toward Abby, and she moved closer to me.

The larger one, Ted, pointed his finger at me and laughed. "You're already dead meat. But Mitch and me, we made a deal. We led these guys through the swamp, and now we get to spend a little time getting to know you, Abby."

He reached for her arm, but I'd had enough. Without a second thought, my fist crashed straight into his nose. Caught off guard he went to the ground. I turned to Mitch; my foot went straight for his groin. When he bent over in agony my fist landed on his chin in a classic uppercut. They were both on the ground sniveling, at least for the moment.

I was surrounded quickly by angry men who grabbed my arms and held me tight. The man with the gun was laughing, hadn't moved a muscle.

Ted and Mitch slowly got to their feet, ready for revenge. I was about to get the butt whipping of my life when I heard a gun blast and a shout, "Enough!"

It hadn't come from the man with the gun. Struggling to turn toward the sound, I saw a tall man walking toward us. His rifle was aimed directly at Ted.

"Let go of him, and back away slowly," he said calmly, like he had all the time in the world.

No one loosened his grip or even moved. I caught sight of a hawk circling in the distance, looking for prey; time seemed to have stopped.

The man with the handgun broke the silence. "Now don't do anything stupid, whoever you are. Look around. There's ten of us here and more waiting with the cars. Lower your gun and walk away. You don't want to get killed over something that's none of your business."

The tall man didn't flinch or lower his weapon.

"I don't think you understand. Abby is my business, and you're on my property without permission. Now back away, all of you. I'm not going to warn you again."

"I think I like our odds—twenty to one, at least," responded the leader. His gun was still pointed directly at my chest. "And guess who I'm going to shoot first."

I figured the man with the rifle must be Abby's friend, Cary. It was easy to understand why she'd had a crush on him. His features were chiseled, with a deep tan; he reminded me of the guy in the fancy car commercials. I appreciated his intervention, but he was about to get us both killed. I wondered what he thought he could accomplish. Then I noticed the telling red dot from a laser scope on the chest of the man with the handgun. Cary was not alone.

I heard a bit of a shuffle and turned to see a big man striding down the boat ramp. Clovis was followed closely by six guys who were dressed in camo and armed to the teeth. The man with the gun no longer looked so confident.

Clovis stopped at the bottom of the ramp, his deep drawl about as threatening as any gun. "If I were you, I'd do as Cary says. Those fools back at the cars are sitting on the ground, all tied up and wishing they were anywhere else. There's a laser scope aimed directly at your chest, and if even one of you reaches for a weapon, you'll all be dead before you can blink an eye. Now do what Cary said: step away and lower your weapon."

After the initial shock, the men did as they were told and soon found themselves handcuffed to the dock. The man who had held the gun on me, the leader of the pack, so to say, smiled and gave me a little salute. I tried to ignore him, but his attitude was more than a little disconcerting: he didn't look the least bit concerned. Abby gave me a quick hug and ran to greet Cary. I tried to look nonchalant as I walked toward Clovis and reached out to clasp his hand.

"Glad you could make it. I was a little worried you might not."

He laughed, "Stella got the email from Dr. Broussard, but she could tell someone had modified it to say you were going to Terry's Landing, wherever that is. It took Stella no time at all to figure out that you were alive and headed to Cary's when the storm subsided.

"I sent for Brian and Big Mike, and they recruited the rest of these guys. Given the weather, our biggest worry was getting here, but it worked out okay."

Brian Hattoy works for me as a paralegal, while Mike works for the security agency that protects Walter Matthews, my good friend and owner of Bridgeport Life. In another life, they had worked together as snipers in the special forces.

"Thanks, guys—I sure am glad to see you! Now what should we do with these guys?"

Cary spoke in a deep Cajun accent. "The sheriff's as crooked as a snake, and Clovis told me you were worried about the FBI in New Orleans. I called a friend with the FBI in Houston. He and I used to play ball—he's as clean as a hound's tooth. A team of his field agents will be here any minute. I'm comfortable they'll put these guys away for a long time."

Right on cue, Cary's friend drove up and took charge. After he had taken our statements and his team had carted the bad guys away, I turned to Abby. "I'm worried that Ted and Mitch will get word to the sheriff, and he'll come after you before the FBI can find him. Why don't you come to DC with me?"

She smiled. "That's a tempting invitation, but my work here in the swamp takes priority. I have at least three months' worth of data to record after this storm, and flesh-eating bacteria to capture, catalog, and analyze—heaven knows what else. You know, all the fun stuff. Besides, Cary will be all over the sheriff if he so much as looks crossways at me."

Leaving Abby here with Cary didn't seem like such a good idea to me. He was a good-looking man who obviously cared for her more than his mother. But I sure wasn't going to stay here in the bayou, so… Clovis was already waiting by his car and frowned when Abby pulled me aside. She gave me a long, lingering kiss, reminding me that we had a date the next time I came to New Orleans. Feeling much better, I walked toward the car's open door. Shaking his head in disapproval, Clovis slammed the door behind me and off we went.

14

CLOVIS WANTED TO FLY DIRECTLY BACK TO DC, BUT I insisted we spend the night in New Orleans so we could meet with Royce and Thibodeaux. Besides, the guys had earned a night in the Quarter.

We met the next morning in a conference room at the Royal Orleans. Tom greeted us with a smile and offered coffee from a silver pot as well as tiny croissants and beignets. After the usual niceties, he turned to Royce, who hadn't said a word, waving away even the beignets.

Clearly angry, Royce went after Clovis almost immediately. Why hadn't Clovis contacted him when he found out where Abby and I were? Royce wanted to take care of the kidnappers without involving the FBI. He kept shouting that my abduction wasn't anyone's business but the syndicate's. Clovis kept his cool, totally unruffled by Royce's verbal onslaught. Thibodeaux didn't stop him, so I let him vent for a while. His reaction was exactly why Clovis hadn't included him in his plans. The last thing either of us wanted was for the kidnappers to be found at the bottom of some swamp with their throats cut.

When Royce finally calmed down, I told them what I had learned—there was a traitor in their ranks who thought Thibodeaux should be replaced as the head of the syndicate. I repeated word-for-word what my gun-pointing kidnapper had told me. I expected the big man to explode, but his poker face gave away nothing. Royce peppered me with questions, but Tom remained silent.

When Royce finally ran out of questions, Tom raised his hand and spoke quietly.

"Jack, I hope you will accept my apologies. I want you to know that I never, not even for one minute, thought you had left New Orleans on your own volition. I am horrified to think what you have been through these last few days. Without Dr. Broussard's timely rescue, you would surely be dead. You came to New Orleans as my guest, and my men failed to protect you. They will be dealt with appropriately. My organization has become sloppy. That will change." He glanced at Royce who swallowed hard.

"Now that you've made me aware of the situation, I will take every step necessary to protect my family and my organization. I will not forget your bravery or your service."

"Thank you," I responded. "I do have one favor to ask. I owe my life to Dr. Broussard. As you noted, I'm alive, standing here with you, because of her. I feel sure she's returned to her home on the bayou, ready to continue her research. But I'm concerned for her continued safety."

Thibodeaux raised his hand, palm forward. "Say no more. You can be sure she will be able to live her life and conduct her research in total safety."

Tom was a man of few words, but now I could leave Louisiana knowing Abby was under his umbrella of protection. Considering what I owed her, it was the least I could do.

Turning to Royce, Tom smiled. "Royce, I would like to spend a few minutes alone with Jack. Perhaps you could offer Mr. Jones a second cup of coffee."

Royce looked uncomfortable but didn't argue. Tom opened a door to what I had assumed was a closet but turned out to be a smaller room furnished with only two club chairs. We both sat down, and I waited.

"Something is worrying you, Jack," he stated calmly. "Something you didn't want Royce to hear."

Tom was more insightful than I had realized.

"The people who hired those thugs will surely be angry when they learn I'm alive and that I still intend to represent your grandson. I'm afraid they might target my daughter."

"I have already foreseen that possibility. Your daughter and her fiancé will be safe, as safe as if they were my own children. I've sent a specialist to St. Louis, a person who can raise the level of security they already enjoy. Royce is aware of your concern for your family. So—please tell me what is really bothering you."

Thibodeaux had read my mind, and for the next half-hour I told him what concerned me. He listened carefully, interrupting only to ask for clarification. When I finished, he remained silent, as did I.

"Your suspicions and concerns speak well of you. What you and I have discussed will remain between us until we talk again."

When we returned to the larger room, we found Clovis sipping his coffee and Royce pacing back and forth.

Our conversation was at an end, so I thanked Tom for putting us up at the Royal Orleans last night and for treating the guys to dinner at Dickie Brennan's. I mentioned that we'd like to stop by Theo's on Magazine to get pizza and wings for the plane ride home. That got his attention.

"How on earth do you know about Theo's? My wife gets take-out at least once a week. She always orders the Expert."

"Excellent choice," I replied as Clovis opened the door and we walked into the lobby. Let him wonder, I thought. I was ready to go home.

Thankfully, the flight to DC was uneventful. While we munched on pizza, Clovis told me what I'd missed while I "was enjoying the scenery in Cajun country." Brian tried to bring me up to date on office matters, but I couldn't seem to focus.

My mind wandered to the kidnappers. Who had hired them? I personally knew several of the lawyers representing the internet companies. I couldn't begin to imagine them condoning a kidnapping, much less murder. I also couldn't believe the government was involved. Why bother? They could easily drown me with paperwork.

I also thought about the extra protection that Tom was providing for Beth and Jeff. Was that favor a black hole sucking me further into an obligation I could never repay?

And what as it about David's small company that had caused such an extreme reaction? Internet companies use tried and true methods to crush competition. If they couldn't destroy David, why wouldn't they simply buy him out? And the government could easily make mincemeat out of any small business that caught its eye. Indicting David and seizing his business was surely a bit dramatic.

Clovis tapped me on the shoulder. "Hey, anyone home in there? I bet a dollar to a doughnut you're daydreaming about Abby Broussard and wishing you were still with her in her fortress on the bayou, storm or no storm."

For once, I had no answer.

15

LISA ECKENROD, head of Walter Matthews' day-to-day security operation, was waiting on the apron where our plane landed in DC, along with a half a dozen security officers. Lisa had impressed me with her toughness and smarts the first time we worked together. Walter had a keen eye for talent; it wasn't long before he elevated his former head of security, Martin Wells, to the board room and promoted Lisa. I hadn't expected to find her waiting but wasn't surprised when I saw Big Mike. When I asked about the show of force, she frowned.

"Let's see—you were kidnapped, almost killed, and left in a swamp to die, before you were rescued by a beautiful scientist during a fierce tropical storm. What do you think? You're lucky we weren't told to pick you up in an armored van. Maggie's orders were to bring you straight to the office. I think you have some explaining to do." But her frown had turned into a smile, followed by a grin as she took my arm.

Maggie Baxter and I had been friends and partners for many years, long before she became Maggie Matthews. She wasn't an attorney, but she knew the law and she understood what made people tick, an invaluable asset in any profession. Her marriage to Walter had been icing on the cake for all three of us.

It wouldn't be easy to explain why I had agreed to represent David Ruple without consulting her, not to mention why Clovis and I had been in New Orleans in the first place. For someone who supposedly wanted to back away from our practice so she could spend more time with her husband, she sure kept an eagle eye on me. But how could I complain? She'd saved my bacon more than once.

Maggie was sitting at the reception desk when we walked in. Lisa and Big Mike waved and made a hasty exit. Maggie turned to me and said coolly, "Why don't you, Clovis, and Brian meet me in a few minutes in the conference room. I've got a couple of things to clear up, shouldn't be more than a minute or two."

I had decided evasion might be a good course of action.

"Take all the time you need. I need to call Red about his stadium deal, and Clovis needs to get back to Little Rock."

"Don't even think about it, Jack Patterson. Into the conference room, all of you." She walked into her office, closing the door firmly behind her.

Maggie only addresses me as "Jack Patterson" when I'm in hot water. The three of us tucked our tails between our legs and did as we were told. She took her own sweet time. I was about to remind her who was boss when she backed through the door carrying a tray that held three cups of coffee and half a dozen blueberry muffins. I jumped up to take the tray, and she took the chair opposite me. Clovis looked relieved, but there was to be no chit-chat; she was all business.

"First, Jack. Both Micki and I are aware that Novak hired a New Orleans 'family' to protect Beth—with your blessing. We've known for some time but decided not to raise the issue. Neither of us approve of the choice you made, but Beth is your daughter, and so far, she and Jeff are still alive and well, so…" She paused, but since I basically agreed with her, I said nothing. Obviously still irritated, she continued, "Now that we've got that out of the way, please tell me why someone wired $100,000 into our trust account this morning. And who is Gloria Ruple? I have a feeling she may replace Red Shaw as my least favorite person in the world. She is one pushy woman."

I apologized for keeping her in the dark, explaining that I had no idea we'd have a new client until after the lunch with Tom Thibodeaux. I reminded her that I'd been otherwise occupied until yesterday, avoiding any mention of Abby.

Her brows shot up at the name Thibodeaux. I had no doubt she would ferret out all the details of my recent adventures, probably sooner rather than later. My escape was only temporary.

"Okay, Jack." Her tone indicated just the opposite. "Stella is on her way to DC; her flight should touch down any minute now. One of Lisa's people will bring her here directly from Dulles. Clovis, I've booked a room for you at the Madison. You and Stella can work from this office—you'll need to stay in DC for—well, at least until this case has been resolved. Stella is already working to update our phone and computer security. You and Lisa are meeting this afternoon to discuss Jack's protection."

I tried to interrupt, but Maggie cut me off.

"You have no say in this matter, Jack. Surely you don't think your adversaries will just go away?" She focused a frosty glare on me but didn't wait for a response. "Once again, you've taken a case from a dubious source who you know engages in, shall we say, "shady" practices. I've decided we'll take no chances. Clovis and Lisa will make sure you're guarded twenty-four hours a day until this case is over. Lisa has also upgraded my security. I assume you've already made similar arrangements for Beth and Jeff. Or do I need to do that as well?"

"No, I've already made the call," I replied. At least I'd done one thing right.

"As for the new client, why don't you tell me what you know. All the Court documents are under seal, although I understand Clovis has a box for Brian to organize. Your meeting with Mrs. Ruple is at the Willard at four o'clock. You're lucky that she didn't meet you at the airport."

Relieved to be off the hook, I recounted what I had learned from Royce and Lula. Hoping to regain some control of my troops, I assigned the first tasks that came to mind. Maggie agreed to begin the process of getting me into the jail to meet David. Brian would contact David's former partners and interview his girlfriend.

I didn't look forward to meeting Gloria, especially before I met with David. The last thing I needed was an overprotective and demanding mother who could easily make matters worse. Then again, I cautioned myself, "You haven't met the woman yet; don't make assumptions."

The day had caught up with me; I could feel myself slump,

exhausted more mentally than physically. Clovis bluntly advised me to take a nap and left to meet Stella at the Madison. Brian followed almost immediately, carrying the box of files under his arm. Maggie produced a bottle of Perrier from the wine fridge, and we toasted our friendship. She told me how angry she'd been at first, and how worried she and Walter had been when I went missing.

"At least you're still alive. We couldn't help but wonder…" Her voice trailed off.

I knew she wanted to ask about Abby. Maggie tended to be overprotective when it came to the women in my life; she had good reason. I didn't volunteer, and she changed tactics.

"Jack, we have a nice law practice. Red Shaw's issues alone could keep us in the black without taking on any new clients, especially those who might get you killed. I can't do this anymore. You've got to promise me this one is the last!"

She was right. I didn't need to be putting myself or her at risk, much less for a client whose 'family' didn't blink an eye at a little extralegal behavior. But I couldn't promise. How could I have seen this coming? I didn't even know David Ruple existed before New Orleans, and I could hardly have refused the invitation.

My 'Big Business' clients can cause serious economic damage to the competition and even to our country, but as far as I know they don't kill people or traffic young men and women. Every lawyer worth his salt dances on the edge of his conscience from time to time. If we don't engage in criminal behavior, our code of ethics gives us license to defend just about anyone or any entity. But the edge has its hazards, requiring good judgment and thoughtful decisions. Maybe this time… but no. It was simple: I owed Tom Thibodeaux.

After Maggie had finished lecturing, and I had apologized for about the thousandth time, I did call Red about the stadium in San Antonio. He already knew what had happened. Somehow, he always did. He gave me bloody hell for a few minutes, then told me to be more careful. Red never minced words.

"What in the hell? There's bound to be a woman involved. When will you ever learn, and do I get to meet this one before she gets you killed?"

I promised to introduce him to Abby when the Lobos played the Saints later this year. I wondered how he and Maggie knew so much. Maggie always complained about Red's brusk manner, but I felt sure they got along better than she let on.

She left to call Walter, and I managed to get a quick nap before Mike arrived to drive me to the Willard. I told him I would much rather walk; he could meet me there.

"Sorry, Jack, but no way. Mrs. Matthews orders. I'm to stick to you like glue until this case is over. It's my job, not to mention what Lisa would do if I let anything happen to you, so please cooperate."

I gave up. But he did let us walk; it was only a couple of blocks.

I love the renovation of the Willard; the lobby is fabulous, but I'm not a big fan of the bar. It's a favorite of tourists, lobbyists, Congressional staffers, even the occasional Member. But it's too small, noisy, and crowded for my taste, a poor meeting place if you want to hear what your companion has to say—not that anyone really listens. I didn't know what Gloria Ruple looked like, but when I walked through the doors, I had no difficulty recognizing her—at four in the afternoon, she was the only woman in the room.

She was seated at a very visible table near the round bar: a dark-haired woman wearing sunglasses, bright red lipstick, and a black cocktail dress; an enormous red Chinese scarf was draped around her shoulders. A half-empty martini glass sat on the table in front of her. She didn't move a muscle when I approached her table.

"Mrs. Ruple?" I hesitated. "My name is Jack Patterson."

She lowered her glasses, giving me a slow once-over, then lowered them into place, took a sip of her martini, and said, "Well, don't just stand there; sit down. It's about time you showed up.

"I hope you're a better lawyer than the usual mouthpieces Royce hires, or my boy is in deep shit." She raised her hand and snapped her fingers, "Keith, bring this man a martini with extra olives. Hendricks okay with you, Jack? Or do you want some of the fancier stuff. Did you know they make gin in Vermont with honey? Not for me!"

I thought about declining. A martini at four in the afternoon was too early even for me, but I sensed the martini was part of a test. "Hendricks is fine, thanks," I agreed. "And, no, I didn't."

The bartender delivered my martini, along with a separate bowlful of olives, obviously not for me. Equally obvious, it wasn't Gloria's first encounter with the bartender.

After he left, Gloria asked, "Now, what have you done to get my son out of jail?"

"So far, nothing. I haven't even met him yet."

16

SHE CALLED FOR KEITH AGAIN, telling him to bring us a charcuterie plate and two more martinis. When I objected and asked for a pinot noir, she glared but didn't argue.

She took a long sip of her martini and said, "Look, Jack. I'm not stupid. I know David is in serious trouble, but I don't know why. So please tell me what happens next—in terms that I can understand." We waited in glum silence until Keith brought my wine. I was glad to have time to think.

"Gloria, I know how hard this must be for you. And you are right to be worried. To be honest, I can't tell you exactly what will happen next or when. I need more information before I can devise a strategy. But I can give you some basics."

The bar was still almost empty, no one obviously listening. I told her what I could. First, I would interview David and consult with the U.S. Attorney, asking him to release David on his own recognizance or at least with minimum bail. Next, I would reach out to the Romatowski law firm to discover what their clients hoped to accomplish with the civil litigation. I didn't emphasize the hurdles I would face, but I didn't sugar coat them either.

Gloria listened, or at least didn't interrupt, but she seemed more interested in the extra olives than what I had to say. When I asked what she could tell me about David's girlfriend, she frowned and called her "nothing but a gold-digger, no class at all." Abandoning the girlfriend for the moment, I turned to David's work.

"I don't understand the first thing about computers or what he does with them, but I do know that David is a genius. I'm certain he will make us a fortune," she answered.

I was curious about her reference to "us a fortune." Royce had said no one in the family was an investor. So, I asked.

"I'm his mother; we are very close. Why should I need to invest my money in his business? He saw how my father treated me. He treated David the same way, for that matter. No, I am not an 'investor.'" Her icy tone made her opinion very clear.

She rose from the table, handing her empty glass to a waiter who had appeared at exactly the right moment. As I watched her weave her way to the restroom, I couldn't help but wonder how much of her performance was an act. I asked the bartender if she would be alright.

"Don't worry," he replied. "Some bigwig is paying the bills. Hotel management makes sure she gets back to her room safely every night. Most of the time she drinks her martinis, eats her olives, and is escorted back by one of the bellmen. Sad, don't you think?"

I wondered why Gloria was even in DC. Sure, under these circumstances any mother would be worried about her son, but to spend your whole day in a hotel didn't seem productive. I almost asked the bartender what she did during the day, but it was none of my business. Besides, I did have things to do and chatting with my client's mother and drinking martinis wasn't one of them. When Gloria returned, I made my apologies and left her with a fresh martini, a bowl of olives, and a promise to stay in touch.

I found Mike waiting outside the bar. He agreed we could walk to the Madison where I would meet Clovis and Stella for an early dinner. Maggie had texted to tell me that a new laptop and a briefcase full of work and messages had been delivered to my home. No more martinis for me.

The renovated bar area at the Madison is terrific. The bar at The Mayflower, whose dark booths and tables are always full of power brokers, senators, congressmen, and lobbyists, is more well-known. The Madison is geared more toward businessmen. Its bar is light and contemporary, a site for easy networking after a long day.

Stella and Clovis were waiting at a table in the restaurant area of the bar. She was easy to spot, even without Clovis. She was tall and, well, my mother would have said 'statuesque.' She changed her look on an almost weekly basis. Her short, spiky hair was now a bright pink, which contrasted with a white blouse, black leather pants, and stiletto heels. Her piercings were silver, somewhat subdued for Stella, but she stood out in the Madison.

We chatted about this and that while waiting for menus. Clovis told me Gloria had already called Royce to complain. I hadn't offered her dinner, and she was sure I was the wrong lawyer for her son. I hadn't worn a proper suit, and "no one came to our table to introduce themselves the whole time we were talking." She demanded that Royce fire me and hire the high-powered firm of Williams and Connelly. A young attorney at the firm had bought her drinks the night before and told her that he'd never heard of me.

Clovis cut off my response with a raised hand. "Royce was delighted with her reaction—told me he hoped you had better things to do than dine with Gloria. He also didn't bother to tell her that W&C are one of the firms suing David."

Stella tried to explain the steps she'd taken to protect our phones and computers since my kidnapping, but she was speaking Greek as far as I was concerned. She continued with bad news, "There's no sense trying to deal with your credit cards, bank accounts, or change all your passwords. Whoever abducted you has every bit of that information and would know about any changes in a heartbeat. It's not worth the effort to try to get around their monitoring. I don't think they have any interest in stealing from you. I think we should play possum, but be ready to move quickly if anything changes.

"Don't text or email anything or anyone you don't want the government or the opposition to see. I'll monitor everything, but these guys are good, maybe the best I've seen so far. Any clue who might be behind all this?" she asked.

I took a few minutes before answering. "Well, I don't think it's the government. They always seem to be playing catch-up when it comes to technology. By the time they get through appropriations, budgets and their procurement procedures, any computer or software is already out of date. The government is light years behind private industry when it comes to IT. Anyone sophisticated enough to earn your praise wouldn't be working for the government. They'd make five times more working in private industry.

"I also don't think we can lay the blame on the lawyers. They don't have to cheat to win. And I know several of the lawyers at Romatowski. They would resign if they thought their clients had taken part in my abduction or were accessing my personal information. So, the short answer is no, I have no idea.

"Stella, Brian will give you a copy of the pleadings in the morning. Maybe they can give you some sense of what our client has done and why the government and the computer world want to put him away for good. My gut tells me the key lies in whatever software he's developed. Someone either wants it for himself or wants to make sure it's destroyed.

"Look, it's time for us to quit worrying about whether I should have taken this case and focus on defending my client. Let's eat— I'm starving."

After we had ordered dinner, I changed the subject by asking about mutual friends in Little Rock and what was new with their respective businesses. Clovis' detective agency had grown by leaps and bounds, and he was considering a merger with a national group. He said he needed the administrative help, especially since he was spending more and more time in DC. Red Shaw had employed his company to keep tabs on his star ballplayers, some of whom were easy prey for scam artists.

Walter had recently hired Stella as a consultant on computer issues, and Lisa had called on Clovis more than once when she faced a sticky problem. One of the things I liked about Lisa was that she had no reservations in seeking help when she needed it. Stella still operated her cross fit gym and complained that all the travel and computer security work for Walter Matthews was making her fat.

Over dinner, I came back to the difficulties we faced in representing David. To keep me from direct access to my client, the government would probably claim he was a risk to national security. They would oppose his release on bond for the same reason. The civil case would not demand the same urgency, but could be a thorn in my side, requiring our time and effort to respond to their lawyers' discovery requests. We discussed whether I should engage another firm to help, and I raised the possibility of asking Micki. Micki Lawrence had been my co-counsel in several major criminal cases in Little Rock, and we worked well together.

Clovis said, "Micki is overwhelmed with work right now. Little Rock's new U. S. Attorney is using the office to puff her own political profile. She has sued at least ten doctors in the last month for Medicare fraud, is investigating the local congressman for campaign finance violations, and to top it off, she's subpoenaed the Razorback Foundation's donor records for NCAA recruiting violations. She has a PR professional on staff and holds a press conference at least once a week. Micki represents several of the targets and has threatened to choke her new adversary—anything to shut her up. But if you called, I'm sure she would find a way to help."

"My money's on Micki, but I won't ask her yet. At this point, we don't even know what crime David is supposed to have committed."

17

⊷━━━━━⊶

CLOVIS AND I RETREATED TO THE BAR AFTER DINNER. Stella declined our invitation, claiming she needed her beauty rest. At my raised eyebrow, she noted that her workday would begin at four o'clock tomorrow morning, when she would begin scanning the Internet and her clients' computers for threats. Apparently, computer hackers do most their work while we're asleep, happily unaware of the dangers they pose.

I wasn't ready to go home to an empty condominium. Over a glass of Port, I filled Clovis in about Abby and the concerns I had raised with Thibodeaux. I trusted him implicitly, and my instincts told me he needed to know everything. He listened carefully but said nothing in response.

"Okay, Clovis," I sighed. "What's bothering you?"

He didn't beat around the bushes.

"Jack, your adversaries have been a step ahead of us the whole time. They had access to your meeting with Thibodeaux and knew about the guards Royce had hired at the hotel. Your identity was stolen, and you were lucky that Stella was able to interpret the message you sent from Abby's house. Otherwise, you'd be swimming with alligators right now. I bet they won't let Stella best them again. I wouldn't be surprised if they knew exactly what was said between you and Mrs. Ruple this afternoon."

I laughed, "All they learned from this afternoon was that Gloria has a large appetite for olives and gin."

"It's not a laughing matter," he frowned. "We've faced some dangerous people and circumstances together and always managed to come out alive. But this time… I've got a bad feeling."

"You're assuming there's only one person or group. I suspect we're dealing with at least three."

"Three," he paused. "Three?"

"Three. The government, the corporate entities who want David to disappear, and someone inside the Louisiana syndicate."

"You mean someone who wants to oust Thibodeaux?"

"I don't know who, or why. But someone within the syndicate is up to their neck in this business. I have no idea whether that person is working alone or is in cahoots with either the government or the tech companies. What I do know is the answers lie with David Ruple, whether he knows it or not."

Clovis asked, "Do you think the government will allow you access?"

"Experience tells me I'll have to jump through several hoops, but eventually they'll have to. You can't lock someone away, deny them counsel and their day in court forever. Not in America, at least not yet. The obvious exception, of course is Guantanamo. But to charge David as a terrorist would be more than a little far-fetched. From the little I know, David has designed a piece of software that has rocked the boat for both big business and the government. But it's not like he's blown up a building or shut down a pipeline. Hopefully, Stella will soon be able to tell us what all the fuss is about."

Clovis responded, "Stella may be able to figure out what we're dealing with, but she won't know the 'who.' You mentioned your meeting with Gloria Ruple. Did you learn anything?"

"She likes her martinis dry, her olives on the side, and does her best to make sure you know she's a sad specimen who's lonely and clueless."

"Royce seemed nervous about the meeting. It doesn't sound like he should have been concerned," Clovis commented.

"Oh, I think there's much more to Gloria Ruple than gin and makeup. Our meeting was a carefully orchestrated performance, contrived to throw me off guard. Only time will tell, but something tells me that Gloria Ruple is as smart and ruthless as they come. We need to keep our guard up with that one."

"You sure you're not a little paranoid?" Clovis asked.

"It's possible, but then, maybe I should be."

I watched Clovis as he absorbed what I had told him. He was usually quick on the uptake, and I valued both his intuition and his judgment. But the last few days had taken their toll on both of us. I needed sleep, and this conversation would have to wait. Like magic, Big Mike showed up.

On the way home, Mike explained that Lisa had arranged for someone to check out my condominium, sweep it for bugs, and stand watch during the night. There would be no abductions on her watch. Mike would drive me to work and be my primary protector during the day and early evenings.

"Is all this necessary? What if I want some privacy?" I grumbled.

"It may seem like overkill, but neither Lisa or Maggie are taking any chances, and this time I agree with them."

"Why?" I asked.

"Well, we were followed on the way to the Willard and trailed by two men when we went to the Madison. Please don't look, but there's a car on our tail right now. You've been followed since the moment your plane touched the ground, and not by us. Lisa is pulling her hair out trying to figure out who's so interested in your comings and goings, but so far, no luck. Whatever this case is about, someone is devoting a tremendous amount of time and resources to keep an eye on you."

I was tempted to flip the bird to the car following us but thought the better of it—a childish gesture unlikely to have a positive result. Best not aggravate the unfriendly. The question was why? I had been kidnapped and now followed before I knew squat about the case or had even met my client. Why the intense focus on me? So far, my adversaries were big businesses and the government. I hardly posed a threat to either.

Mike insisted on accompanying me into my building and handing me off to the man who was charged with guarding me tonight. I stopped at the front desk as usual to get my mail from the night clerk. She was an attractive woman in her thirties training for the Boston marathon. We usually engaged in a little harmless flirting and banter, but tonight there was no mail and no night clerk. It wasn't like her to be absent, and I was oddly disappointed. I missed her sweet "Goodnight, Mr. Patterson."

We took the elevator up to my floor; as soon as the door opened, we both knew something was wrong. The hall lights were out, and the door to my condominium was wide open.

Mike stuck out his arm to prevent me from going ahead of him and called out. "Jerry, everything okay?"

There was no response. Mike pulled his gun and approached the front door slowly, continuing to call out for Jerry. I followed at a healthy distance. He gave the open door a good kick—to frighten whoever might be in there, I supposed. No one appeared, but it was evident that someone had ransacked my home. Mike handed me his phone, told me to call nine-one-one and report a break-in. I was not to leave the entryway; he would search for Jerry.

The dispatcher was polite and quickly responsive, telling me the Metropolitan police were on their way. Mike returned with his gun holstered, assuring me that the bad guy or guys were gone. He'd found Jerry on the floor in my bedroom, unconscious, but alive. He took the phone from my hand and asked the dispatcher to send an ambulance. My home had been completely trashed. Every drawer had been opened; papers were everywhere. Yet my laptop sat on my desk undisturbed, and nothing seemed to have been stolen. I felt like I was watching a movie, that this was happening to someone else.

While we waited for the police and the medics, Mike called Lisa to give her a report and ask for backup. I wanted to go downstairs to check on the woman at the front desk, but Mike insisted I stay put and let the police find her.

The police and the medics arrived at about the same time. Fortunately, Jerry would be fine. He had no memory of what happened, but the huge gash and lump on the back of his head spoke for him. The medics insisted he go to the hospital. Questions by the police would have to wait. I must have looked as queasy and unnerved as I felt, because one of the medics asked me for my name and birthday and offered to get me a blanket. I asked about the woman at the front desk. The police had found her gagged and bound in the custodian's closet. She was terrified, but okay. Somehow three men in ski masks had been able to override security, enter the building, and snatch her in a matter of seconds.

Lisa arrived with three other security officers. She told me the police would take over the condo as a crime scene. She had arranged for me to stay at the Madison until the police had finished their work. While I packed, I asked her what they could have been after. They hadn't taken my laptop, and I usually keep my current work papers with me.

"I have no idea. Looks to me that whoever they are wanted to send a signal: You aren't safe. We can get you anytime we want!"

18

NEEDLESS TO SAY, I spent a restless night. Getting to sleep was tough enough, but waking up to the presence of a large, unfamiliar security guard in the room was too much. The least Lisa could have done was choose a guard who was as attractive as she was. Of course, I wasn't serious, but lack of sleep had left me in a bad mood.

I joined Clovis and Stella for breakfast. The food was a little fancy for my taste—I had no use for "poached eggs served over arugula with yogurt and chili oil." But the coffee was hot, and I managed to talk the waiter into pancakes with sausage, so my mood improved.

Over a second cup of coffee, I told them what had happened last night and how Lisa had reacted.

"She's probably right," Clovis said. "The intruders left your computer intact as a message. 'We can get to you whenever we want, and we don't need your computer to access every bit of information you have.' Jack, this must be the computer companies playing mind games."

"That's the most logical conclusion. I just can't believe reputable lawyers would stoop so low. I'll ask Maggie to call them the first thing this morning. It's amazing what people will admit to a woman with a British accent. Stella, is there any way to protect our information?"

"I've cleared the decks and put my other clients on hold until I find a solution, except for Walter. He's in constant fear that the company will become a target of someone seeking ransomware. He's glad I'm in town," she answered.

Clovis added, "Lisa has asked Martin to join us this morning to discuss everyone's security. We can use his expertise. I'll alert Royce. I want to make sure Beth and Jeff are safe."

"Right. You know, it occurs to me that we've fallen into their trap. We're so focused on security we've neglected our primary focus—defending David Ruple. By the way, when you meet with Lisa—no offense to last night's fellow, but can you ask for a better-looking guard?" I grinned.

"Now, whose mind is distracted? You should be ashamed." Stella replied sternly.

I noticed Mike standing at the hostess desk, waiting to escort us to the office. He wasn't happy when I suggested we walk. But it was a beautiful morning, and I think better strolling the streets of DC, rather than dodging cars and bike couriers.

Maggie already had coffee brewing and her tea kettle was whistling. As a welcome back treat, she had ordered muffins and pastries from her favorite Georgetown bakery. Clovis and I munched happily while Maggie and Stella caught up. We had decided to split into two groups. Brian, Maggie, Stella, and I remained in the conference room, while Clovis, Martin, Lisa, and Big Mike gathered in the spare office to talk security. We divided the croissants as well.

Maggie began, "Jack, you and I are scheduled to meet with the lawyers for the computer companies at eleven this morning at the Dooley law firm."

"I thought Romatowski was taking the lead." I said with a frown. "I was just about to ask you to call them about what happened last night."

Brian answered, "When I called a paralegal I know at Romatowski to schedule the meeting, she said they had withdrawn their representation. She and I are old friends, and after much cajoling she told me the partners had held a very hush-hush, closed-door meeting a few days ago. She didn't know what was discussed, but after the meeting Pete told her to package up all the files and send them to the Dooley firm."

"I bet they got wind of what their clients were up to and wanted nothing to do with them or the representation," I mused. "It would mean a huge financial hit to the firm, but you can't buy integrity. Good for them."

Brian asked, "Do you want me to try to find out more?"

"No. The files are already out the door, and they won't gossip about it. Not to you or anyone else. Who's the lead lawyer from Dooley?"

Maggie answered, "That's the bad news. It's Jordyn Duarte."

"Damn," I mumbled. Jordyn was one of the country's most successful trial lawyers, but no one enjoyed working for her or against her. Her nickname was "The Ice Queen," and her staff lived in constant fear of her explosions. Associates assigned to her had zero social life and seldom lasted more than a few months. The only time she was charming was with a trial judge, when butter wouldn't melt in her mouth. Opposing counsel quickly learned that she took no prisoners: make even the tiniest procedural mistake and she would seek sanctions and report the offender to the Bar's ethics committee. I should have expected her to be the lead in a case of this magnitude. I had yet to face her in court, but her reputation was formidable.

"Well, okay. Now at least we know who we're up against. What else, Maggie?"

"Take your pick: the meeting with Jordyn, your appointment with the client, or the latest from Gloria Ruple? We can wait a while to discuss the call Walter received, or what you are going to tell Red this afternoon."

"I have a feeling I need to hear it all. Let me get another cup of coffee, and a blueberry muffin, and I promise you'll have my total attention, no interruptions."

I left before she could object. I didn't need another muffin nearly as much as I needed a few minutes to recover from the Jordyn Duarte news. I fussed with the coffee and returned with the remainder of the muffins and pastries.

Maggie refused my offerings and resumed her recital of bad news.

"The Duarte meeting is at the Dooley firm because it's one of the few DC firms with a conference room large enough to hold all the lawyers who've demanded to attend. Jordyn is the lead, but every client wants their own counsel in attendance."

I said, "They call a flock of crows a murder. I wonder what the term is for a room full of lawyers?"

That brought a smile even to Maggie's face.

She continued, "The good news is the U.S. Attorney's office has no objection to you meeting with David. They scheduled the meeting for two o'clock this afternoon."

"Well, that's interesting—a bit of a puzzle. I felt sure they would invoke 'national security' and try to limit access."

"It's certainly unexpected. They also said we could read the indictment after you sign a confidentiality agreement. They're supposed to email it over this morning. They would like to meet with you late this afternoon to talk about a convenient time to hold the arraignment. They even mentioned discussing bail terms this afternoon." Maggie continued.

"Really? I thought we'd have to do battle on every single item. This news is almost too good to be true."

Maggie gave me a knowing smile. "Well, there is one problem."

"I knew it. How bad is it?" I asked, wondering how much worse it could get.

"That depends on your point of view. Gloria has engaged a lawyer to represent David. Apparently, she wasn't happy after your meeting with her at the Willard. Not only did she call Royce to complain, but she also called her friend at Williams and Connelly. He told her his firm had a conflict but did give her a recommendation. She had dinner with the lawyer last night and called early this morning to let me know that you've been fired. Both the Cooley firm and the U.S. Attorney received similar calls this morning."

I smiled. "That's not the end of the world. The ultimate call on attorney representation is David's. I'm getting tired of being followed, and the threats on my life are getting old. If David's happy with Gloria's choice, we can politely bow out. I'll make it right with Thibodeaux. Who is the lucky lawyer?" My day had suddenly gotten a whole lot better.

Maggie answered, "That's the bad news. Duke Madigan."

It took a long minute to absorb the shock. Duke Madigan wasn't just a piece of work; he was a terrible lawyer. He had been disciplined by the DC bar at least half a dozen times. He always wore a buckskin coat and cowboy hat in court and chased after every camera and talk show host in town. I had no doubt he had charmed Gloria, but he was the last lawyer you'd want if you were in real trouble.

"Boy, Maggie, you sure know how to turn good news into bad, and in a hurry!" I sighed. "I feel a headache coming on."

"Now you know why the Dooley firm and the U.S. Attorney are suddenly cooperative," she said. "You're a formidable opponent, but you would never attempt to try this case in the press and the talk shows. Madigan has already called this morning. He wants to come by before his press conference to arrange for an 'orderly transition'—his very words."

"He's holding a press conference before he's even met his client?" The man's conceit knew no limits.

"I told him your schedule was very busy, that I doubted you'd have the time to meet with him."

"I really wouldn't mind turning this matter over to another attorney, but I can't in good conscience let David engage this jerk without at least a warning. Time to call Royce," I sighed.

Maggie interrupted, "Before you dig yourself a deeper hole, you promised to listen. There's more."

"More?" I asked. What else could there be?

"I was followed home last night. And Walter got a call yesterday suggesting that he encourage us to not take the case. Of course, the caller may be having second thoughts now that Gloria has intervened. Red got a similar call, but his came from the Pentagon. He said not to worry, that you should represent 'whomever you damn well please.' But he did call. When you get a minute, you might return the call. Apparently, Lucy was approached as well."

Lucy Robinson is the junior senator from Arkansas and is married to Red Shaw. I've known Lucy since college; we've had a sort-of love-hate relationship over the years. It didn't help that my best friend murdered her first husband, or that I defended him in court, but that's another story.

"You know I promised Walter that I wouldn't involve you in

another dangerous case. Brian and I can take it from here."

Maggie scowled. "I'll make the decision about if or when I should I walk away. I'm okay and so is Walter, at least for now. Besides, if Gloria has her way, you and I will be out of work by this afternoon, with plenty of time to spare."

"Anything else? Any more surprises?" I asked, not sure how much more I could stand.

"I think you have quite enough on your plate," she answered.

"Okay," I took a deep breath. "First, I'll call Louisiana. They warned me that Gloria would be a pain, but if she has her way, David could be looking at a train wreck. I've never known Duke to end up with a satisfied client. He may be a dandy on the talk shows, but his clients end up breaking rocks. Let me see if Royce and Tom have any suggestions.

"Brian, please go over the confidentiality agreement with a fine tooth. I'd like to be able to sign it, but I don't want to give away the farm. Maggie, ask Stella to do her best to keep our systems secure. But more importantly, she needs to continue to scour the civil complaint. I'm counting on her to figure out why David's software has everyone so riled up."

Stella looked up from her computer. "While Maggie's been giving you the bad news, I've been scanning for bugs and malware. Something very sophisticated has infected your systems. The good news is that I don't think anyone can listen to your conversations, but I suspect any document you review online is compromised. I'll do my best to figure it all out, but it may take a little longer than usual."

"Thanks, Stella. I bet that's why they, whoever they are, left my laptop in the condo last night. They can already download anything they like, and probably already have. Fortunately, there's nothing on that laptop that pertains to this case. We haven't had time to scan even Lula's information yet. You sure my phone calls are safe?"

"As sure as I can be. But I'm..."

"That's good enough for me." I said with a smile.

In fact, none of us had ever heard the slightest trace of doubt from Stella before now. It was more than a little unnerving.

"Okay," I said after a minute's silence. "Let's move on. We only have an hour before we're supposed to be at the Dooley firm. Maggie, let Mike know we need to leave a little before eleven. Brian, why don't you come with us. The other side will bring an entire 'murder' of lawyers, so we might as well and show up in full force. Besides, you've never met the 'Ice Queen.' You're in for a real treat."

19

ROYCE ASSURED ME that David seldom listened to his mother and would never hire Duke. He said that David was anxious to meet me and understood that I had been hand-picked by his grandfather. I told Royce that the U.S. Attorney seemed to be a reasonable person and might be agreeable to bail. Royce wasn't counting his chickens but was excited about the possibility of bail. As for Royce talking sense into Gloria, that was another matter.

"I've tried, but she's not taking my calls. Maybe you'll have better luck, headstrong is where she begins. Try to find a way to keep her happy."

"Great," I thought. "You've asked me to handle a case that's impossible to defend, thrown in a few people trying to kill me, and given me a wild card mother who cares more about herself than her son. And I should 'keep her happy.' Can you make my job any more difficult?"

Maggie, Big Mike, and I were soon headed to the Dooley law firm. Brian begged off; he was knee deep reviewing the confidentiality agreement sent over by the U.S. Attorney's office. Apparently, it wasn't a boiler plate form.

The Dooley firm's offices were not what one might expect from a large traditional law firm—no paneled walls or deep leather chairs. Instead, the office looked more like a startup technology company with large yoga balls and bean bag chairs in the lobby. The receptionist, Brandy, didn't sit behind a desk but roamed the lobby wearing jeans, tennis shoes, and a tight, V-necked sweater. I could see wireless ear buds hanging from her ears. She was very friendly and smirked at Maggie's obvious disapproval.

Brandy escorted us to the second-floor conference room. I was relieved to see a large, contemporary table and chairs; asking Maggie to sit on a ball chair would have been a bit much. There was no sign of a coffee pot or the pastries I had hoped for. We politely declined the Kombucha or Green Juice Brandy offered. The look on Mike's face was priceless.

As expected, big law firm dynamics were in full force. Brandy closed the doors as she left, and we sat in silence. I decided to give them ten minutes. We had just pushed back our chairs to leave when the door opened, and a team of young associates entered in single file. They remained standing, backs against the walls; no one said a word. I noted that the male associates were empty-handed, while each female carried a legal pad or file. I glanced at Maggie, who was trying her best not to laugh.

Next, a cadre of attorneys who must have represented the plaintiffs marched in and took their seats at the conference table. The men gave me a casual nod and tossed business cards down the table. The three women were a bit more polite, offering smiles along with their cards. Maggie gathered the cards while we waited for the curtain to rise. I chose to ignore the smiling young woman who had been strategically placed directly across from me at the table. Any attempt at small talk would have been absurd.

None of these games and tactics bothered me; I enjoyed playing the underdog. Maggie, on the other hand, was no longer amused, even though she knew the scene had been carefully contrived. I whispered to her, "Having fun yet?" I wondered how they would react if I asked for a Bloody Mary.

Jordyn appeared at the door and walked directly to the head of the table, three more associates in tow. I had no idea how she'd earned her nickname. There had been rumors, but I refused to play that game. I watched as she carefully assembled her papers and positioned her computer before she sat down. She wasn't physically attractive, at least not to me. She was of average height, average build, and wore little make-up. I noticed that her pale brown hair was well cut, and even I could tell her clothes weren't from Macy's. The force of her presence derived not from any physical attributes, but from her keen intelligence and strong determination to win at all costs.

One of the associates held the chair for her and then blended into the wall with the others. I felt sorry for the guy. He had gone to an Ivy League law school, graduated magna cum laude, and now his job was to hold the chair for a senior partner and provide her with ice water with fresh lemon. Surely this wasn't part of his dream when he sat through torts class.

Jordyn didn't waste time. "Welcome, Mr. Patterson. I hope Brandy made you comfortable."

"She was most hospitable. We may go roller skating later," I replied. Maggie couldn't suppress a giggle—Jordyn wasn't amused.

"My associates will give you the discovery requests we have for your client. These include requests for documents, written inter-rogatories, and notices for depositions, none of which should be a surprise to you. But one problem has come to light that we need to clear up first. We received a phone call from Duke Madigan this morning. I assume you know who he is. He claims that he has been engaged by Mrs. Ruple to handle this matter and that your representation had been terminated. I was tempted to cancel this meeting until the issues of representation has been clarified, but my colleagues convinced me to give you the opportunity to explain. Can you assure me that you do in fact represent Mr. Ruple?"

My first instinct was to cry uncle, pick up my papers and walk out the door behind Maggie and Mike. This woman had her game face on, and it wasn't friendly or vaguely collegial. The lawyers sit-ting at the table were waiting for an answer. Charm would not be the right approach.

"I'm scheduled to meet with David Ruple this afternoon," I replied, careful to keep an even tone. "If the meeting goes as I expect, he will sign the requisite engagement letter, assuring you or anyone else that I, and I alone, represent David Ruple. I'll be happy to provide you with a copy.

"I think you're smart enough to know that Mr. Madigan is blowing smoke. Duke has not met or spoken with David, nor does he have an engagement letter. I have no idea what he's up to, but I can assure you that Duke does not represent David Ruple. Let's quit playing games and get down to business. I asked for this meeting, and I appreciate the Dooley firm for providing such an impressive venue. Since the government has brought criminal charges against my client, I hope to work out a stay of your litigation and discuss the possibility of resolving your complaint without costly and extended litigation. The government has already seized all my client's assets. Extended litigation isn't likely to benefit anyone."

My statement brought murmurs from the lawyers at the table. Jordyn's cold gaze soon quieted the room.

"Your naïve expectation reflects a lack of understanding of the litigation we brought. There will be no stay, nor will there be a quick resolution unless your client wants to forfeit the software and sign a cease and desist. I know you are new to this case, but once you understand what your client has done, you'll wipe that smug look off your face and agree to the remedies we have proposed."

I felt Maggie's hand grip my knee. I took a deep breath but didn't respond. Long silences make most people uncomfortable, and the lawyers around the table began to squirm. Realizing I wouldn't take the bait, Jordyn continued.

"Cat got your tongue, Mr. Patterson? You're in the big leagues now, and your tricks or charm won't get you to first base. I suggest you tell that Louisiana thug who engaged you that you've bitten off more than you can chew. Oh, yes—we know who's paying your fees. Don't think for a moment we won't use David's family against him should this case ever come to trial. I doubt a DC jury will have much sympathy for the grandson of a mob boss."

Maggie's grip on my leg tightened. Now I thought she might be the one to lose her cool. I gave her a smile and rose from my chair. I had noticed several cameras in the room and felt sure that the whole charade was being telecast to the clients. Rather than respond to Jordyn, I looked straight at the camera above her head.

"You know, Jordyn, I've been thinking. All these lawyers must cost your collective clients a pretty penny. I bet your hourly rate alone would choke a horse. If this farce cost my client, say—five hundred

dollars for the hour it has taken, I bet all these lawyers doing absolutely nothing must have cost your clients at least fifty thousand
dollars. That's a lot of money for twiddling thumbs and dirty looks.
Frankly, I'd be embarrassed to charge my client for this exercise in
futility. What d'you say, let's agree not to charge our clients for this
meeting since nothing was accomplished. Do we have a deal?"

"What we charge our clients is none of your business," she
snapped.

I returned her scowl with a big smile and turned to Maggie.
"Come on, Maggie, we have work to do. You're correct, Ms. Duarte.
How much you charge your clients is none of my business, but I will
say one thing I like about this case so far—I like the odds."

"Odds? What odds?" She looked genuinely confused.

"Five hundred to fifty thousand every hour we spend together is
one hundred to one. I like the odds."

20

ON THE WAY BACK TO THE OFFICE I pondered the fact that the opposition knew about my arrangement with Thibodeaux. I wasn't worried that David's case could be harmed. Who paid my fees was irrelevant to any part of the case. Any judge would throw out an attempt to sully the case by raising Thibodeaux's reputation. I was concerned because I was now certain that someone inside Thibodeaux's organization was leaking to the opposition. Who and why?

"Maggie, when we get to the office, please tell Stella that Jordyn knows all about our arrangement with Thibodeaux. I'll call Royce. We need to discuss confidentiality, sooner rather than later. It's going to be hard to defend David if the opposition is aware of our strategies before we can put them into action."

*****

I found Brian sitting at a small table in my office, reading the agreement the U.S. Attorney had sent over.

"It's not like any agreement I've ever seen. It's more like a gag order than a confidentiality agreement," he said. "It's as if the government is more concerned about the public discovering that David's software exists, rather than its purpose. They ask you to agree not to make any public statement about the litigation and to limit any discussion about the case to your client, attorneys, and staff who have signed the agreement—and of course the judge.

"They've asked the court to place all pleadings under seal and to close any hearings to both the press and spectators. I don't know how this is going to work with a civil suit going on at the same time. But they do hold out quite a carrot if you agree to their terms."

"Okay, I'll bite. What's the carrot?"

"Unrestricted access to David, beginning this afternoon," he replied. "They'll also support David's release from custody without bail if he agrees to their conditions regarding use of computers and compliance with the confidentiality agreement. Of course, the judge will have the final say about bail, but they assure me they're not playing games."

"Hmmph—sounds too good to be true. But I can't agree to waive David's rights without his permission. Will they let me meet with him before I sign the agreement?"

"They didn't want to, but I reminded them that you couldn't very well sign something your client hasn't even seen. If you and David are willing to go forward under their terms, they'll ask the judge to schedule an arraignment and bail hearing. Our meeting with David is at two o'clock this afternoon. You get one hour with him. Next, we meet with the U.S. attorney and his deputies. They seem to have quite the team working on this case."

"Okay, work with Maggie on an engagement letter. I'll go over the confidentiality agreement to see if I can live with its terms. From what you describe, the judge will probably have more trouble with the closed courtroom than I do. Jordyn can deal with him on that issue. I still want to look the U.S. Attorney in the eye before I sign anything, but at least we'll be able to meet David and get this ball rolling. Jordyn was her usual charming self today, but I can't imagine the judge will let the civil case go forward until the criminal case is concluded, no matter what the Ice Queen wants."

Brian and Maggie went to work on the engagement letter, while I tried to follow the terms of the confidentiality agreement which I found to be a poorly crafted document. Government attorneys are used to litigating, not drafting agreements. Moreover, this instrument was trying to keep confidential a criminal process that is designed to be public and transparent.

More troubling were the conditions the government wanted to impose on David. How could he agree to limiting his use of computers since they were his livelihood? The gag order applied to him as well. Would he agree to refrain from even acknowledging the existence of his software in exchange for freedom?

Time flew, and before long we were going through security at the federal courthouse to finally meet with David Ruple. We were escorted to a small conference room where a deputy U.S. marshal explained the rules of the interview. As I had expected, the rules included the prohibition of phones, computers, or any other electronic device. I agreed and added that we hoped to have David sign an engagement letter.

Brian offered both the letter and a pen to the deputy, who inspected both, nodded his approval and said he would remain just outside the door in case we needed him. His easy-going attitude came as a pleasant surprise. The last time I had represented a defendant with national security implications, the FBI had insisted on sitting in during my initial interview.

David entered the room escorted by another deputy. He was wearing the typical orange jumpsuit with chains attached to his wrists and ankles. To my surprise the deputy quickly unlocked the chains and left the room with the other deputy. So far, the U.S. attorney had kept his promise.

Slight of build and bookish in appearance, David evidenced no kinship to his grandfather. His dark, curly hair was long on top, but almost buzzed on the sides. He wore thick wire-rimmed glasses. Yet he had a winning smile, and when we shook hands, his grip was firm. He didn't appear to have suffered any indignities in jail, but I had to ask how he was holding up.

He gave me a rueful smile, rubbed his cheek, and replied, "I'm okay, mostly just bored. And I guess I could use a shave."

I gestured toward the small table, and after we were all as comfortable as possible, I began, "David, we only have an hour, so let's cut to the chase. Your grandfather has asked me to represent you and has offered to pay my fees, but the ultimate decision regarding a lawyer is yours. Your mother has engaged a lawyer to represent you as well, and if you're interested, I suggest you interview him too. You may also know a totally different attorney you'd prefer to use."

David held up his hand to stop me.

"I'm already aware of my mother's attempts to control this process. When I heard that grandfather had chosen you, I did some research in the jail library. I can't imagine why you'd take my case, and frankly, I don't want to know what hold my grandfather has on you. But if you're willing to represent me, I'd be a fool not to accept. Thank you.

"There is one condition. You must tell grandfather that I'll repay him. The marshal told me the government has seized my business and bank accounts. I want him to know that once this is over, I intend to pay back every dime if it takes me the rest of my life. I have never asked my family to support me, and I don't want to be beholden to any of them, no matter what the circumstances. Do you understand?"

I was impressed and told him so, adding, "David, if you're uncomfortable with your grandfather paying my fees, we can work something out. You're the client, no matter who pays my bill, and I will take my direction from you."

"No, I'll feel better if you're paid upfront," he replied. "I don't understand what I'm supposed to have done, but I know I'm in deep shit. I was an independent contractor myself, and I know that when I wasn't worried about being paid, I didn't think about cutting corners. I need you to pull out all the stops, hire whatever experts you need, without being worried about money. My grandfather understands this. My mother wouldn't. She'd expect any lawyer she hires to do it on the cheap."

I offered to go over the terms of the engagement letter, but he declined, took it from my hand and signed it on the spot.

"Now can you please tell me why I'm in jail?

I couldn't. But I did my best to explain what little I knew about the government charges, the civil complaint, and the confidentiality order the government wanted us both to sign. By the time I'd finished, our hour had slipped away. Brian gathered the papers, and I waited while David gathered his thoughts.

"Mr. Patterson, I'd do just about anything to get out of here. The software is no big deal. How could it be? I designed it as a favor for my cousin. If they'll let me go back to my business and my girlfriend,

I'll gladly let the government have it. But something tells me there must be more to it. Have you talked to Rita? Is she okay?"

The marshal had opened the door quietly and was now waiting patiently.

"No, I haven't talked to Rita, but she's next on my list. From what Royce tells me, she's okay, but frightened for you. Let me start the process of getting you out of here. We'll have plenty of time to talk about the software and how we might resolve this matter quickly."

We shook hands and the marshal escorted David back to his cell. I called Royce on the way to the U.S. Attorney's office. I told him that our meeting had gone well, and that David intended to pay Tom back every penny.

"No surprise there," he said. "I'll tell Mr. Thibodeaux about David's condition to your representation; he won't be surprised either. David's desire for independence is one reason the young man is his grandfather's favorite. But you have a bigger problem: Gloria. She's demanding that we pay Madigan's fees, including a two hundred-thousand-dollar retainer."

"David has signed an engagement letter with me," I responded. "She'll calm down, and Duke won't hang around when he knows he isn't getting a retainer."

Royce responded, "I hope you're right, but I wouldn't bet on it."

2 1

The U.S. Attorney for the District of Columbia works for the Attorney General, but his offices aren't at "Main Justice," the enormous Robert F. Kennedy Department of Justice building on Pennsylvania Avenue. Rather, the federal government rents space at Judiciary Center on 4th St. for DC's U.S. Attorney.

Brian and I found security at this building to be much more intrusive and thorough than it had been at the courthouse. As I was being frisked and prodded, I wondered if all the increased security worked. I suppose we'll never know what horrors might have been thwarted, but our daily routines have certainly been altered. I miss being able to walk straight into a building or onto an airplane wearing my shoes. Maybe the terrorists have already won.

The reception area presented a sharp contrast to the Dooley offices. The receptionist's desk was an old metal desk, the kind you usually see in car repair shops, and the chairs were the cheap metal chairs found in every government building around the country.

The receptionist greeted us with a gravelly voice, "Have a seat. Someone will be with you soon."

Unfortunately, all the chairs were currently occupied by other lawyers and their clients waiting to meet Mr. or Ms. Someone. Brian found an empty corner, and we stood watching the receptionist at her job. She greeted each person who came to the desk with the same tired, chain-smoking voice: "Have a seat, someone will be with you soon." As we waited, I wondered how long she'd had this job and whether she had nightmares about arriving at the pearly gates and being told, "Have a seat…"

Just as I had decided that not another soul could fit in the reception area, a young woman opened the door and said, "Mr. Patterson? Please come with me."

We followed her down a series of winding halls with closed doors until she opened one, and we were ushered into a good-sized room with a walnut conference table, comfortable chairs, and tall windows with a view of downtown DC. Having worked at the Justice Department I knew the government had plenty of windowless conference rooms with scarred tables and wobbly chairs. This conference room was for the big dogs, and I didn't mean me.

My instincts were proven right when U.S. Attorney George Deacon, two deputies, and a chief deputy from the Justice Department's Criminal Division strode into the room. I introduced Brian and they introduced themselves, each giving Brian a business card. He gave them one of mine, thus fulfilling the time-honored procedure when well-schooled lawyers meet. Deacon opened the conversation.

"I appreciate your coming here to meet with us. I understand you met with Mr. Ruple. I take it from your presence that you will represent him in this matter?"

I knew exactly who was on his mind: Duke Madigan. "David signed an engagement letter with my firm this afternoon. I will represent him in this matter as well as the civil case. If you need a copy of the letter, we'll either fax or email a copy to your office later today. I'll give Mr. Madigan and David's mother the good news after we conclude our business this afternoon. But let me assure you that my firm alone represents David Ruple."

The relief on their faces was apparent. "Thanks! That *is* good news," said the U.S. Attorney with a grin.

At that point the deputy from Main Justice took over. Although I had never dealt directly with William Stanford, I knew him by reputation. The Attorney General almost always called on him to take the lead in complex criminal cases, especially those involving espionage or terrorism. David's case was clearly a matter of high priority.

Stanford was Harvard educated, both undergraduate and law.

He was known for being tough, thorough, and totally prepared. The phrase "take no prisoners" comes to mind, except that was exactly what he did. The unlucky souls he prosecuted usually spent the rest of their lives behind bars. The government had brought in the "A team" against David Ruple.

He didn't waste any time. "I take it that you have read the confidentiality agreement that was sent to your office. Are you and your client willing to sign the document?"

I answered, "Yes, we are. But I foresee one difficulty. Until a judge stays the civil proceedings, I must do whatever is necessary to defend that litigation. I met with Jordyn Duarte and her associates this morning and got the clear impression they're unwilling to stay their litigation. Until we get a Judge to slow her down, I need you to modify your confidentiality agreement so it doesn't tie my hands."

Stanford replied, "I feel sure we can come to a compromise with you regarding the civil litigation. Let me give it some thought. We'll send you a revised agreement tomorrow morning."

"Brian has told me that you won't oppose reasonable bail for my client. Is that true?" I asked.

Stanford responded, "That's correct. If your client signs the confidentiality agreement and consents to reasonable restrictions on the use of computers, I see no reason to be a horse's ass about bail. I feel sure the judge will want some financial security, and your client will need to surrender his passport, maybe wear an ankle monitor. But as of now I see no reason for him to be held behind bars before trial or a guilty plea.

"We can schedule an arraignment in a couple of days. Once the confidentiality agreements have been modified and executed by you and your client, we'll provide you with a copy of the indictment. We're currently examining your client's computers and bank accounts to determine his source of income. If we don't discover anything sinister, we'll release his bank accounts so he can live until trial."

I returned his genial smile, wondering if we had landed in Wonderland. His reasonable attitude should have been reassuring, but I felt sure the other shoe would soon drop. I decided to push for a little more generosity.

"Thank you. I know David will appreciate being able to sleep in his own bed. While we're at it, perhaps we should begin a conversation about how to resolve this matter."

His eyebrows came together in a frown and his tone took on the seriousness of a father's lecture.

"Mr. Patterson, you are clearly unaware of what your client has done. If I were you, I'd wait until you've read the indictment before you start plea negotiations. Please don't misinterpret my willingness to be reasonable before trial as anything other than a show of good faith. We fully intend to prosecute your client to the fullest extent allowed by law."

SO MUCH FOR GENEROSITY. I had no desire to linger, so I glanced at Brian who, with instinctive timing, had already gathered his papers. I thanked Stanford for the meeting, nodded politely at the others, and we were soon out the door. Stanford hadn't engaged in any trash talk or bragging. He had portrayed confidence and professionalism while emphasizing the gravity of David's situation. He appeared to be a reasonable man, but neither his words nor his manner had lessened my concern for David's future.

Big Mike joined us as we walked back to the office. He confirmed that we had been followed again. "It's strange—They haven't tried to hide or avoid detection. And Maggie asked me to let you know that Duke Madigan's been calling the office. He's still asking about the transition of the files."

I sighed: One more thing to deal with—the checklist was growing. I wanted to consult with a patent and trademark expert about how to protect intellectual property such as software. I needed to meet with his girlfriend before I saw David again. And I had neglected my regular clients for far too long, especially Red. My next few days were going to be packed.

I turned to Mike. "Call Maggie and ask her to get us a table in the back room at Tony Sharp's. We need to get organized and might as well enjoy a good meal while we're at it."

Tony Sharp's had become one of my favorite watering holes in DC. Tony had converted the first floor of an older office building into a barbeque restaurant with tables both inside and out on a shady patio. I'm of the opinion that no one in DC produces real barbecue, the kind that's tended for hours in big wood-smokers, but Tony comes damn close. The aroma from his smokers drives people crazy, and his sides are just what you'd expect at a southern barbecue joint—cole slaw, onion rings, grilled corn on the cob, fresh butter beans, okra, and first-rate hush puppies—crispy on the outside and light as a feather inside. He serves only two desserts: banana pudding and soft serve vanilla ice cream. Either is the perfect ending to a meal of chopped brisket, pulled pork, or dry rubbed ribs. I'd known Tony for years and never had any trouble getting a table.

Mike looked worried. "Do you think that's a good idea? All of us in one location?"

"Mike, if we aren't safe with you, Lisa, Brian, and Clovis at our table, then we aren't safe anywhere. Tell Maggie to make sure Lisa joins us. We won't get anything done if we're looking over our shoulder all the time."

Clovis and Stella were the first to join us. I'd introduced them to Tony's long ago, and they'd quickly become regulars. We used to kid Tony about his rules for finding good barbeque. "Never eat barbeque at a place that serves asparagus. Never eat barbeque at a restaurant that gives you little white napkins," and my personal favorite, "never eat barbeque at a place that doesn't have at least five pick-up trucks in the parking lot." Tony never served asparagus and made sure there was a large roll of paper towels on every table. As for the pick-ups, Tony said parking in DC was scarce and too expensive for most folks. Tony's clientele came via the Metro, cab, bus or even limousine.

Maggie and Lisa soon joined us, and we ordered a rack of dry-rub ribs, fried okra, and hush puppies for starters. It had taken Maggie a good while to get used to the idea of eating ribs. She still ate them with a knife and a fork, ignoring the stares of less dainty diners. But she'd taken to the idea of fried okra almost immediately, declaring that anything so strange must be healthy. We all have our little rationalizations. Without them, how could we eat anything in good conscience?

The corner of my eye caught a sudden movement just outside

the front door. A child could have recognized the two men as security guards.

"Lisa, let's ask your guys to join us. They're bound to be hungry," I suggested. "It's early, and we can pull up some more chairs."

"Not a chance, Jack," she snapped. "They're on duty. And by the way, one of their duties is to be obvious. Maggie told me you'd insist on meeting in public—though why on earth is beyond me! Mike did tell you, didn't he, that you've been followed all day?"

"He did," I replied, trying without success to keep a neutral tone. "That's exactly why I decided we should meet out in the open air. This gathering is meant to signal that we will not be intimidated, that we will conduct our business as usual. Besides, I'm hungry for barbecue, Tony's barbecue. Any questions?" I waited, but she had no response. "Now can you please give me an overview of what you and Clovis have worked out regarding security. Not the details, just an overview."

Clovis cleared his throat and responded. "Well, we decided your request for better looking guards would be tough to fulfill, so Stella and I will move into your guest bedroom this evening. At least one of us is better looking. Lisa has also arranged for a detail to watch your building twenty-four seven."

"I'm sure my neighbors will be grateful," I commented with a frown.

He chose to ignore my sarcasm and continued.

"Big Mike will oversee your security and transportation during the day. He'll decide how much back-up he needs depending on the circumstances. Maggie and Walter already have their own detail, and Lisa has told them of the increased danger. Stella, why don't you tell Jack what you've discovered so far."

Stella spoke up before I could complain. "All of our phones and computers are being monitored by as complex and sophisticated a technology as I've ever come across. First, I'm going to create a cone of silence in your office so you can talk without being overheard. Next, I'll see what I can do to protect your computers—all our computers, for that matter. That could take a while, hopefully not more than a day or so. I've ordered some burn phones so we can communicate without worrying about eavesdroppers."

Lisa interrupted, "Do you think my phone has been compromised?"

"I wouldn't be surprised. I need to check all our phones, as well as those of anyone else who is guarding Jack or Maggie. And Brian, of course—he's both a guard and a colleague. Jack, I doubt you talk business with Beth, but I can check her phone remotely if you like."

I told her that wouldn't be necessary. I didn't want a public discussion about my daughter's security. I would pull Clovis aside later.

I waited while our server delivered our chopped pork sandwiches and sides. "Okay, Stella. Sounds like you're doing all you can. For now, we must assume everything we say and do is being monitored. It's damned irritating, but we can work around it. Let's focus on the job at hand. Brian, get in touch with David's girlfriend, Rita Gonzalez. Ask her to meet us at the office tomorrow, preferably tomorrow morning, and arrange for us to meet with David again. We need to prepare him for the arraignment, discuss the terms of his release, and get some inkling about what his software does.

"Maggie, email the engagement letter to both Jordyn and the U.S. Attorney's office. And follow up with hard copy, please. Work with Brian on the revised confidentiality agreement to make sure we can live with its terms as we try to deal with civil litigation and a criminal indictment at the same time. I don't mind being gagged, but I won't be handcuffed.

"Clovis, please call Royce to give him an update. Stella, once you've made us as safe as you can, I need you to turn your attention to the software. What exactly does it do, and how can David make it less offensive to the feds. Despite what Jordyn said, if we can get the indictment dropped, I feel sure we can come to some compromise with the tech companies. Now, let's enjoy this feast. Lisa, please pass the ribs."

Maggie asked, "Haven't you left someone out? What will you be doing while we work our fingers to the bone?"

I smiled, "I'm going to meet with Duke and Gloria. Anyone want to trade places?"

There were no takers.

2 3

—◇—

I WAITED UNTIL AFTER DINNER to call Duke Madigan, using Lisa's phone. He insisted we meet for breakfast at the Willard. No, Gloria wouldn't be joining us. Apparently, she wasn't an early riser. I allowed myself a small sigh of relief, feeling much like George Deacon had the day before. Duke and I agreed to meet at nine o'clock, giving me ample time to pick up a copy of the engagement letter at the office and think through what I was going to say.

We went our separate ways after dinner. Clovis and Stella were serious about spending the night in my guest room, so Mike drove the three of us back to my place. Once we were settled, a thoughtful Stella departed for the condominium's gym so Clovis and I could relax. I knew that several of Martin's men were on duty in the building, but thankfully they were unobtrusive, almost invisible.

I pulled a bottle of cabernet from the wine fridge, poured myself a glass and handed Clovis a Wicked Weed Pernicious IPA—his current beverage of choice. I nodded toward the den, and we sat for a while in silence, nursing both our drinks and our thoughts. I was the first to voice mine. "Look, Clovis, I'm sorry I gave Lisa a hard time. But this emphasis on protection is making me nuts. I can't help David or anyone else if I don't have space to think. Lisa and Martin have got to find a way to give me some freedom. Do whatever you need to do for Maggie and Brian, but I will go batshit crazy if you're all walking in my footsteps."

His harsh response stopped me cold. "Okay, Jack, but you take care. You can't help David, or anyone else, if you're dead. Didn't you learn anything in that swamp?" He took a deep breath. "Sorry. I'll see what I can do. We all may need space to do some extra thinking."

He busied himself with getting me another glass of wine and himself another beer, leaving me to do my own thinking. I was relieved when he returned, plopped down on the sofa, and resumed our conversation in normal tones.

"Speaking of security. I had a strange conversation with Royce. He said Thibodeaux had told him not to worry about Beth's safety in St. Louis. It appears that Thibodeaux is handling her protection personally. Royce is freaking out and wants to know what I know about Beth's protection. Thibodeaux has assured Royce it's not a reflection on either his abilities or loyalty but won't tell him anything else. I told him I didn't know about any changes, but he clearly didn't believe me."

I smiled. "I'm sure you're familiar with the phrase 'plausible deniability'? When I met with Tom after my abduction, I told him I was worried the bad guys might go after Beth. Tom assured me he would see to Beth's protection personally. I couldn't ask questions, and so far, he's been a man of his word. He was pretty upset with Royce over the kidnapping. I think he's keeping him in the dark on purpose, letting him squirm a little."

Clovis asked, "Any idea what Thibodeaux has changed? Who he's added to the job?"

"The St Louis 'family' is still in charge of protecting both Beth and Jeff—they did a good job during our last case. Tom told me he had decided to send a special person to St. Louis until David's case is over. That person knows to contact you should there be any risk of harm to Beth."

Clovis took a long sip of beer before asking, "If I get such a call, how will I know it's real, that he's really Tom's person?"

"I asked Tom that very question. His answer was 'He'll know. I've trusted this person with my own life on several occasions. I promise your daughter is in safe hands.' Let's hope you never receive his call."

We turned the conversation to news and gossip from Little Rock, tossing in various strategies I'd thought of for David's defense. Clovis' specialty was investigation and protection, but over the years I'd grown to rely on his common sense and instinct. Except for Maggie and Walter Matthews, Clovis was my closest friend; there were no secrets between us. Stella returned from her workout, and we turned the conversation to who might be behind all the surveillance, and what could be done to create a zone of privacy.

When I was a young lawyer, I would have been shocked to learn that an opposing lawyer had tried to learn my strategy or eavesdrop on conversations with clients or witnesses. Now I seem to spend as much time protecting sensitive information as I spent gathering it. I had learned the hard way that corporate espionage and eavesdropping are as commonplace as paper towels in washrooms, and that attorney-client privilege and work product confidentiality are considered old-fashioned.

I turned to Stella, "It'll be a relief if you can protect our conversations from being wire-tapped, but don't spend too much time on the effort. The most important thing you can do is figure out what David's software does and why it's got everyone in such a tizzy."

"I've already read the civil complaint," she replied. "It's the biggest compilation of legal gobbledygook I've ever come across. It accuses David of theft of intellectual property, violation of patent and copyrights, unfair competition, and on and on. But nowhere does it mention what the software does."

"Surely David knows," I mused. "He said he developed it for his cousin. It can't be that complicated."

"Wait a minute," Clovis interrupted. "I don't get it. You've got a group of companies who say David stole their software and violated their patents. Then you've got the Feds saying David's software violates U.S. criminal laws. Well, if it's a crime for David to develop and own the software, why isn't it a crime for the companies to develop and own the same product?"

"Good question, Clovis, one more that I can't answer." I was totally frustrated. "Nothing about this case makes any sense. I was kidnapped before I'd even met my client. Why hijack the lawyer in the first place? David is sitting in jail, but no one will tell us what he's alleged to have done or even what his software does. We're being followed, our phones and computers have been hacked, and

God knows what wrenches Gloria and her lawyer are about to throw into the works. To top it off, the prosecutor seems to be a nice guy, which is weird in itself, and the lead attorney on the civil side is not. In fact, she seems to delight in being a total jerk. Everyone involved seems to have a hidden agenda or is playing a role for which they are miscast. It's like a jigsaw puzzle with no straight edges—I don't know where to start."

Neither of them said a word. I needed a minute or two to calm down, but I felt better after my little tantrum.

"Okay—so far all we have is questions. Tomorrow, we need to start getting the answers. But right now, I'd like to take you both into my confidence on a different matter."

They remained silent, faces expressing both confusion and expectation.

I took a deep breath and began, "I'm seriously considering closing my law office. Defending David might be my last case."

Now they both looked, well, shocked. At least I had their attention.

"Let me explain. Red wants me to go in-house as general counsel for his companies—the Lobos alone already take up more than half my time. Maggie and Walter would like to travel more often, and Walter and I have had some heart-to-hearts about how dangerous my practice seems to have become. Brian is more than welcome to come with me, so it's not like I'd be leaving anyone searching for a job."

Clovis pulled another beer from the fridge and gave Stella a long look before responding. "I don't know, Jack. I can't see you working for anyone full time. Red isn't the easiest person in the world to work for, and then there's Lucy. I think there's more to this turn around than you're letting on."

"You're right, Clovis, but it's less about me than it is about Beth, Maggie, you, Stella, the whole team. I don't know what happened to my nice, quiet, cut-and -dried anti-trust practice. Sure, it wasn't all that interesting, but at least I didn't have to hire protection for my daughter every time I took on a new case. We've had some close calls, and I worry that it's just a matter of time before someone gets killed. I don't know that I could live with that kind of guilt. This last abduction might have been the last straw.

"I can honor my obligation to Tom, defend his grandson, and hopefully dodge any further bullets. But when it's all over, it's time to stop putting my daughter, friends, and myself in such unpredictable situations. Red will pay me well, keep me busy, and Lucy and I can have fun getting on each other's nerves."

Clovis smiled. "I understand how you feel, but somehow, I don't think your life is meant to be that simple. I appreciate your telling us, and we'll have plenty of time to talk again. Right now, let's figure out how you can get Tom's grandson out of the mess he's in."

He was right of course. But I felt better for getting my hatchling idea out in the open.

Stella looked at Clovis and said, "Time for you two to head to bed. You've got lots to do tomorrow, that's for sure. I do my best work when the only people awake are hackers and bitcoin miners. I'm going to spend some time trying to figure out what David's idea is all about. Until we know the answer to that question Jack's retirement plans are nothing but a pipe dream."

24

I WAS EARLY FOR MY BREAKFAST WITH DUKE. The Willard's dining room is lovely, but much too formal for a real breakfast, at least for me. Give me Formica countertops, a couple of fried eggs, and coffee in a mug any day, but the venue choice wasn't mine. As I waited for Duke, I scanned the room. Every table was occupied by men and women wearing suits and deep in conversation. I wondered how many submarines and tax subsidies had been inserted into legislation over egg white omelets and biscuits hard as brick.

My waiter had just poured my second cup of coffee when Duke appeared at the restaurant's entrance. There was no doubt it was him. He stood about six feet two, clad in jeans, a fringed leather jacket and boots, with a well-worn cowboy hat perched on his head. His hair was long and grey, pulled back in a ponytail. I'd seen him on TV several times, but this would be my first in-person meeting. To my eyes he looked ridiculous.

Duke took his time crossing the room, slapping people on the back, and stopping at any table that seemed to want to meet him. There weren't that many. He finally made it to my table and extended his hand. His grip was surprisingly clammy, not firm nor as confident as I'd expected.

After we'd howdy-dooed like old friends, he took his seat and said, "Let's order before we talk business. I'm starving."

Our waiter appeared at his side on cue. Duke slipped him a twenty and said, "My usual, Sean, but tell the cook that when I ask for my steak to be cooked Pittsburg rare, I mean for it to be so rare it's almost bleeding. And no damn fruit or vegetables in my Bloody, you hear? No room for the vodka when it's full of that crap. Jack here wants the same thing."

Sean, who had a poker face worthy of Vegas, merely replied "Yes, sir," and turned to me.

I asked for eggs over easy, bacon, sourdough toast, and a mimosa, anything to keep Duke from making a scene. We played the game of "who do you know" while we waited to be served. I like a hearty breakfast, but mine was meager compared to Duke's steak, fried eggs, and pancakes which he washed down with a succession of Bloody Marys. The man must have a stomach of iron.

I wasn't quite finished when Duke pushed his plate back and threw his napkin on top. The waiter appeared almost immediately and after our plates had been cleared Duke got down to business.

"I can have a runner come by your office to pick up the files on this case. What I'd like to do this morning is pick your brain. There's got to be a way to plea bargain with the government so David doesn't end up spending forever in prison. As for the computer companies, I see a gold mine. With a counterclaim and the right publicity, I'll have them begging to settle. A million bucks each is chicken feed to those companies. The press will be all over this case. It's classic David versus Goliath. Get it?" He roared with laughter at his own joke. "You sure you don't want something stronger than that sissy drink?"

I was already sick of this guy and tempted to stand up and walk away, but I didn't want to create a scene. Besides, something told me to go carefully with Duke and Gloria. I didn't know enough about David's case to antagonize either his mother or her wild hair attorney.

"No thanks," I replied. "You think the best strategy is to plea David out even if it means prison time, and try to settle the civil litigation using threats of bad publicity?"

"No offense, pardner, but a silk-stocking lawyer like yourself doesn't have a chance in hell of pulling off what I can. I've spent twenty-five years building a reputation of being unreasonable and a pain in the ass. People hire me just to prevent me from being on the other side. There isn't a lawyer in DC who wants to see me across the table."

That much was true, but perhaps not for the reasons Duke thought. I decided to ask a few questions before I broke the bad news.

"Rather than discuss settlement strategy, let's talk a little about how much Gloria knows about the case against her son. The civil complaint is eighty pages of vague allegations and conclusory mish-mash. What does she know about the software he developed and why it's got everyone so worked up?"

It took Duke a few seconds to swallow the last bit of his Bloody and order another.

"Hell, son. You've met Gloria. She hasn't got the foggiest idea what her son's software is about. She smells money, and so do I. We have every major tech company joined at the hip to keep David's idea from reaching the market. It doesn't matter what it does or even if it works. The beauty is that big business understands economics, and big business don't give a tinker's damn about principles. Instead of paying their lawyers, they'd just as soon pay millions to get their hands on whatever David's come up with. When I hit them with a big counterclaim and subpoena all their senior executives for days of depositions, their wallets will open right up."

The strategy Duke had just described was right on point. Every time a publicly held company makes a mistake or a prediction that doesn't pan out, a gang of lawyers race to the courthouse to file complaints on behalf of the company's shareholders. After the dust settles, these cases are settled with the attorneys getting richer and the share-holders receiving pennies. Sound like legal blackmail? You betcha.

Shareholder actions are just one form of legal blackmail. Our judicial system has many flaws, and lawyers like Duke have found hundreds of ways to use those flaws to line their own pockets. Courthouses are full of attorneys who use the cost of litigation as a roadblock to justice. Court sanctions and fines have little deterrent effect on even the worst abusers.

Duke interrupted my soapbox daydream.

"When can my boy pick up the files?" he asked. "I don't want to let any grass grow…"

"Well, there's a bit of a problem," I interrupted, trying my best not to smirk.

"A problem? What problem?"

"I met with David yesterday. He wants me to represent him, and he wants his mother to go home."

No explosion, no ranting, no nothing. Duke merely finished his drink and sighed. "To tell you the truth, I expected as much. Tell your client that Gloria isn't going to leave town or give up on the fortune she's entitled. She sees whatever software he's created as the only way to get out from under Tom Thibodeaux's controlling thumb. You know damn well that my plan is the only chance David's got. But if he's dead set on spending the rest of his life in jail, we'll simply proceed on our own."

Proceed on their own? I had no idea what he meant and wasn't about to ask. I was just glad that he hadn't lost his famous temper.

"Duke, please tell Mrs. Ruple that I'll communicate your concerns and suggestions to David. I'll also find out to what extent he wants to keep both you and her in the loop. But I'm telling you what I had to tell Mr. Thibodeaux: David is the client, and he calls the shots."

Duke didn't respond except to snap his fingers at the waiter and demand a refill to his Bloody. I thanked him for breakfast, shook his hand, and left him to his drink, trying not to run.

With my mind a million miles away, I started to walk back to my office. I knew Mike was supposed to escort me, but it was a beautiful day, I was ready to get to work, and Mike was nowhere to be seen. I had just reached Lafayette Park, when someone walked up behind me and stuck something hard against my ribs. I tried to turn, but he pushed me toward a bench and whispered, "Take a seat, Jack. It's time you and I had a talk."

25

I RECOGNIZED THE VOICE IMMEDIATELY. After we sat down on a park bench, I turned to meet the man who had led my kidnappers in the Louisiana swamps.

I said, "Put the gun down. You're not about to shoot me when we're only a few yards from the White House."

"You're probably right. But it did get you to sit down, so I think I'll just keep it handy for a while longer. Wondering what happened to Big Mike? Maybe you should ask who else we might target to get you to cooperate. If we can subdue Clovis and make Mike disappear, who might be next—Stella, Maggie, or your precious Beth? No one's been harmed yet, Jack, not even you. What happens next is entirely up to you."

"What do you want from me? And who exactly is 'we?'" I demanded.

"It's simple. David Ruple's software must never see the light of day," he replied. "As for your second question, you'd better hope you never find out."

"And how do I manage that?"

"You complicated matters by surviving the swamp and taking on David's defense. Now that Thibodeaux can't possibly believe you simply flew the coop, the job has become a little more complicated. Listen carefully: this is how you'll manage it. You will lose the civil litigation, and his software will belong to the business entities suing him.

"You have a reputation for pulling rabbits out of an empty hat. Not this time. Your chances were already minimal, and my clients have gone to some length to make sure you won't win. But this case is too important to give you even a tinker's chance. You will lose, or you will all pay with your life. Don't doubt our resolve even for a minute.

"In addition, David must never dabble with computer software that affects these clients again. He and his girlfriend can fix broken computers and write code until kingdom come, but anything related to this software is off-limits for the rest of his life."

"Why can't I just stop representing him? Tom has many friends; he can find another lawyer. That was your plan when you took me to the swamp. Why isn't it good enough now? And here's another thing—do you have a name? Or can I call you whatever makes me happy?"

"Oh, Jack, please don't lose your cool now. Please remember who's in charge, and who is not. And yes—my name is Hans, and you are welcome to use it if it makes you feel better. Just think—you and I on a first name basis. As far as you quitting, what's to keep you from blowing the whistle once you think your daughter and Maggie are safe? Your bowing out would raise too many red flags. The quickest and simplest way to accomplish our goal is for you to lose the civil case and convince David to plead guilty."

"How in the world could I let David rot in jail for the rest of his life?" I asked.

"Why should he? Once you lose the civil case, I think you'll find the government to be receptive to a plea deal. David might have to spend a few years in prison, but he doesn't have to die there. At least not if he keeps his mouth shut. You're a creative lawyer. I'm sure you can come up with a solution."

"How do you know the government would accept a plea deal?" I asked.

"I told you. Nothing, and I mean nothing, has been left to chance."

"And if I don't agree to go along with your new scheme?" I asked.

"Don't even think about it, Jack. We have ways to get past any security Clovis could put in our way. Stella Rice is good, but we're better. Your computers, your phones, and your conversations are constantly monitored. Either David and his software disappear for good, or else—well, I think I've made the consequences clear."

As quickly as he had slipped up on me, he was gone. I had

watched FBI agents arrest Hans and his cohorts at Cary's Landing. How could he be here now? And why had he switched to "we" rather than "they?" Who was "we" and was Hans more than just a hired gun? No security my team had in place had prevented them from doing exactly what they wanted. I felt like the proverbial sitting duck. Could I really put Beth or Maggie, or any of us for that matter, in such a dangerous position? Yet was I willing to purposely lose a case to save my own skin? I had no answers.

I also had no time. Big Mike, face in a panic and breathing heavily, was running across the park toward me.

"Take a seat, Mike. Catch your breath. To be honest, I totally forgot to wait for you after breakfast and started walking to the office as usual. Guess this case has made my brain fuzzy." My attempt at sounding sheepish sounded suspicious, even to me. "When I realized I'd left you behind, I decided to wait for you to catch up. I was about to call to let you know I was here in the park. I don't think Lisa needs to know we got separated."

Mike's face relaxed. I don't know what relieved Mike more—my apparent safety or that I had no intention of telling Lisa.

He had regained his breath, and said, "I was watching you and Duke when three hotel security people surrounded me and started asking questions about what I was doing and why had I brought a gun into the hotel. I had cleared my carrying with their boss earlier, but they claimed there was no record of any such approval. By the time I convinced them that I had indeed followed the hotel's protocol, you were gone."

"No harm," I answered. "I was enjoying the fresh air, trying to clear my head after breakfast with Duke."

I wasn't about to tell him or anyone else about my conversation in the park, at least not yet. My mind raced as we walked back to the office. With the odds stacked so heavily against me, I was bound to lose the civil case no matter what I did. But could I live with myself when the jury returned a verdict for the computer companies? And how does a lawyer guarantee a loss?

And while I was busy losing the case, who would protect my team? Who was safe—David, his girlfriend, his mother? I couldn't very well send them to Mars. Yet not only did I have to figure out how to lose on purpose, but I also had to figure out how to get us all through this alive.

I glanced at Mike, who hadn't said a word. Maybe he was still embarrassed about losing me. Maybe he thought I'd lost my mind. Either way, an idea began to formulate in my sluggish brain.

"Mike, do you mind if we keep walking?"

"Not at all. Good for both of us," he smiled.

"Good. Please call the office. Ask whoever answers to have everyone meet us there in an hour."

The more we walked, the more my mind raced. My fledgling strategy had almost no chance of success and would require a great deal of trust from a diverse set of people. But since Hans had said I could never win, what did I have to lose?

I would have to scramble. I would have to convince Tom, David, and even Gloria that I knew what I was doing. But the toughest nut to crack would be Maggie. If I could sell her on my strategy, maybe it could work. It was a long shot, but all I could come up with during an hour's walk.

26

WHEN WE FINALLY REACHED THE OFFICE, everyone had already gathered in the conference room. They were enjoying coffee and pastries, expecting me to report on my breakfast with Duke and hand out assignments for the day. I poured a cup of coffee and sat down across from Maggie. I didn't say anything, and before long their voices grew silent, their faces watchful. I took a deep breath and began.

"Most of our meetings are pretty free-wheeling, and I usually welcome interruptions, but not today. This isn't easy, so please let me finish what I have to say. I also want to meet with each of you, individually, after we break up.

"Stella, despite all your efforts I've learned we have a larger audience listening to this conversation, as well as monitoring our computers. You all need to realize that anything you say in this room is going straight to the lawyers for the computer companies."

I could tell Stella wanted to object, and the others looked uneasy. I continued before they could interrupt.

"So here we go. I've decided to close the office, leave the practice of law. David Ruple will be the last man I defend in court. Red has offered me a full-time position with the holding company that owns the Lobos and his other businesses, and I've decided to take it. Brian, if you agree, I'd like you to help me transition our remaining clients and join me at Red's company. I've already cleared my request with Red, who's happy to have you. To sweeten the pot, the move will mean a substantial increase in salary for you."

Brian was Red's favorite nephew, and he'd been more than

willing for Brian to come with me when we'd talked about the possibility of my joining his operation. Brian nodded but said nothing.

"Lisa and Mike, I appreciate all you've done for me, but as of tomorrow I won't need your protection. Lisa, I'd like you to join me when I explain my decision to Martin. Can you please arrange a meeting? A lawyer with no clients or cases hardly needs protection.

"Stella, God knows how many times you've pulled my sorry ass out of the fire, but this time we're up against experts who have an unending source of money and resources. I know you'll be upset by my next request. Please dismantle all the protections and encryptions you've put in place. I mean all of them. I'll explain more over dinner tonight, but after you've finished turning everything off, you and Clovis will be free to go home."

Stella wouldn't be able to hold her tongue for long, so I didn't slow down.

"Clovis, please call Royce. I need to meet with Tom in person, tomorrow if possible. See if we can borrow Walter's plane, or Red's, if need be, because I need to get back to DC as soon as possible. We can drop you off in Little Rock on the way home." I sensed mutiny and kept talking before it could erupt.

"As you can tell, I'm dead serious about closing the office. I am just as serious about trying David's case the old-fashioned way—going out in style. That means no months of depositions, no motion practice, and no delay tactics. I intend to ask the Judge to set the case for immediate trial at the court's earliest convenience."

Mouths flew open at that latest sentence. None of them knew that my announcement about a quick trial was said for the benefit of those listening. I hoped they would fall for my first trap. Now came the hardest part.

"Maggie, you've been by my side for every trial since I left the Justice Department. This time, I'll be on my own. Please call the Mayflower and ask for a reservation for two for a late lunch today. Better yet, make it for three and ask Walter if he can join us. I need to explain to both of you why you can't play a part in defending David Ruple. You can help Brian shut down the office, but otherwise it's hands-off.

"My intention is to defend David on the cheap and then close the door and take down my shingle. I know you've all got questions, and I'll do my best to answer them when I meet with you individually, but right now I need to call Red."

I rose and left a room full of hurt faces and open mouths. My hope was that Hans had heard every word and believed I'd decided to comply with his demands. He would understand my need to talk to Thibodeaux. I hoped I could find a way to prevent Hans from listening in to that conversation. I'd come up with the bare bones of a plan just an hour ago. I was flying by the seat of my pants, and I knew it, but it was time to put it to the test.

He answered on the first ring, and I decided not to beat around the bush. "Red, I've decided to take you up on your offer. How soon do you want me?"

27

I WANTED HANS TO HEAR THE CALL TO RED. It was important for his clients to think that David's case would be my last. I chose the Mayflower restaurant for several reasons. It would be difficult to plant a listening device there on short notice. I seldom ate there, and it was usually crowded with diplomats, lobbyists, and governmental officials. And Hans would understand my need to explain more than I already had to Maggie. It was worth the risk: both Maggie and Walter were important to my budding plan.

Maggie didn't say a single word to me as we walked from the office to the Mayflower, her anger almost palpable. The restaurant was full of diners and busy waiters. I crossed my fingers that Hans hadn't found a way to listen to our conversation. Walter and I exchanged pleasantries until the waiter had taken our orders. Maggie still hadn't said a word except to the waiter.

I gave her a stern look and said, "What I have to say can't leave your ears. It really is a matter of life and death." I had their attention.

"This morning I was instructed to throw David's case. If I refuse, none of us, not Maggie, not me, not Beth, 'will ever see another birthday.' The threat was real. Those were his exact words." Maggie turned pale but remained silent.

I went on to explain about my encounter with Hans at Lafayette Park. I didn't leave out any details. Our waiter brought our salads just as I finished, which gave us all a few moments to think.

"Have you called the police?" Walter asked.

"No, I haven't told a soul. I'm pretty sure no one would believe me. Besides, I think the enemy has just about everyone in their back pocket. Hans and his gang walked away from the FBI after my kidnapping. Why would I think a police inquiry would scare them?"

"The main bad guy finally has a name, Hans? Wasn't there a movie—"

Maggie interrupted with a "Walter!" and a scolding glare.

Walter's grin quickly disappeared. "Sorry, Jack. I see your point. I'll ask Martin to raise everyone's security."

"I'm meeting with Martin this afternoon. I'll ask him to step down my protection, except for Maggie. My adversaries must believe they've gotten to me, that I'm totally spooked. If I were to ramp up my protection, they might think I plan to cross them. By losing my protection I hope to get them to lower their guard—at least a little.

"Walter, you and I have had some candid conversations about how some of my cases have put Maggie in danger. This case turns out to be the one we both feared. I want you to increase her protection. Send her out of the country to visit relatives—whatever. But she can't be part of this case."

"Don't I have a say?" Her tone was frosty.

"Of course you do, but think for a minute. Hans and his clients know you'd never let me do anything unethical. When they see you aren't involved, they'll think I've caved. Maggie, you and I have been the perfect team for a long time. I can't imagine trying a case without you, but your life and reputation mean far too much to risk. Sadly, the possibility of winning David's case is minimal anyway. I'm going to try this case on my own."

Walter asked, "I appreciate your concern for Maggie, but from what you've said, Hans' threats are designed to get you to throw the case. He didn't say anything about Maggie's appearance at trial. Maggie is at risk whether she helps you or not."

"That's correct," I agreed. "And if it were up to me, she'd already be on her way to London for an extended family visit. These guys mean business. And I'm not just worried about Hans and his clients. I'm afraid this case could be the tip of the iceberg. Whatever David's software does, if it's enough of a threat to bring this level of scrutiny from the Feds, imagine who else would stop at nothing to make sure it's destroyed."

We all took a minute to let that prospect sink in.

"I do have a couple of favors to ask."

"Name them," Walter replied quietly.

"Use of your jet would be the first one. I need to be in New Orleans tomorrow and return to DC as soon as possible. Next, after Stella and Clovis return to Little Rock, can you come up with a reason for them to return to DC? I know they've done consulting work for you in the past. I need their help, but it must look as if they're here strictly on your business."

"Done. The plane is at your disposal. I'll call the pilots and tell them to be on standby for your call. And I'll make the appropriate arrangements for Stella and Clovis as soon as I get back to the office. Not a soul will suspect anything; it's the perfect cover."

"You're not going to lose the case after all, are you?" Maggie broke in. "Why am I not surprised."

"I didn't say that. The odds of winning are slim to none, but you know me better than to think I could ever throw a case. My goal is for everyone to think I'm the most incompetent lawyer on the planet, while giving my client his best opportunity to win."

"And just how do intend to do that?"

"Honestly, Maggie? I don't know, haven't gotten that far. I only know that I need to do everything I can to convince Hans and anyone else who's interested that I'm going to lose the case. I'll have to figure out how to win later."

Walter chuckled, and Maggie asked, "How can I help when I can't work on the case?"

"Well, here's a way which should be easy for you. I know you won't go to London, so when you return to the office write a letter to me on the office computer giving me two weeks' notice. Include something about how if you didn't know me better, you'd think I was trying to throw David's case. Say something to the effect that you'll use the next two weeks to help Brian close the office, but my behavior has created a real obstacle for any continuing friendship."

She looked doubtful, and more than a little obstinate.

"Maggie, listen to me—please," I begged. "The more Hans thinks we are estranged, the safer you'll be. It's a simple as that. I can't focus my attention on David's case until I'm comfortable that you and Beth are safe."

"What about your own safety? Why are you dismissing your own protection?" she asked, her voice trembling. I felt like a real jerk.

"I'm trying to create an illusion for Hans and his clients. Yes, I'm taking a risk, but what better way to convince them that I'm cooperating than to act as if I have nothing to fear."

Walter handed her a tissue, commenting, "That's one hell of a risk, my friend."

"Well, maybe, but Clovis will be back in a matter of days, and I'm not really terminating Lisa or Mike, despite what I said earlier. I'm meeting with Lisa and Martin this afternoon to work out the details."

"Are you telling me that everything you said this morning was meant to create a false impression? That none of it was true?" Maggie's stiff tone radiated disapproval.

"Sorry, Maggie, but yeah, pretty much. It was a performance for Hans and his clients."

Walter frowned and said, "Let me get this straight. You want to look like you're trying to lose David's case on purpose. But your real intent is to win, hoping no one notices your ploy until it's a fait accompli?"

"In a nutshell, yes." I smiled.

"Why not do as they ask? Why go to all this effort to win a case you say is already lost? I gather that Hans and his cohorts already have the judge, the federal government, and the facts on their side. Why not throw in the towel?" Walter was perplexed.

"Walter, I can't. I can't throw David to the wolves. And I just can't throw a case. That's not who I am."

28

WALTER OFFERED TO GIVE MAGGIE A RIDE back to the office. I was sure they had a few things to discuss outside my presence, and I wanted to walk back so I could clear my head. I reminded myself to be more alert, hoping Hans and his gun wouldn't try to waylay me again. I wasn't at all sure Lisa and Martin could pull off what I wanted, but I needed the chance to ask.

Brian was waiting in my office. I knew the office had been bugged, so I chose my words carefully. Brian was bright; I counted on his ability to see through my ruse. One slip and we might alert the enemy.

"While I'm in New Orleans, please schedule meetings with David, Jordyn Duarte, David's girlfriend Rita, William Stanford and another person who might come as a surprise. Call Duke and tell him I've had a change of heart. I want to meet with both him and Gloria to see how we can work together. The order of the meetings doesn't matter, but the sooner the better after I return from New Orleans."

Brian's eyebrows lifted when I mentioned meeting with Duke, but he didn't question my reasoning. If Hans was listening, he wouldn't be happy at the possibility of my working with Duke. Neither Duke nor Gloria posed any threat to their scheme, but Duke was a wild card they hadn't foreseen. I hoped they would turn their attention to Duke for at least a little while. I needed some breathing space to put my evolving plan into motion.

Brian passed me a scribbled note. "Are the bad guys listening?"

I wrote, "I hope so," and handed it back to him.

My response brought another eyebrow raise, but no questions.

It was time to meet with Lisa, Martin, and Mike. Lisa drove us to a location she assured me was safe from any form of electronic eavesdropping. Martin was to meet us there. She drove over the Roosevelt Bridge into Virginia and took the exit to Falls Church. We circled a block of office buildings a couple of times before entering an underground parking garage. She parked quickly and led us into an elevator. I watched her push the button marked P6.

We exited to a reception desk where a very unfriendly guy demanded our photo IDs. After running our names through some database, he escorted us to a room with no windows. The room was empty except for a small conference table, chairs, and Martin, who was sipping on a bottle of water.

"Welcome to Langley Annex, Jack. We're six stories underground, and the room is lined with lead, just like the Skiffs at DOJ and State. If your opponents can listen through these walls, then God save us all. Now why the need for such secrecy, and why did you fire these two?"

Martin wasn't one to mince words. Without pointing a finger at Big Mike, I told them I had received credible threats on the lives of Maggie, Beth, and my client, not to mention myself.

"No criticism of Mike or Lisa, but these guys have been able to breach any form of security we've placed in their way. I can't give you any details yet, but my best form of protection is to appear to have none. At the same time, Maggie needs extra protection, and my client's girlfriend needs round-the-clock protection."

"What about you?" Martin asked.

"Unless you can be invisible, I'll have to take my chances. Brian is a former Ranger and has helped with security in the past. I'll be with Clovis tonight. I must appear to be unafraid, even confident. The truth is I'm scared shitless."

"Walter has already called," he replied. "He didn't say why, but he was most insistent about Maggie. Do you mind stepping outside for just a minute? Otis has hot coffee ready for you both. He's not as gruff as you might think."

Otis proved to know more about the Washington Nationals than a DC sportswriter, but it wasn't long before Martin opened the door and said, "Come on in, Jack."

He closed the door carefully. "Mike will be in charge of Ruple's girlfriend, unless that interferes with your plans."

I thought a minute.

"No, it shouldn't. Hans would expect me to protect her, and he knows he can't use her to get to me. But, Mike—I have yet to meet her. What if she objects?"

"Leave that to me," he replied with a smile. "She'll be fine."

Martin continued, "And Lisa will continue to provide your protection."

I objected. "No, no, a thousand times, no. I need our opponents to think I have no protection."

"Unless I have to act, they'll never even know I'm there," she said.

"Sure. An attractive blonde carrying a big gun is going to be invisible."

She smiled. "Thanks for the compliment, but I'll bet you two tickets to a Commanders' game that you'll never know I'm even close, much less spot me."

"Better yet. You pull this off, and you and Mike will be my guest in the owner's box when the Lobos play the Commanders."

"You're on." Her smile exuded confidence.

29

I WAS LEERY OF LISA'S ABILITIES, but it felt good to know she'd have my back. We spent some time working out how we would communicate and then headed back to DC. By the time we got through traffic, I had to rush back to Kalorama to make my appointment with Clovis and Stella.

We had agreed to meet at the Lebanese Taverna, one of my favorite restaurants in the city. Angie and I had eaten there on many occasions, for both celebrations and one that would alter the course of history. The décor had changed over the years, but the quality of the food had not. Their fattoush and shawarma were irresistible. I spotted my friends at a booth near the kitchen, sat down and tried to loosen the tension with a tired joke about baba ghanoush. Stella wasn't buying, and Clovis didn't try to stop her.

"Cut it out, Jack. I promise you no one can listen to our conversation, but what the hell? I've now dismantled all the protections I just installed on your phones and computers. God knows why. What on earth is going on?" Her tone was just above a whisper.

Fortunately, a waiter I knew well appeared, and we quickly placed our orders. I spent the next half-hour telling them about my meeting with Hans at Lafayette Park, my lunch with Maggie and Walter, and my trip to Falls Church. Clovis was more confident about Lisa's ability to remain in the background.

"I'm more impressed with her every day. You might just lose that bet," he commented.

"I'll be glad to pay up. But let's talk about your roles in my theater of the absurd."

My plan was for Clovis to travel with me to meet Thibodeaux. On the return flight to DC, the plane would drop him off in Little Rock. Stella would take a commercial flight to Arkansas tomorrow. Walter would call Stella a couple days later, asking her to return to DC for consulting work. Yes, she could bring Clovis along.

"Walter knows the consulting work must be real and that it can't raise any red flags. Meanwhile, Stella, please try to solve the puzzle of David's software. What exactly does it do? And forget what I said about Hans' abilities. I know you can find a way to protect our conversations and computers from the bad guys."

"I'll do my best, but those are tall orders," she answered, looking pleased as punch.

"Clovis, you and I can talk on the plane. I don't think even Hans or his clients can listen to a conversation aboard a private plane."

"Please put your phones on airplane mode," Stella grinned. "Fasten your seatbelts and be sure your seats are in their upright and locked position."

Clovis wasn't amused. "Jack, are you sure you're going about this the right way? You still have friends at Justice. Surely, they would believe what you know about Hans and his threats. Do you really think you can outsmart him, his thugs, and a gang of high-powered lawyers? All by yourself? Wouldn't it be better and safer to turn everything over to the authorities?"

"Don't think that thought hasn't crossed my mind. But where does that leave David? Something tells me the computer companies and the government are in cahoots, despite outward appearances. The timing of the lawsuit and the indictment couldn't have been just coincidence. I may be wrong, God knows I often am. But I feel sure the key to this case is David's software. Once I know its purpose, I'll be a long way toward developing a defense."

Stella asked, "Can't you just ask him?"

"You'd think so, right? So far, my time with him has been limited, but when I see him again, you can be sure I'll ask. But I don't think his answer will tell us much. His software probably does exactly what he created it to do, and as such isn't a threat to anyone.

"But what if it does more than he intended? More than even he realizes. What if the computer companies and the government see another use? An unintended consequence, so to speak. Maybe, maybe not. But I know one thing—David's adversaries are scared to death, so frightened they're willing to put David behind bars for years and threaten to kill his attorney and anyone else who tries to help him.

"Stella, I need you to find out not only what the software does on the surface, but also any other applications it may have—that bigger picture."

Stella was slow to respond. "You know I'll do whatever I can, but what if I discover that David did indeed steal someone else's software and claim it for his own? What if the government's claims are valid, that David is a hacker out to destroy the internet? Sorry for my exaggeration, but…"

"I can deal with that," I interrupted. "Not easily, and don't ask me how. But I'd bet my life he didn't steal anyone's software and is not any kind of threat to the government. If another company originated this software first, why would the other companies be party to the lawsuit? No, they all want a piece of what he created. If David had copied someone else's work, he would have received a cease-and-desist letter, not a seventy-page complaint."

Clovis objected, "Sounds to me like you're betting your life on someone you've met only once at the request of a mob boss. I still think you're much better off to tell Thibodeaux to get another lawyer. Martin and I can keep you safe from any type of revenge he might seek."

Why didn't anyone seem to understand? I knew they were only trying to protect me, and to be honest, themselves. Maybe I hadn't been clear. I decided to try again.

"Clovis, I didn't take this case because I was afraid of what would happen if I didn't. I took on David's defense because for many years Tom has protected my daughter, and defending his grandson is the least I can do in return. Now that I've met David, I believe he's innocent; he has no idea why he's been charged and no sense of having done anything wrong. The odds are stacked against him, and he needs help. I know lawyers who would take his case, plead him out, and give away his software.

"But think about it: reputable lawyers don't hire thugs to kill the opposing attorney. The FBI doesn't release kidnappers and turn a blind eye from a laundry list of crimes and criminals unless they have orders from way above. A young man doesn't become the target of the best and brightest at the Justice Department without a single leak to the press. Hans has told me, more than once, that both the criminal action and the civil suit are sure winners, no way they can lose. So why did he kidnap me, steal my identity, and leave me for dead in a swamp? Why have they followed me, invaded my home, tapped our computers and phones, and now threatened to kill those I love if I don't lose the case?

"There must be a logical reason behind this behavior. It's a question of motive—when we know the 'why,' we'll have answers to those questions and be able to provide David the defense he deserves."

I had tried to keep my voice down, but I noticed that other diners were looking our way or trying not to. Fortunately, the waiter appeared with both coffee and the bill, giving me time to calm down.

Stella had been stirring her thick, Lebanese coffee. "You basically fired us all this morning. What was all that about? The team is in place, we just need to be more careful in how we communicate."

"I wish it were that simple. I still must prepare the case on my own, and the threats against Maggie and Beth are very real. How do I look like I'm throwing the case while I'm really trying to win? I haven't figured that part out yet. This morning was a diversion, in hopes of getting Hans and others to lower their guard. It probably won't work, but it might buy me some space and time. I need both."

We let the subject drop, made our goodbyes, and went our separate ways. It was hard to believe that this time tomorrow I would be in New Orleans, maybe even about to head home again. My day had begun with Duke telling me how he would defend David. I wondered where I would be if I had just given in. Would Hans have issued his threats? I certainly wouldn't be flying to New Orleans to explain why Tom Thibodeaux's grandson should remain in jail a while longer.

30

THE FLIGHT TO NEW ORLEANS WAS UNEVENTFUL, the best you can wish for any flight these days. I was able to explain to Clovis what he needed to do when he returned to DC. He still wanted to argue with me about my strategy, but I was deaf to his reasoning. My night's sleep had been constantly interrupted by my own second guesses and reservations, but I'd met the morning with no better options.

"Listen, Clovis. My plan could get squashed if Thibodeaux doesn't agree. We'd be back to square one. The odds are better than fifty-fifty that he'll fire me on the spot. Your job is to get me safely out of town if he does."

Clovis grew silent at that prospect and remained so as we drove to a midtown restaurant where Tom and Royce were waiting. I wasn't at all sure we were at the right place. The building looked like any other house in a small neighborhood. I couldn't see any signs or advertising of any kind, and the only parking was on the street. Our cabbie demanded his fare, swearing this was the place. We walked up the old sidewalk, entered through a front door in need of a new coat of paint, and found ourselves facing an older woman sitting at a small desk. She was tiny, well-dressed, and greeted us with a smile.

"Do you have a reservation?" Her voice was low and sweet.

"We're here to meet Mr. Thibodeaux," I answered.

"You must be Mr. Patterson. George will show you to his table. He's running a few minutes late. George!" She shrieked in a voice that made me jump.

We were led to a table in the back of a small room. The entire room held only about ten tables, and I wondered how they could make a profit on such a small space. But all the tables were occupied except Tom's. The clientele was older than one might expect, and the room was neither crowded nor loud. George failed to give us a menu, but quickly returned with a glass of wine for me and a beer for Clovis. He placed a bottle of Mountain Valley Water and two small, clean glasses in the center of the table, then disappeared.

I decided not to ask for a menu, but did try, with little success, to see what other guests were eating, but the tables were too far apart, and Tom's was tucked in the back of the room. Clovis sipped on his beer, remaining unusually quiet. My wine was an Italian Red that I didn't recognize but enjoyed.

It wasn't long before I noticed Tom and Royce at the front door. Tom didn't need George to bring him to the table, and he took his time stopping to speak to people he knew. He worked the room like a politician, and I noticed that every table looked genuinely pleased that Thibodeaux had acknowledged them.

After they arrived, we made the usual greetings. George immediately brought a glass of wine to Tom and straight bourbon on the rocks to Royce. Two more glasses were added to the center of the table in case anyone wanted water.

Tom said, "Let's wait to talk until we've eaten. Their gumbo is the best in the city, and the shrimp po-boy isn't far behind. But they'll make you about anything you want, within reason of course."

I joined Tom in ordering a cup of gumbo and the po-boy. Clovis asked George what he would recommend and took his suggestion—blackened red fish. Royce ordered turtle soup and a dozen grilled oysters. He was indeed a strange guy. We never saw a menu.

Tom was right about the gumbo, and the po-boy smothered in brown gravy rivaled any I'd ever eaten. Royce ordered yet another dozen oysters. It helped the mood of the lunch that George kept our glasses full, except for Clovis who had switched to water. Thibodeaux kept the conversation light, quizzing me about the Lobos and touting the Saints chances next season.

After the table had been cleared and dessert declined, George filled our glasses one last time, and Tom spoke, "Before we begin, I want you to know you can speak openly in Royce's presence. Whatever concerns I may have had about his loyalty have been resolved. You may speak freely—nothing you say will leave this table."

Royce turned beet red, and Tom quickly continued. "You asked for this meeting, and I suspect you don't bring good news. Please don't pull any punches. Good news can always wait, bad news is best served fresh. So go ahead."

I answered, "I fully intend to shoot you straight about David's case. With David's permission, I've come to ask for your help. But first, let me bring you and Royce up to date."

I told them everything that had happened since I'd returned to DC, including my meeting with Gloria and breakfast with Duke. When it came to my conversation with Hans, Royce began to fidget. He clearly wanted to jump in but managed to hold his tongue. Tom must have told him he should remain quiet. Tom asked a few insightful questions, but for the most part listened attentively.

When I had finished, I took a sip of wine and waited for Thibodeaux's response.

"You say you need my help. Royce thinks you've decided to withdraw from the case, going back on your offer to help David." He had lowered his voice. "Is this true?"

"I have no plans to withdraw."

Tom gave Royce an "I told you so" look and continued, "I wouldn't be surprised if you did want out. Your representation has placed you, your daughter, and your friends in danger."

"I won't withdraw unless David himself asks me to do so. He is the client."

Royce couldn't help himself. And I couldn't help but wonder why.

"Oh, yeah—you'll go to court, but you'll blow the case to save your own skin."

Thibodeaux turned on Royce with a nasty glare, and I replied before he could respond.

"You're wrong, Royce. I'll do everything I possibly can to win David's case, to see him walk out of court a free man. But I admit my method will be unorthodox. People will think I've lost my marbles, that I'm intentionally trying to lose the case. I'm not doing this to save my neck, but to save David's."

This time Royce looked at Tom for permission to speak, and he nodded.

"How do you plan to carry out this unorthodox plan of yours?"

"Well, a lot depends on today and whether Mr. Thibodeaux is willing to help out."

"You need more money." His contempt was obvious, and again I wondered why.

"No, I don't," I replied.

"You need someone taken out?"

"No."

Before Royce could ask another stupid question, Tom interrupted.

"Enough, Jack has put both his life and the lives of those he loves on the line. We owe him the courtesy to listen to him, not to insult him."

I thought Royce might cry at Tom's harsh tone and waited until he calmed down.

"My first request is a tough one. Royce has assured me that David is safe in DC's jail. If David agrees, I think he will be safer there than on the streets. Hans has made it clear that his 'clients' don't want David to ever touch another computer. I wouldn't put it past him to kill David to make sure he doesn't. Before I ask David if he's willing to remain in jail until and during the trial, I need to know—will he be safe?"

Tom asked, "How long are we talking about?"

"If my strategy works, we'll be in court within a few months. If not, we'll have to rethink."

"I assure you that David will be safe; please assure him that I said so. I'm sorry to tell you this, but I am far more comfortable about his safety than I am about yours." Once again, Royce's quick smirk was erased by his boss's glare.

I raised my hand, palm forward. "Wait—please don't agree to anything until you've heard my other requests. I've come to under-stand that your relationship with your daughter is, at the least, estranged. Her lawyer is a snake oil salesman, that's for sure. Yet I think they can be useful, and I'd like to enlist their assistance."

"My daughter has been a disappointment, but she is David's mother. You don't need my permission to ask for her help."

"If it becomes necessary, I want to be able to say that you asked her to help. I know it's a tough ask, and I will only use it if it's absolutely necessary. But I need your consent in my holster."

You could tell he was hesitant about using Gloria. When he spoke, he didn't mince words.

"My daughter cannot be trusted. She chose her no good husband over family and conspired with those who would like to see me step down. We haven't spoken in more than a year. I need to think about your request. What else do you need from me?"

He was obviously irritated, and I took a minute to consider how to phrase my final request.

"You are a man of your word, and you've given me your word that my daughter and her fiancé are safe. But I need your assurance that no harm will come to them. I'll do my dead level best to help your grandson. I will put my own life on the line, but I can't do my best unless I know my daughter won't be harmed, not now, not ever. There you have it."

I waited while he absorbed the meaning of my request and decided how to respond. I would hear no off-the-cuff promises from this man.

"Well, Jack, it seems we have something in common," he said with a smile. "Your daughter is your weakness, as my grandson is mine. I assure you that Beth and Jeff are as safe as the President, maybe safer. And she will be as long as I draw breath. As to enlisting my daughter in your efforts on behalf of her son, you have my permission to ask her whatever you like—I won't deny anything you've requested. But be careful. She's much craftier than one might think. And please tell David that I said to listen to you."

Royce blurted out, "But..." He was quickly caught short by Tom's stare and didn't say another word. I wondered if I would ever know the reason behind his animosity and suspicions.

I had no more requests, so I thanked him for lunch, and we quickly left the restaurant, a somewhat humbled Royce leading the way. I thought the woman eating a bowl of gumbo with short black hair looked familiar. But who could I have recognized in New Orleans? I must have been mistaken.

31

THE FLIGHT FROM NEW ORLEANS to Little Rock took just long enough for me to tell Clovis how he could help when he returned to DC. He wanted to be at my side but having him close would defeat the scenario I was trying to create. I insisted we stick to the plan.

We dropped Clovis off at McKelvey Air, a new facility at the Clinton Airport in Little Rock. Stella was waiting, and the three of us chatted while the plane was refueled. The pilot soon signaled, and we were off to DC again. I watched as Little Rock disappeared below the clouds and settled down to review my nascent strategy again. I couldn't seem to think of anything to improve it, so I quit trying. My mind turned to Royce's odd behavior, and I drifted into sleep in seconds.

I woke with a jolt when I felt the plane begin descending into the DC area and Reagan National on the Potomac River. For the longest time I had objected to the addition of the former president's name to my favorite airport. But my opinion has changed of late—its name could be worse.

The late evening view of DC from an airplane on descent into the airport is one of the most beautiful sites in the world. As the fading sunshine yields to evening, the monuments, the government buildings, the museums, the White House, and the U.S. Capitol convey a majesty and grandeur that rivals none other. Our country has lost respect for the institutions that are housed in those magnificent buildings, and in part, rightly so. I hope I live long enough to see Americans come together to elect leaders who will restore the honor those institutions deserve.

I walked from the plane to the hanger. No one was one waiting for me. It had been my decision, but it still felt odd to wave goodbye to the pilots and cram myself into an Uber. I think I'm in pretty good shape for an old guy, but at six-three with big feet to match, fitting into the back seat of an ordinary Uber is a challenge, especially when the driver ignores my request to move the front seat up a bit.

The rush hour traffic crawled, especially over Key Bridge, and I wondered what awaited me at my condominium. Would it be empty and quiet, or would Hans or one of his henchmen be waiting to confront me? Maybe I should have let Clovis come with me after all.

We finally arrived at my front door, and to my relief my home was empty, no sign of intruders. I wasn't hungry, there was no game on TV I cared about, and my call to Beth had been forwarded to voice mail. I took a shower and went to bed. Who knew what tomorrow would bring.

Up early the next morning, I stood at my front door considering my options. I was used to seeing Big Mike waiting; most days we walked to my favorite breakfast joint before going to the office. Today, the last thing I wanted to do was drive into work during morning traffic. I walked to the nearest coffee shop and tried to relax for a few minutes before braving the Metro. I'd forgotten how cramped and crowded the Metro had become and decided that tomorrow I would take the bus, a much more civilized means of transportation.

I found Brian in the conference room making a pot of coffee. He said Maggie had called and would be in later, answering my silent question.

"She sounded angry, said she had given you notice. You're not really going to let her leave, are you?"

"I don't know that I have any choice. It's her decision." My tone was cold, but I'd scribbled two words on the note I handed him, "no way."

"What's our schedule for the day?" I asked, glad to see his smile.

"Well, there's been a new development," he answered as he threw the note in the trash. "The judge has scheduled a status conference for three o'clock this afternoon. He's been assigned to both the civil and criminal cases."

He saw my frown, paused, and said, "Sorry, but there's more, a lot more. Both Jordyn and Mr. Stanford have begged off meeting with you until after the status conference; the jail has denied our request to see David; and David's girlfriend hasn't returned my calls.

"You have a meeting this morning with Duke and Gloria at Barker's. Gloria balked at going to Barker's, but Duke was excited at the prospect. I got the impression he's applied for membership. I think he convinced Gloria by telling her that Barker's is exclusive and that very few women are allowed."

"Hah!" I replied with a grin. "Hell will indeed freeze over before Duke Madison gets into Barker's."

Barker's was the perfect meeting place. DC is full of clubs with good food and pricey booze for those who can afford the entrance fee, but few are as truly anonymous as Barker's. A member can entertain Congressmen or high-ranking government officials without having to read about their conversation in the *Post* the next day. Any member who flouted the rule would be expelled immediately; no excuses allowed. I'd spent some time there during one of my more significant cases, and their rule of anonymity had saved my skin. Hans could not have planted listening devices in Barker's.

I told Brian I had skipped breakfast and suggested that we head to a nearby Starbucks. I wasn't really hungry, but we did need to be able to speak in private.

I ordered us both a latte and slice of pumpkin bread and joined Brian at a corner table.

"This status conference could be a trap," I began. "It's hard to believe that Jordyn has a federal judge in her pocket, but my trip to New Orleans may have spooked Hans and his cohorts. Who's the judge?"

Brian sighed. "Judge Greg Moorman, a Trump appointee. Originally from Beaumont, Texas, he went to Liberty U for his undergraduate degree. After law school at Regent in Virginia Beach, he somehow got himself appointed to the staff of the Judiciary Committee, where he toiled away for years in relative obscurity until he was appointed federal judge. He would never have been confirmed if the Democrats had controlled the Senate. He's never practiced law or even taught law school, not for a single day. His pro-business reputation and lack of experience make him a very unlucky draw for this case."

Of course, I thought, the same sort of appointments happened no matter which party was in charge at the time. Judicial appointments have always been an easy political payback. This one seemed to be particularly egregious.

"Five will get you twenty that luck had nothing to do with the draw. You've got to hand it to the opposition: they've touched every base. This afternoon should be interesting. If I can convince Duke to play ball, maybe we can throw them a few curves this afternoon. Let's head over to Barker's."

I had arranged for Duke and Gloria to meet us at the grill in the basement. I'd thought about reserving a conference room for our meeting, but decided an early lunch in the grill with my client's mother would attract far less attention. If the bad guys had listened in to my conversation with Brian, they already knew I was going to meet with Duke and Gloria again. What I didn't want them to know was what I was going to ask of them.

The grill was almost empty when we arrived, and Duke and Gloria soon joined us. Duke was wearing his normal uniform: designer jeans with a belt buckle larger than a police badge, a bolo tie, and a fringed leather jacket. Gloria had toned down her make-up and looked great in a conservative dress and heels; she could have been one of a hundred well-to-do female lobbyists. She did order a Ramos gin fizz when the waiter came around to take our order. Duke tested our waiter's knowledge of single malt Scotch before ordering a double on the rocks. Brian and I settled for iced tea, declaring we had to appear in court that afternoon.

"Okay, Patterson," Duke said in a low voice. "You called this meeting. Have you come to your senses? Are you ready to turn over David's representation to me?"

"Not quite, but I have come up with a way for you to both protect your client's best interests and help her son at the same time."

"I'm dubious, but I'm willing to listen," he replied. Gloria said nothing. Sipping her gin fizz and stifling a yawn, she appeared to be totally bored.

"Why don't you intervene in the civil litigation, asserting that Gloria has a silent interest in David's software. Your motion can state that you have no knowledge about the merits of their claim or the government's claim of criminal conduct, but that Gloria does own a significant part of his intellectual property. You'll have a seat at the table during the litigation, but you won't expose Gloria to civil damages or criminal liability."

"I don't have any criminal liability." Gloria interjected in an oddly detached voice. Maybe she wasn't so bored after all.

"Maybe not, but Duke will tell you that if you claim to own a portion of David's software, the government might threaten to indict you as a co-conspirator. Prosecutors threaten mothers and family members every day to use as bargaining chips against a defendant. If the court grants Duke's motion to intervene, the computer companies can't settle the case without you. Duke has told me that merely getting rid of him alone would be worth millions, right Duke?"

Realizing that I was using his own strategy against him, he smoothly tried to change the course of our conversation.

"Rather than get involved, why don't we simply claim that Gloria's interest in the software was based on David's promise to give her part of the profits when he sold it. She and I can look on from the gallery during the trial. If you lose, we're no worse off, and if you win, Gloria's son will be generous."

I went straight to the point. "Because you're a trial lawyer, and you're dying to participate. If I lose, and you aren't one of the parties, Gloria won't see a plug nickel, and neither will you. More importantly, I need you. You can be a thorn in the side of both parties by shouting that I'm incompetent, obviously trying to lose the case."

"I get it. You think David doesn't have a chance. You want to lay the grounds for incompetency defense."

I didn't respond. I knew that some criminal defense lawyers miss deadlines on purpose or make spurious arguments so their clients can appeal, claiming they had incompetent counsel. That wasn't my intention, but it was fine with me if that's what Duke wanted to think.

Gloria looked up from her drink and hissed, "I don't trust you, Jack Patterson. Why should I do anything for you? I bet that snake

Royce Peters came up with this stupid idea. I won't have any part of it!"

It was time to pull out what I hoped would be my hole card.

"Because your father is asking you to." I didn't elaborate.

Gloria's face paled. She demanded another drink from a passing waiter and responded, "You're lying! My father wants nothing to do with me. And I want nothing to do with him." Her voice was full of bitter anger, and she quickly jabbed away an unwanted tear.

For all her blustering, I had a feeling that Gloria still loved and missed her father. The waiter arrived with her drink, and I let her have a minute to regain her composure.

"Gloria, if you doubt me, why don't you call him and ask. I was in New Orleans with him yesterday. He specifically asked me to tell you he was asking for your help. You know that David and Tom have a special relationship. Whatever came between the two of you is none of my business, but isn't it time to bury the hatchet, especially now when David needs your help? My impression is that he wants his daughter back, that he wants to work with you to get David out of this mess."

She said, "My father said that? 'Tell her I'm asking?'"

"His words exactly." I didn't mention that I had put the words in his mouth.

"Duke, do whatever he says," she whispered and returned to her drink.

Duke was clearly suspicious, not inclined to cooperate. But he came around when I told him that Tom had agreed to pay his expenses and legal fees within reason, and better yet, that I would ask Barker's management to show him around the club after lunch.

I let the two of them order lunch on me, then excused myself— simply no time with all the work left to do. No one was disappointed.

I had no idea how either the judge or Jordyn would react when Duke showed up in court this afternoon, but at least no one could accuse me of trying to win David's case. I was confident that Duke would do his very best to dispel any doubts. Now to get ready for the trap Jordyn and the federal government had laid.

32

THE STATUS CONFERENCE HAD BEEN moved to the largest courtroom in the federal courthouse. Apparently, Jordyn Duarte would speak for all the plaintiffs, but all the interested parties had insisted on their counsel's presence in the courtroom, costing the consortium more than a pretty penny. The government never shows up in court without a cadre of lawyers, paralegals, and assistants. The poor defendant, David Ruple, had yours truly and his paralegal, Brian. Duke was a no-show when the marshal called us to the bar. I was surprised to see that the gallery was empty; I was soon to learn why.

The judge entered the courtroom with a flourish. Before I could object to my client having to wear the orange jumpsuit and shackles in court, Jordyn was on her feet to address the court.

"Your Honor, thank you for closing this hearing to the press and public. Several of our clients would have liked to be here in person, but they appreciate the sensitive nature of these two cases. I believe you have already reviewed the motion and brief filed by the U.S. government about how this case is critical to this country's national security." It wasn't a question.

Normally I would have immediately stood to object to a motion that was filed without my receiving a copy or having a chance to respond. But since I was supposed to be throwing the case, I didn't.

Jordyn proceeded as if I weren't even in the room. "Your Honor, normally when both a civil and criminal case arise out of the same set of facts, the criminal case takes priority. However, for reasons outlined in my motion, I suggest we go to trial on the civil case first.

Mr. Stanford has authorized me to say that the U.S. government has no objection."

The judge queried, "Is that true?"

'It is, Your Honor. These cases are essentially the same in nature; it matters not who proceeds first."

The old me would be screaming bloody murder. There is almost no circumstance in which a civil case should take precedence over a criminal case. Fifth amendment rights were the first and foremost reason for objecting. When the judge asked me if I had anything to say, I replied meekly that I had no objection. Both the judge and my client, neither of whom had any idea what was happening, looked at me as if I'd lost my mind. Maybe I had.

At that very moment, I was saved by the bell. Or should I say, saved by a cowboy.

Duke shouted from the back of the courtroom, "I object, Your Honor."

Almost in unison, the judge, Jordyn, and Stanford spouted, "Who are you?"

"Duke Madigan, Your Honor. I represent the defendant's mother, Gloria Ruple. Earlier this afternoon I filed a motion to intervene on her behalf in the civil case pending before this court. My client has an economic interest in the intellectual property at issue. Moreover, she has no confidence that Mr. Patterson has either the qualifications or expertise to protect my client's interest. His failure to object to what Ms. Duarte has requested is clear evidence of his incompetence."

Duke walked through the rail and over to our table with a swagger, pulled up a chair and gave me a wink. The judge looked at Jordyn to rescue him.

"Your Honor, we're not privy to Mr. Madigan's filing or whether it has any merit. I suggest that Mr. Madigan be allowed to sit with Mr. Patterson on this side of the rail, but that we proceed without his participation until you've ruled on his motion."

Judge Moorman was upset that the script had been altered, but he recovered well.

"Mr. Madigan. Once all the parties have had an opportunity to review your motion and file a response, I will rule on it in a timely fashion. You may sit at the defendant's table, but I suggest you limit your participation unless and until I say otherwise. Otherwise, you'll find yourself escorted out of the courtroom. One last thing: I expect you to appear before this court in proper attire. Jeans and a string tie may be appropriate in a beer hall, but not in my courtroom. Do you understand?"

I couldn't help but wonder if he was as old and stodgy as he sounded. I'd figured him to be about forty-five, but his testy voice sounded much older.

Even Duke knew he had overstepped. His meek response of "Yes, Your Honor" was all he could say. Now came Duarte's next surprise.

"Your Honor, for reasons set forth in our motion we suggest an expedited trial. There is no need for discovery. My clients will expedite any document request the defendant might make."

"We concur, Your Honor," Stanford announced. It was disheartening to hear the Justice Department concur in this railroad job.

The judge looked at me. "I suppose we should get your input, Mr. Patterson."

I wanted to scream, "Get my input?" We had been given no opportunity for discovery, were facing a criminal indictment, and had yet to even see the various motions filed by Jordyn and the government. I took a minute to think maybe the rush to judgment could play into my hands.

Hans wasn't present, but I think even he would have been surprised to hear me say, "No objection, Your Honor. We are ready for trial whenever you empanel the jury."

I had just thrown the first grenade into my opponent's carefully orchestrated strategy. I felt sure that asking for a jury trial would catch Jordyn, Stanford, and the judge off guard. Any reasonably competent lawyer would want the court to try a complex intellectual property case. They had forgotten that I wasn't supposed to be a competent lawyer. I was a lawyer who had been told to do his best to lose the case.

Duke interrupted again. My opinion of him was beginning to change.

"Your Honor, why the rush to judgment? My motion to intervene is still pending. If I didn't know better, I'd say Mr. Patterson simply wants to collect his fee and head off into the sunset. We need months if not years of discovery, depositions, and motions."

Normally I would have been outraged by Duke's characterization of my motives, but he was doing a bang-up job of convincing anyone who was listening that my client had a fool for a lawyer. I caught Jordyn and Judge Moorman exchanging a furtive look. Neither one wanted this case to drag out for years.

She gave the judge the out he needed.

"Your Honor, my clients want this matter resolved as soon as possible, but Mr. Madigan is entitled to have his motion heard before we go to trial. We can review his motion this afternoon and respond expeditiously. Could the court hold a hearing on his motion this Friday? In the meantime, both parties can work to find trial dates that don't conflict with anyone's schedule."

She was buying time, and probably giving Hans time to pay me a visit. I didn't want that to happen. Duke rose again to address the court, thankfully giving me a minute to think.

"Your Honor, with all due respect, what she has proposed is outrageous. Mr. Patterson should be on his feet objecting to high heaven. This is a complex intellectual property case that requires the testimony of experts. Mr. Patterson is acting like it's a fender bender."

Duke had given me the perfect opportunity.

"Your Honor, now I object. Mr. Madigan has impugned my integrity and thrown doubt on my competence. I know exactly what I'm doing. The plaintiffs claim the software in question belongs to them. So let them prove it. I don't think Ms. Duarte would have filed her complaint unless she had all her ducks in a row. If she and her clients think the software in question belongs to them, let's tee it up. If they aren't ready to prove the software is theirs, they should never have filed the complaint.

"My client is sitting in jail, waiting for justice. If Ms. Duarte and Mr. Stanford want to trade places, I have no objection to slow walking to trial one day. But if Mr. Ruple is to remain behind bars, I demand a quick trial, whether it be the civil or criminal case.

"Moreover, since I'm already standing, how about setting a

reasonable bail for my client? He's no axe murderer."

The judge looked to Stanford for rescue, and he complied.

"Your Honor, I regret that I may be responsible for the confusion regarding bail. I had hoped Mr. Patterson and I could agree to a reasonable bail, and I told him so. But information has recently come to our attention that confirms Mr. Ruple is a risk to our national security. I fully intended to advise Mr. Patterson that the U.S. government would oppose bail for his client. If he wants a bail hearing, I suggest he file a motion. We will respond, and the court can set a hearing on the matter in due course."

Suddenly the government wanted to slow walk bail. I wondered why, but I wasn't going to object. As I had explained to his grandfather, David was safer in jail than out on the streets. However, it was time for me to act the incompetent lawyer again.

"Hogwash, Your Honor."

"Pardon me," responded the judge in glacial tones.

"Hogwash. David Ruple is as much a national security risk as I am. Opposing counsel is doing everything she can to slow down the inevitable jury verdict that David's software belongs to him. If they were so confident about their case, they would consent to Mr. Madigan's intervention and join me in asking that the court set this matter for a jury trial as soon as possible."

"Sit down, Mr. Patterson. You are out of order. You are not in charge of the court's calendar—I am." Judge Moorman had finally decided to take charge.

"If you want bail for your client, file a motion. If you want a trial, file a motion. Even Mr. Madigan understands that's how things work in this court. Do you?"

"Yes, Your Honor, I do. May I ask how to get access to my client?"

"File a motion," the judge repeated. "Speaking of motions, Ms. Duarte I believe you have several motions pending."

I couldn't help myself. "Your Honor, my office has not received one motion from Ms. Duarte."

"May I explain, Your Honor?" she asked.

"I certainly hope so," Moorman answered, idly flipping through the pages of his calendar.

"As Mr. Stanford has advised the court, we are dealing with a defendant who is a national security risk and computer software that is proprietary. We've filed several motions to ensure that matters before this court don't find their way onto the front page of the *Post* or in the hands of our nation's enemies. The court might note that so far there has been no publicity about either the civil or criminal matter.

"We did not want to serve Mr. Patterson with our motions until after this hearing. We've asked that he be placed under a gag order. The same will apply to Mr. Madigan, now of course, as well as all other parties involved. We appreciate the court closing the courtroom to the press per our motion."

I wasn't concerned about a gag order. I don't believe in trying one's case in the press. Duke, on the other hand, loves the cameras. I did wonder what other motions had been filed under seal. I had a feeling I was about to find out.

Duke stood. "Your Honor, may I respond."

"No, we are going to proceed my way. I am going to rule on the plaintiff's motions which are all procedural. After you and Mr. Patterson have reviewed the motions, either of you may file a motion to reconsider. I assure you that I will keep an open mind."

Duke sat down. He knew neither he nor I were going to get anywhere with this toady of a judge.

"First, as to the plaintiff's motion for a gag order, the motion is granted. The details will follow the recommendations outlined in Ms. Duarte's motion. The gag order applies to all parties, counsels, and employees of the respective law firms. Let me warn counsel that this court will not look favorably on any breach. What is said and done in this courtroom stays in this courtroom. Am I clear?"

We all heard a surreptitious, "Crystal, Your Honor."

Even Moorman laughed, clearly tickled by Duke's movie reference. He waited for the obligatory chuckles to die down. "All pleadings, motions, etc. will be filed under seal. Mr. Madigan, your motion will be sealed, and any other motions or pleadings you wish to file will be as well, even though you aren't yet a party. The gag order applies to you and your client, as well."

The train was leaving the station.

"Plaintiff's motion that Mr. Ruple's applications for intellectual property protections before the U.S. Copyright Office and the U.S. Patent and Trademark Office be stayed is granted. An order consistent with Ms. Duarte's motion will be forthcoming and served on Mr. Patterson in due course.

"As per Ms. Duarte's motion to close the courtroom to the press, my earlier order will remain in place. Only the parties, counsel, and critical law firm employees will be allowed to gain entrance for any reason regarding this case.

"Finally, Mr. Patterson. you have implied that this court is in no hurry to resolve this case. Nothing could be further from the truth. I fully intend to set this case for trial at a time that's not prejudicial to any party. If you really want me to convene a jury, I expect a motion complete with authority for a jury trial on my desk post haste. This court will not tolerate delay tactics or frivolous motions."

I thought to myself, "Truth is this court won't tolerate motions or delays unless the request come from Ms. Duarte or Mr. Sanford."

Duke nudged me under the table, rose, and asked, "Your Honor, would the court entertain a motion to remove Mr. Patterson as counsel for the defendant? He's clearly in over his head."

Moorman had had it up to his ears.

"Until your motion to intervene is granted, this court will not accept or entertain any motion you file, Mr. Madigan."

With a bang of his gavel, Moorman gathered his robes and left the bench for his chambers.

33

DUARTE AND STANFORD LEFT THE COURTROOM QUICKLY, giving me no chance to ask the thousand questions I had. They were probably in chambers right now deciding how to deal with my demand for a jury trial and Duke's motion to intervene. Only Duke remained.

"That was fun," he said with a grimace. "But I don't think anything we say or do is going to make one bit of difference. You're up against a stacked deck, my friend. They won't even let you talk to your client. Maybe my strategy is our best chance."

"Brian was able to give David a note telling him not to worry. Today was all theatre, and I do have a plan, although God knows what it is at this moment." I felt miserable, wondering if maybe he was right.

At that moment Brian reappeared in the courtroom. He had bolted out when the judge banged his gavel. He looked troubled, and I waited for the bad news.

"David's girlfriend is in the hospital. She came to court hoping to see David, but they wouldn't let her in. As she was leaving the courthouse, two thugs grabbed her and tried to force her into their car. She put up a good fight, and fortunately Big Mike got there in just a few seconds. He knocked one of the attackers to the street and they both jumped in the car and sped off. He took her to the hospital and is with her now. I'm pretty sure they went to George Washington; it's the closest. I've got a car waiting if you want to see her."

I told Duke we would talk later and followed Brian to the waiting car. I had no idea how Brian knew all this, but now was not the time to ask. Hans and his gang had gone too far. It was time to take off the gloves.

Mike met us at the door to Rita's room. He told me she had suffered bruises from trying to get away and scrapes from the pavement but would be okay. The ER doc had decided to keep her overnight as a precaution. Her room would be guarded by two of Mike's men.

I thanked him for his quick action, but he looked unusually flustered, so I asked him why.

"Well, could you try to convince Rita that I'm one of the good guys?" he asked. "She doesn't know who to trust, and who could blame her?"

I knocked softly before slowly opening the door to her room. The young woman I saw dozing in the bed had long, dark hair and petite features. She was propped up by several pillows, and I noticed a bandage on her forehead. She woke with a start almost immediately, and I quickly tried to reassure her. She didn't seem the least bit frightened, and smiled when I pulled up a chair and said, "Rita, my name's Jack Patterson. I'm David's lawyer. We were in the courtroom today when you were attacked. Mike is one of my men, a good guy," I said with a smile. "They're here to protect you, although I heard you did a pretty good job of defending yourself. I hope you'll let him and his colleagues do their job. David will be relieved to know you're in their care."

"I know who you are," she answered with unexpected poise. "Royce told me you'd been hired and to expect a call. I googled you so I know a little bit about you and recognize you from the pictures on the Internet. I appreciate what Mike did for me today, but the men who tried to grab me also said they worked for you. I shouldn't have come. I knew I should stay in hiding, but I thought if I could only see David..." Her voice trailed off. She suddenly looked very lonely.

"I know he feels the same way, Rita. When I saw him in jail, your safety was all he cared about. The government is taking a tough stance about allowing him visitors, but I'll do my level best to get them to make an exception for you. In the meantime, listen to Mike. He'll keep you safe."

"What on earth do they want? David is no criminal; he wouldn't harm a soul."

"I was about to ask you the same question. Apparently, the charges relate to software he's developed. When he made application for intellectual property protections for this software, several major technology companies sued him, claiming he'd stolen their creation. More of these companies have joined the suit in the last couple of weeks. I'm not a patent lawyer, nor do I understand the creative process or terminology, but that's the crux of what the civil lawsuit is about. Simply put, these companies want to get their hands on whatever software David has developed.

"I'm less sure about why the government has brought a criminal charge. I haven't seen the indictment yet—it's all been very hush-hush so far. But I do know it involves the same software. What do you know? Did you work on it?"

"No, I didn't," Rita replied. "We work on projects together all the time, but always for clients, not on our own ideas. Any software we develop usually belongs to the client. That's part of the contract, and we have nothing to do with intellectual property rights, except to answer patent lawyer's questions."

"David said something about helping his cousin. Said it was no big deal."

"Oh—that. Now that you remind me, I do remember. His cousin Tony was having trouble getting a job because he had a record. David had an idea he thought might help, but I'm pretty sure nothing came of it."

"So what was his idea," I asked, trying to be patient.

"He said something about expungement, whatever that is. We didn't pursue it, and he didn't bring it up again. You don't know David, but he's always getting new ideas. He writes code like other people doodle or knit. Like, we'll be at a Nat's game, and you think he's keeping score. In fact, he's writing code all over the scorecard. He says it relaxes him. He files away most of his doodling in a storage box, and that's the end of it."

"Do you think he followed up on his idea for his cousin? You know, developed software to fix his problem?" I asked.

"I don't think so. Like I said, he never mentioned it again. But even if he did, it can't have been a big deal. There's no way his idea for his cousin was more than just talk, no way it could be what these big companies want. One thing I do know is that David would never steal or copy someone's work." Her words were strong, but her voice wasn't, and her eyes were beginning to droop.

"Rita, you've been through a lot today—the ER doc told me you need to rest. We'll talk again soon, and I'll try to get you in to see David. Will you do me a favor? After you're discharged from the hospital tomorrow, Mike will take you to a safe place where you can stay for a few days. He'll take you by your place first to get some clothes and whatever else you need. While you're there, can you grab that storage box, that is unless the government seized it when they took his computers."

"They didn't, and sure, no problem," she said. "Do you think I can get my computer back?"

"I'll try. In the meantime, tell Mike what kind of computer you need."

"I built the one they seized myself. It's unique, and I really hope they'll give it back."

I knew the chances of getting one's computer back from the government were about zero, but I didn't want to disappoint her.

"I've got a friend who can get you just about any computer you want until yours is returned. Tell Mike what you need, okay?"

"Thanks. Tell David I love him, will you?" She turned her head into the pillow. I watched her for a few seconds before closing the door.

I told Mike to be sure to take the storage box to the office. I had no idea what was in it, but at least the government couldn't get it. We also talked about where Rita could stay for the time being. Maggie had built her dream home on acreage she and Walter owned in Maryland. It wasn't far from Walter's company headquarters and would be a good place for Stella to meet with Rita to go over the contents of the box.

Mike wanted to drive me home, but I declined, once more emphasizing the need to stick with the plan. I didn't tell him that I'd decided to ignore it.

I figured Hans would be waiting for me somewhere, and I thought I knew where. Sure enough, I found him in Lafayette Park sitting on the same park bench we had sat on just a few days earlier. Today the park was full of tents for some protest or the other, but he was all alone on the bench. I joined him, and for a few moments neither of us said a word. Hans broke the silence.

"I thought you fired your security team."

"For me. I'm not going to quit protecting my clients or my loved ones. I'm not going to ask how you know I fired Lisa and Mike. By the way, you try to harm Rita again and any thought of me losing the case is out the window. The same goes if you try to go after David or anyone else for that matter."

He shot back, "Rita isn't part of our deal."

"We don't have a deal. You threatened to harm my daughter unless I lose this case. I think I'm doing a pretty good job of it so far. But if you try to harm me, my family, my friends, or my clients, you will find out what a good lawyer I can be."

"Not if you're dead," he rebutted. He'd made his point, but so had I.

I was tired of playing games and for a quick minute thought about telling him to go ahead and get it over with. I didn't, afraid he might call my bluff and do it. Which gave me an idea that I kept to myself.

"Speaking of losing the case," he continued. "What's the deal with encouraging Duke Madigan. He's a nutball and a nuisance."

"He could make it difficult for both of us if he's on the outside shouting at the press and anyone else who'll listen. If Gloria is a party, she and Duke are both subject to the gag order. I don't know if she has a piece of David's software or not, but what's the saying? 'Keep your friends close, and your enemies closer.'"

He gave me a look but chose to ignore the irony of my comment.

"I hadn't thought about the gag order. Makes sense, but still. And what's going on with asking for a jury?"

"You didn't tell me how to lose the case, you just ordered me to do so."

"A jury introduces an element that's difficult to control. So does

Madigan. He makes you look bad."

"Isn't that the point? What difference does it make anyway; this is the last case I'll ever try."

"You mean all that going to work for Red and closing the office is true?" He confirmed once again that my office was bugged.

"Absolutely. Do you really think I could live with myself after losing David's case and selling him down the river to the Feds?"

Hans asked, "Then why do you care what we do to him and his girlfriend?"

I took a deep breath. "I care because they're just two young people who created a computer program. That's all they've done, that's it. I can live with losing their case, but I cannot and will not be complicit in their murder. You've said you don't make threats. Well, I do. You touch one hair on their heads, and you will have grabbed a tiger by the tail. A tiger who will do everything in his power to see that you and your clients are brought to justice."

Hans stood up. "Don't be so testy. You do your part of our bargain, and David and his girlfriend will be just fine. They're in plenty of trouble without my interference."

I don't know if he heard me as he walked away. "We don't have a bargain."

34

I SAT ON THE PARK BENCH A LITTLE WHILE LONGER, just thinking. I was faced with a Hobson's choice. If I somehow managed to pull off a win for David, Hans would make sure I was dead by the end of the day, and no telling who else. If I lost as planned, David would spend years in prison and Hans would probably kill me anyway, and no telling who else. I still found it hard to believe the lawyers for the opposition knew about Hans. Well, maybe Jordyn. But he was still a hired hand; I wanted whoever was pulling his string. It was time to dust off my backup plan.

I walked back to the office and found Brian poring over all the motions Duarte had filed now that we'd finally been given copies. It was good to see Maggie at her desk. She was doing a good job of pretending to be mad as hell about my closing the office, or maybe it wasn't an act after all. I announced that Rita was okay, and that Big Mike would take charge of her protection. I couldn't tell Maggie where Mike was taking her until we were away from our wider audience.

I thought about calling up an old friend of mine who still worked at Justice, asking her out for drinks. She was bound to be aware of the case, might even have approved the filing. If that were the case, she probably wouldn't come without bringing Stanford with her, and that would defeat the purpose. I knew her well and felt sure she didn't know anything about the threats or attempted kidnapping. For that matter, I really didn't think Stanford did either. In the end, I realized she couldn't help and that it would be unfair to ask; I was picking at straws. It was time to face whatever lay ahead.

I put Brian to work on the first draft of our request for a jury trial, suggesting he call Grant Roney for help with the legal research. I'd called him on Stella's burner phone before leaving to find Hans at the park. Grant assured me I was correct in believing that my right to a trial by jury was inviolate.

I had no chance of winning if Moorman adjudicated the facts. Hans had made it abundantly clear that Moorman was in his pocket.

Maggie and Brian were both hard at work, but I couldn't clear my mind, couldn't be still. When Maggie looked up and gave me a glare, I knew it was time to leave before I said something I shouldn't. I decided not to go straight home and took the Metro to Nanny O'Brien's in Cleveland Park. Nanny's is an Irish Pub and was a regular hangout both when I was in law school and when I had worked at Justice, but not so much these days.

I took a seat at the bar, and the bartender brought me a pint without comment. I noticed an attractive young woman at the other end of the bar. She returned my automatic smile, but I took a deep breath and returned to the issue at hand. How could I turn this case around? I'd produced several legal miracles in my career, but this time I couldn't see a solution. Frustrated, I ordered brats and another Guinness, and while I ate a little glimmer of a possibility appeared.

I let my mind drift to the imagery of the courtroom. The gallery would be packed with opposing counsel, the judge would be as antagonistic as ever, Jordyn would be aloof, and Duke would be obnoxious. But none of them mattered. I saw only myself and twelve jurors. If I could get to that point, David had a chance.

"One for the road, Jack?" the bartender asked.

"No thanks, Colin. It's been a long day. By the way, who's the woman at the end of the bar? She looks familiar?"

"Don't know. Want me to find out."

Another night I might have bought her a drink, and who knows… but not tonight.

"Nah, just curious." I gave him a generous tip, crossed the street, and throwing caution to the wind, hailed a waiting cabbie who drove the few blocks to my condominium in silence.

I opened the front door with trepidation, but there were no bur-
glars, no kidnappers, only a few dishes in the sink and an empty bed.

The next morning, I woke early after a night of dreaming
about ways to force the judge into a jury trial, all of them brilliant.
Unfortunately, I couldn't remember a single one. I knew I would
win that argument at some point; the question was when. Time was
not my friend.

Brian had left a draft of our motion for a jury trial on my desk.
He must have worked all night. Once again Maggie had called to say
she would be late. I poured a cup of coffee and spent the next hour
editing his work. I found him in the conference room organizing
folders for trial and handed him my edits.

"Nice work. Was Grant helpful?"

"More than helpful. Most of the work is his. He said you owe him
dinner at DeCarlo's."

"Gladly—I owe him more than dinner. Make sure he sends me
a bill."

Brian asked, "No matter how right we are on the jury issue,
what's to keep the judge from ruling against us?"

I wasn't comfortable discussing strategy in my office. I put my
fingers to my lips.

"I haven't had breakfast. Let's go across the street for an egg
sandwich."

I nixed the McDonalds around the corner. Brian snagged a cab,
and we headed to Barker's instead.

We picked up coffee and pastries from the reception area, and I
found a small conference room where we could talk in private. "Our
opposition is opposed to a jury trial, but they also don't want to give
us grounds for an appeal. Your brief is ironclad, and they will know
it. My bet is they'll slow walk their response and encourage the judge
to put our request on the back burner. David is stuck in jail without
a computer, and so far, the lawsuit has received zero publicity. I've
got to come up with a way to get them to change their strategy, to
ask for a jury, or at least not object to our request."

"What about publicity?" Brian suggested. "You have friends in the media. Can't you talk to them off the record?"

"I've thought of that, but involving the media is almost always a risky tactic, even off the record. Besides, the judge has issued a gag order. David hasn't got a prayer if I'm held in contempt."

"Do you have to be the one to tell them what's going on? Isn't there someone else who'd be willing to speak to a reporter you know?"

"Brian, you're a genius, and I know the just the right person. Make lunch reservations for two at Joe's Stone Crab. I can't think of a more visible restaurant in town these days. Then find a way to call Duke without tipping off good old Hans. Tell him I suggested that he might want to drop by our table. Not a word about the case, just a friendly stop to see a friend. Tell him he'll enjoy meeting my guest. And feel free to imply that she's a she."

Brian grinned and was gone before I could pick up my phone. Although we hadn't talked in months, I knew Cheryl would take my call, and I felt sure she'd meet me for lunch. I sure wished I could see Hans' face when he heard my call.

Cheryl Cole was a reporter for CNN. I'd known her in college, and for a brief time she was married to my friend, Woody Cole. When Woody was charged with the murder of Arkansas's newest senator, I'd used her obvious need to get a scoop to my advantage, and her stock rose when the publicity went national. We ended up collaborating on a couple of other cases, but I was always careful to keep Cheryl at a healthy arm's length. Her recent affair with a Belgian prince had raised East Coast eyebrows, and CNN had reduced her airtime accordingly.

Joe's Stone Crab was already packed when I arrived. I noticed Cheryl sail through the door just as the waiter was seating me. I couldn't help but admire my old friend as I watched her work the room. Maggie would have sniffed and said something like "well, she obviously keeps her plastic surgeon busy." She might have been right, but Cheryl looked great to me. She was dressed to the nines, and I enjoyed watching her work the room like the pro she was.

I rose as she approached our table. She gave me a peck on the cheek and told the waiter to bring "her usual" as she seated herself in the chair I held for her. In the old days, her 'usual' meant vodka in a coffee cup. Now, it meant a pricey chardonnay disguised in a tinted glass as "lemonade with no ice."

After a few exchanges about mutual friends, she brusquely changed the subject. "Okay, Jack, to what do I owe this pleasure? I hope you've got a story worth my while."

Cheryl was always direct, and I did have one hell of a story. But since I couldn't reveal even a single word of the truth, I lied. "I'm as boring as ever, but it's been a while, and every time I see Woody, he asks about you."

"Dear Woody—I do occasionally miss him." She dabbed at an eye, and I had to bite my lower lip not to laugh. "But Jack—you're a terrible liar. What's the real reason for asking me to lunch in the most visible restaurant in town? You want to be seen with me, but you don't want to tell me why, which means there's a juicy story behind this charade. Come on, time to fess up."

The jig was up, but Duke saved the day, strolling up at the perfect moment. He greeted me as though we were fast friends, but quickly turned his attention and Texas charm on Cheryl, who hadn't been around a cowboy in a long time. He never mentioned David's case, but easily directed the conversation to a class action he was about to file against several drug companies. Before you could say ten-gallon hat, she was batting her long lashes and asking how she could help. Why sure, she'd be happy to interview his whistleblower.

My presence was clearly superfluous, so I left them with their lemonade and bourbon, my purpose easily accomplished.

With any luck, Jordyn would soon be on the phone railing that I was in contempt. I would deny, deny, deny—hoping she'd worry about leaks to the press. She knew that if the press heard even a rumor about David's software or the twin lawsuits, she'd have hell to pay. Maybe that worry would lead her to change course, pushing for a rapid resolution.

Walking back to the office I checked in with Big Mike to make sure Rita was safe and secure.

He told me they'd settled in at the farmhouse, that she seemed to be okay. The storage box had been retrieved, and she'd spoken to Stella about her computer needs. He also mentioned that Clovis and Stella were already on their way back to DC. I smiled to myself; Walter hadn't let any grass grow under his feet.

I deliberately chose to walk past 'Hans's' park bench in Lafayette Park and was surprised to find it empty. This fact was strange in itself as much of the park has become either a home for the homeless or a relatively safe spot for them to pass the time of day. But it was a beautiful day, and I had to give my subterfuge time to work. I sat down and wondered who would call first. It wasn't long before I had my answer.

"Jack, Jordyn here. Tell me that I won't have to seek contempt against you for talking to the press. I hear you were lunching with Cheryl Cole."

"C'mon, Jordyn, Cheryl's an old friend. She used to be married to my best friend, and we get together for lunch occasionally. Neither of us mentioned the case. How could she know anything about it?"

"Right. And now you're going to tell me that Duke Madigan's appearance was just a coincidence?"

"It was. I left them talking about Supreme Court judges and their links to corporate America. If you don't believe me, feel free to ask them. Now here's a question for you: are you having me followed? Really?"

I knew Jordyn would never call Cheryl; too many lights would go on: Cheryl was no dummy and could be a bulldog once she sniffed a story. I also knew Jordyn would never admit I was being followed, much less who was behind the hire. She thought about her response for a minute or so, deciding to change tactics.

"I don't want there to be any misunderstanding about this," she said slowly. "My clients have no intention of settling this litigation unless you roll over. But what do you say about meeting with Stanford and me this afternoon? Nothing formal, no gloves on; just a chance to cut through the months of posturing we've come to expect in cases of this size."

This was the opening I had hoped for, but I had no intention of making it easy for her.

"What about Duke?" I asked.

"What about him? He's probably already got your friend Cheryl..." She managed to stop before she went too far. "He's not a party, nor is he likely to be one. His client doesn't care about her son; all she wants is money. Why bring him into the discussion? He'll have his day in court later."

"Why ask Stanford then?"

"He's the one person who can give you access to your client. He can also become very difficult if he feels left out," she answered. She'd scored a good point, and she knew it.

"If we can find a way for me to earn my fee with the least amount of effort, I'm all ears."

This last statement was for Hans and anyone else who was listening. Her sudden gasp took me aback. Maybe she really didn't know about Hans.

She recovered quickly and asked, "How about drinks at The Jefferson? Say six o'clock?" She hung up without waiting for my answer.

I felt suddenly uncomfortable and looked up to see two pairs of eyes staring at me. The young couple were poorly dressed, carried heavy backpacks, and obviously wanted my bench. I handed the woman a twenty and turned toward my office, thanking the Fates again for my undeserved good fortune.

35

I MULLED OVER HER INVITATION: drinks at the Jefferson, the longtime hangout for former presidents and cabinet officials. I wondered what incentives Jordyn would offer to get me to back down from my demand for a jury trial. On the other hand, I needed to convince her of the wisdom of an early trial, the sooner the better. I called an old friend from Justice who agreed to meet me that very afternoon.

Solomon Banks was a retired deputy Attorney General in the antitrust division of the Department of Justice. He later became one of the two founding members of the Banks and Tuohey law firm. Solomon had been my boss at Justice and later recruited me to join his firm. He had retired by the time his old firm and I had a falling out that resulted in my resignation. Solomon now taught antitrust law at Georgetown Law School as a Professor Emeritus.

When twenty competing companies join suit against a lone individual, red flags fly high at Justice. I knew that my meeting with Solomon would give the plaintiffs heart palpitations. We met that afternoon at the law school and talked only about old times at Justice. Once again, my intention was to throw a monkey wrench into their plans, and I bet Jordyn would find a way to bring the meeting up this afternoon.

I knew the office was bugged, so I took every opportunity to broadcast the possibility of hiring co-counsel, getting around the gag order, and turning the case entirely over to Duke, anything to unnerve our opponents. I also mused out loud how I needed more staff and more time to prepare the case. Hopefully, Jordyn would conclude that any delay would benefit me and work against her. I had no idea if my game-playing would have any effect, but at least it made me feel like I was doing something until our meeting at the Jefferson.

Jordyn had reserved a quiet table in a corner of the bar. Stanford was on time and told me he was sorry that Jordyn was running late. He seemed nervous, which wasn't his reputation or the impression he'd had given me before. He already had a beer, so I ordered a glass of cabernet. After we'd exchanged a few pleasantries, I decided to see why he was so antsy.

"I was surprised to hear you agree to Jordyn's request that we try the civil case first. I felt sure you'd expect the criminal proceedings to take precedence."

"I wondered about you, too," he responded. "How are you going to prove the software belongs to your client without his testimony and by waiving his fifth amendment rights?"

I wasn't going to give him my trial strategy, so I fell back on my ruse. "This will be my last trial. The client means nothing to me, so what the hell? I don't care who goes first if I get paid."

My answer clearly bothered him; he remained silent, nursing his beer. I tried to press him.

"When are you going to give me access to my client?" I asked.

"Well, let's see how this meeting goes," he replied.

Why was he stalling? Or was he unaware of the threats and other attempts at intimidation? I tried another tack.

"Are you aware that someone tried to grab David's girlfriend outside the courthouse yesterday? Or that she ended up in the hospital?"

Stanford seemed surprised, but not overly concerned.

"What was she doing there in the first place?" he countered.

"She hoped to see David. Both his mother and Rita need to see David to be sure he's all right. If you won't give me access, at least let him see his family."

He sat up and snapped, "He might try to sneak information to them, that's why. National security is at stake here."

"Oh, come on, Stanford. You don't really believe that David's software involves national security. I still don't know what it does, but it can't be much of a threat."

"The software that young man designed most definitely involves our national security. When you learn what it does and how it affects this country, you won't be so cocksure of his innocence."

Before I could figure out why he was cocksure of David's guilt, I heard the clatter of high heels and looked up to see Jordyn, who seated herself with a confident flourish.

She smiled warmly in Stanford's direction. "William, you haven't given away our trial strategy yet, have you?"

Her comment was meant to be amusing, but she had told me that she and Stanford were on a first name basis, and that they were in cahoots, working together hand and glove—an obvious and unhealthy collaboration between private industry and the Department of Justice as far as I was concerned.

She ordered a glass of wine and continued, "Sorry to be late, but I was just reviewing your motion for a jury trial. Nice work, Jack. but come on. You know a jury trial is simply inappropriate. A complex case such as this will surely involve expert witnesses and software engineering language. You can't expect a jury to understand half of what is being presented by either party."

I repeated what I'd told Stanford minutes ago.

"As I told Stanford, I have no idea what the software does, and I haven't had access to my client to find out. Right now, I don't know what kind of experts I need, much less how to cross examine yours. Maybe if you give me time enough to get up to speed, I might reconsider trying the case to the judge, but for now, the only way I can try this case is by the seat of my pants. And I can only do that in front of a jury who'll be as ignorant about software development as I am."

Jordyn gave Stanford a look which I hoped meant "We got him by the balls. Let's grab them and run."

Stanford followed suit. "Jack, surely you understand. In cases involving national security there are certain protocols and procedures that must be followed, not the least of which requires you to have a security clearance. Anyone who works with you will have to be cleared as well. I understand your need to interview him, but I can't give you access to Ruple until we've jumped through all the hoops."

I wanted to remind him that a few days ago he was willing to give me unlimited access to David and let him out on bail. That was clearly before someone higher up the pay scale gave him different instructions. Besides, I needed a speedy trial more than I needed access to my client.

"I had code word clearance when I was at Justice." What I didn't mention was that my clearance had been renewed on several occasions and was currently valid. If he didn't know, I wasn't going to tell him.

"That was a long time ago, Jack," he replied with an indulgent smile. "You'll need to go through the entire process again, and you know how long that takes. Why, it's worse than renewing your passport."

"Well, I guess we have no option but to put this case on hold for a while," I said, trying my best to sound thoroughly deflated. "You want me to waive a jury trial, and I can't do that without access to my client or experts. I really hoped I could try this case quickly and retire. It's such an obvious loser. Now I'm not sure what to do. Do you think I need to file a motion and get a court order before I even talk to another lawyer about taking my place? Sure do hate to lose my fee."

Neither of them answered my question. Maybe I had laid it on too thick.

I waited and Jordyn finally said, "This wasn't the chat I had wanted or expected, but if you are adamant about a jury trial, I'm not sure we have anything further to discuss."

"The same goes for access," I replied evenly. "There's no way I can waive a jury trial without consulting my client. I'd be disbarred before you could say habeas corpus. I guess we're at a stalemate."

36

JORDYN AND WILLIAM SHOWED NO SIGNS OF LEAVING, so I made my apologies and left. I was afraid I might over play my hand if I lingered. If I hadn't managed to convince them to rush to a resolution, I really would have to play this case straight, which meant interrogatories, depositions, experts, and a mountain of motions that would surely drive our judge to drink. It wasn't my preference, and it risked my client spending a very long time in a jail cell, but I wasn't about to agree to a trial to the court—not before Judge Moorman at any rate. On my walk back to the office, I ran into a sight for sore eyes.

"Clovis Jones, I'll be damned. What brings you to DC?"

He frowned. "Cut the act. Nobody is following you or listening."

"It was an act, but I am genuinely glad to see you. Where are you staying?" I asked.

"We're at the farmhouse. We're supposed to be working at Walter's headquarters which is only a stone's throw away, so it makes sense. Stella has already bonded with Rita, and they're hard at work going through David's box of ideas. Stella told me to give this to you."

He handed me a cellphone, smiled, and said, "You struck a nerve when you said someone was better at her job than she is. She says no one can bug this phone but use it wisely. Your opponents may have bugged more phones than yours."

He continued as we walked.

"I talked to Beth earlier today—she's okay. Her instincts are to come to DC, but I convinced her that if she were here, you'd spend all your time worrying about her. I've talked to Royce and the family in St. Louis. She's well protected, not to mention Thibodeaux's specialist, whoever that is. The St. Louis family wouldn't discuss him, but they know he's in the city."

"Thanks, Clovis. I appreciate your dealing with her in person. She trusts your judgment, and so do I. Thank you."

Clovis also confirmed that I was being followed, but not so close as to constitute a threat. "They're watching where you go, and who you're meeting with. Get used to it."

"Any attempts by Hans or his men to get close to the farmhouse?" I asked.

"So far, no."

"Anything else?"

"Jordyn and Stanford have met with the judge on two occasions. He also joined them at the Jefferson as soon as you left. I expect something will come down the pipe before too long."

"Pull off keeping track of the judge and counsel. What you just told me about their meeting comes as no surprise. I thought I wanted to know if they were colluding, but I really don't. I regret stooping to their tactics; it leaves a bad taste in my mouth. Besides, I have better things for you and your people to do." I gave him new marching orders.

"One last thing. If Stella and Rita come up with anything, have them tell Maggie. She will understand its significance and will find a way to let me know."

"Time to go," he said. "People might think we're talking about something important."

"I sure wish you could join me for a beer," I complained. We'd reached McPherson Square.

"There'll be plenty of time for beer when this is over," he said, turning toward the Metro.

Since I was in the neighborhood, I headed to one of my favorite watering holes. Tonight, I could have a great cheeseburger and crispy fries and make both Hans and Jordyn nervous at the same time. The Post Pub used to be the go-to place for reporters to meet and eat. Sadly, reporters don't indulge in two martini lunches or write their columns at a table anymore. But it's still a great place for a burger in the late afternoon before braving the Metro, and there are always a few reporters who haven't given up old habits.

The Post isn't known for its wine selection, but I ordered a decent Oregon pinot noir and got comfortable at the bar. I chatted with the bartender and caught up on the local sports news scrolling on the large TV overhead. After the first glass, I ordered another and a cheeseburger with fries. What the heck, there was no one waiting for me at home. I debated with the man seated next to me about who the next owner of the Commanders would be, and that was my excitement for the evening. What I wouldn't give to be in Louisiana with Abby Broussard right now.

After my third glass of wine, I knew it was time to go home. I hailed a cab and didn't notice until I'd fastened the seat belt that the driver was Hans.

"Don't try to jump out, Jack. You'll only get hurt, maybe run over. And don't worry—I am taking you home, but I've got a message you won't like."

"I've never thought of you as a bearer of good news," I said.

"You need to fold on your request for a jury trial, and you need to do it tomorrow. A jury trial introduces an element of uncertainty that's unacceptable. This case goes before the judge."

"What happened to 'we don't care how you pull it off?'"

"People are nervous, they're not sure you're on board. Your meetings with old friends have on them on edge."

"I'm supposed to become a hermit?"

"No, but meeting with reporters, former Justice employees, and being friendly with Duke is not the behavior they expected. They smell a skunk."

"What if I want to do it my way? I've never been good at taking orders."

"Maybe not, but this time you'll do as you are told. We have a bargain, and if you want your daughter to walk down the aisle with Jeff, you will do as you are told. You have no other options."

I felt my temperature rising. "Let me say this one more time. We don't have any bargain. What we have is you threating my daughter's life."

"Not just your daughter Jack. Don't forget Maggie, Clovis, and Stella. You'll do as you are told this time, or you'll attend the funerals of your whole team, one by one, before you face the same fate. And if you become too close to anyone else before this case is over, they'll die, too. What's the saying, Jack? 'Not bragging, just facts.'"

The cab pulled up to my condominium and as I stepped out, I turned to face the driver.

"I didn't think you were bragging. I would hope not. My family and friends are important to me. You obviously know that. If they were to be murdered, you wouldn't have to kill me; I would do it myself." I turned and walked into my building, trying not to look back as he drove away.

I'd been careful not to agree to his demand, just as I had made it clear we had no bargain. I needed time to think. I found the phone Stella had given me in my pocket and dialed a familiar number.

"Clovis. Any way you can come to my place without being noticed?"

"I'm already there."

37

CLOVIS HAD SEEN ME GET IN THE CAB and had rushed to my home. He'd swept it for bugs earlier in the day. We could talk freely, and boy did I need to talk to a friend. I told him what had transpired in the cab.

"Sounds like the stakes have gotten a little higher. What now?" he asked.

"For starters, I'd like to punch Hans in the nose. Then I'd like to win this lawsuit and expose every single person behind his threats."

"What's stopping you?"

"I can't bear the thought of something happening, someone getting killed because of me." I almost choked on the words.

"Hmph!" he answered with a snort. "Have you asked even one of us how we feel? We've all gone through this before and…"

"Clovis, you weren't on that island," I interrupted. "You haven't heard this guy. He's a professional; he means what he says. He almost killed me, and he will kill you, all of you."

We both let that sink in a minute. Clovis took his time before responding.

"In fact, we're all professionals, and it's our call whether to take the risk or not, this risk or any other for that matter. I know Walter is concerned about Maggie, rightfully so, but she doesn't feel the same way. She wants to be involved, to be at your side when you try a case. When her first husband left her, you gave her a career and the confidence to remarry. Do you think for a moment that she wants you to tank a lawsuit to protect her?

"Each of us not only owe you, but we also feel better about

ourselves when you put your trust in us. Look at Brian. You took a
gay soldier who couldn't get a job and turned him into a man who
has become the pride of his family. He researched every single
company in the complaint and wrote a brief in less than twenty-four
hours that has totally unnerved the opposition, convinced them that
no matter how they respond, his argument will win. He fought in
the Middle East. Do you think he's shaking in his boots over a jerk
like Hans? When you try to protect us, we're insulted.

"If you give in to Hans, we'll still love you, but as for respect, I'm
not so sure. A lawyer who would lose a case on purpose, whatever
the reason, is not the Jack Patterson we know. To hell with Hans!
We don't want protection; we want you to tell us how we can win."

It was a good lecture, one I needed to hear. But I still wasn't sure
what to do. I expected the judge to call us to the bench tomorrow and
give us a trial date. If I continued to demand a jury trial, there was a
good chance nothing terrible would happen; Hans would wait to see
if I blew the case. But at some point, his threats would become reality.

And Clovis was right. I needed to tell my team how I would proceed and let them decide whether they wanted to participate or not.
So now it was time for me to come to a decision.

He was waiting, by now used to my internal debates. I clapped
him on the shoulder and said, "My friend, gather the troops
tomorrow at the farmhouse. I need to think for a while and then
sleep on it. I'll drive out in the morning."

Clovis smiled. "No, you won't. I'll drive you there in the morning.
I'll be staying in your guest room tonight."

I do own a car, a very nice car, but I seldom drive it. I can't
stand DC traffic and parking downtown is impossible. I leave it in
the garage at my condominium and take it out just often enough to
keep the battery charged. I worried that it might not start the next
morning, but fortunately it purred like a kitten when Clovis turned
the ignition.

We picked up coffee on the way out of town. DC traffic never
ceases to amaze me. Its roads and highways are parking lots in the
mornings and afternoons. Where do all these people work, and why
do they put up with hour long or longer commutes both ways, five

days a week? Do they listen to books on tape, or do they dream of sailing into the sunset? The commuter trains and Metro cars are packed to the gills. So many people crammed into such tight spaces! I suppose it says something about the excitement of the city, its cultural and educational opportunities, museums, and fine restaurants. Or maybe not since these commuters must either prefer living in the suburbs or can't afford DC real estate.

My musings about traffic and commuters could only keep my mind off my dilemma for so long. I was still unsure exactly which course I would follow; so much depended on the judge and the opposition. But in the back of my mind, behind all the musings over traffic, a strategy was beginning to take shape.

"Clovis, find a way to talk to Royce without being overheard. Warn him that if my plans change, Hans may go after David. His clients fear David's computer skills as much as his software. Our chances of winning the lawsuit are slim, but win or lose, David poses a threat to them. If Hans is willing to murder me if I don't cave to their demands, he won't hesitate to arrange a prison suicide for David."

"I'll take care of it." His face was set in grim determination.

My team was already assembled by the time we walked in the front door. I was happy to see them enjoying each other's company as well as the pastries Maggie had contributed. I was also glad to see Rita, who looked none the worse for yesterday's experience. She rose to greet me, and I was surprised by how tall she was, easily as tall as David. Conversation quickly halted, and all eyes looked toward me and Rita. But before I could say a word, Brian informed us all that the judge's clerk had called. I was due at the courthouse at one o'clock. As Sherlock might have said, the game was afoot.

I thanked Brian and began, still unsure exactly what to say. "First, thank you for joining me this morning. Clovis has told me that despite significant threats to your safety, you all want to remain involved..."

Stella interrupted, her tone sharp and impatient, "Cut the intro, Jack. If you're ready to go for the win, we're all in, everyone in this room. Tell us how you're going to pull it off and quit with the worrying about our safety. It's a waste of time, and if you and Maggie are going to make today's hearing, we don't have much of it to waste."

My decision had been made for me.

"Okay. I'm pretty sure the judge will set the date for trial today. I don't know how soon, but Jordyn knows I'm not prepared to defend David in any way, shape, or form. Hell, I haven't even spoken with my client, much less performed discovery or deposed their experts. She'll make one last attempt to get me to waive a jury trial, probably with the judge's help, because she wants me to have less time to prepare. Given more time, I might find a hole in her case."

Maggie asked, "What can we do to get more time?"

"Normally, I would use every trick in a trial lawyer's book. I'd have scheduling conflicts, need more discovery, have an illness in the family, even claim witnesses had disappeared. But nothing about this case is normal, and if I'm right, more time also works against us."

"How's that?" she asked, looking confused.

"Well, I think there may be at least two holes in their case, both pointed out inadvertently by Duke and William Stanford. It will take some digging, but if we can confirm their existence, an early trial date might allow us to use them before Jordyn even realizes she's got a problem."

"Are you going to tell us what they are?" asked Brian.

"No, and not because I'm playing hide and seek. I don't want to prejudice the work I ask you to do. I'd rather give you projects and see what you turn up. Who knows? You might turn up something totally new to me. And don't worry—you'll know what I think long before trial. I'll need your help to devise a strategy to use against them."

No one argued or said a word. I waited a few minutes to gather my thoughts before continuing.

"I know you're all on board, but I need to tell you this. It's likely that this afternoon Hans will finally realize that I won't take orders from him, and you will all be in his crosshairs until this case is resolved. That's another reason that more time works against us. Clovis and Big Mike will meet with Martin to increase our security, so please be careful and listen to them."

"You've said your piece, now tell us what to do. Time's a'wastin!" Stella was ready to go to work. And even better, her enthusiasm was contagious.

"Okay—first, Stella and Rita. I need you to double your efforts to discover what David's software does. See if you can find a note or doodle that could be an early version of the software, especially anything that relates to his cousin. David is bound to have backed up his work on a cloud somewhere; try to find it."

"Will do," Stella answered, trying to stifle a grin. "But Jack, you don't have any idea what you're talking about, do you?"

"Not a clue," I admitted. "The only clouds I understand are cirrus and cumulus. But I've got a feeling there's a doodle or a mustard stain somewhere in that box that will help us win."

Rita wasn't shy. "If it's there, we'll find it."

"Next: Brian. I need you to be in two places at once. We need someone to man the office because Jordyn will surely try to bury us in mountains of motions, and they'll need your attention. At the same time, Maggie and I need you in the courtroom. I feel sure Jordyn has a few surprises up those designer sleeves. So please go to the office now and let me know whatever she's filed so far. Then meet us in the courtroom."

"And if she doesn't bury you in paper this morning?" he asked halfway out the door.

"Check with the court clerk at the courthouse for any filings. She may have conveniently forgotten to send them to us."

I didn't like to think a fellow lawyer might blatantly fail to follow the rules of procedure, but it has been known to happen.

"Clovis and Mike. I can't think if I'm worried about being shot or someone else getting shot or whatever else Hans has in mind. Get with Martin and Lisa—where is she, anyway? Work out our protection for the next few days. Stella, it would be heaven if you could create a bug free zone for us to work in, but don't let it take you away from your research."

"Not to worry—like most women, I can multi-task quite well," she replied.

"Finally: Maggie. We'll have to get ready for court soon. I'd like us to take a walk first."

As we strolled away from the farmhouse, I turned to her and asked, "Are you sure you want to be a part of this?"

"Walter and I discussed it last night after Clovis called. This will be your last case, and Walter knows I couldn't stand not to be with you. He's okay with it; nervous, but okay."

"How do you know shutting down the office and going to work for Red isn't part of my act?"

"Because Red and I talk. We actually get along quite well, but don't tell anyone, especially Lucy. He even offered me a position with his company when you join him, but I turned him down. I want to spend time with my horses, and Walter wants us to travel more often. This is our last case. Now tell me how you're going to pull a rabbit out of this hat?"

As we continued to walk, I explained the weaknesses I saw in Jordyn's case, and the clues Duke and Stanford had given me. Maggie has always been a great sounding board, mostly listening except when I get too optimistic. Now she reminded me that we still had a very weak case, a hostile judge, and no way to confer with our client, the one person who could either confirm or shoot down any theory I might propose.

Maggie also pointed out that we were going into this afternoon blind. I thought I knew what would take place, but for the most part I would be flying by the seat of my pants. When that happens, I tend to get a little cocky. Maggie had a way of pulling me back. She was my restraining bolt, so to speak, the person who kept me from being too full of myself. Most trial lawyers could use such an aide, but Maggie was one of a kind. I felt a lot better about our chances now that she was back at my side.

We walked on for a few minutes in silence; there wasn't much more to say.

She suddenly turned to me and said, "It's time to go."

38

THE COURTROOM WAS PACKED WITH LAWYERS AND PARALEGALS. I thought I noticed a glint of surprise in Jordyn's eyes at Maggie's presence, but I could have been mistaken. There was no sign of Duke or Gloria. Brian met us on the way in and told me that no motions or briefs had arrived at the office. Before I could ask, he added that the clerk of court had told him that several had been filed but were under seal. When he asked to see them, she said he should bring it up with the judge—not a good sign.

More troubling, David was nowhere to be seen. I had hoped to have a brief conversation with him before we were called to order. I asked the marshal where he was and got the now familiar response: "Bring it up with the judge."

The courtroom grew quiet when the clerks came into the room and the marshal told us all to rise. Judge Moorman blew into the courtroom and took his seat. He banged on the gavel and started to speak but I was quickly on my feet.

"Your Honor, I must inquire about the lack of presence of my client."

He peered over his glasses and replied, "I presume he is in his cell. Today's hearing is procedural in nature and does not require his presence."

"I must object, Your Honor."

This time he interrupted me. "Objection noted. Take a seat, Mr. Patterson."

"But Your Honor..."

"Take a seat, Mr. Patterson. You will be afforded plenty of time to speak soon enough."

He paused, then asked, "Is Mr. Madigan present?"

From the back of the courtroom, I heard a good bit of commotion as the door opened and closed. "I'm here, Your Honor. I apologize. I've never seen such traffic." Duke rushed up to join us at the table. Thankfully, Gloria was a no-show.

Moorman frowned but began to read from his notes. "I have reviewed Gloria Ruple's motion to intervene and the plaintiffs' response. The motion is denied."

No surprise there, but Duke was on his feet.

"Your Honor, may I be heard?"

"No. However, I have decided that since Mr. Patterson has no objection to your intervention, you may join him inside the rail, where he can have the benefit of your wise counsel. At subsequent hearings or at trial, you may not address the court or question witnesses, but you may consult counsel."

"But..."

"Sit down Mr. Madigan. May I also remind you that the gag order applies to you until such time as the order is lifted."

"Clever," I thought. Duke is restrained from any of his antics, but he can't argue he wasn't able to provide input.

The judge turned to me. "Mr. Patterson, your request for a jury trial is denied."

Wow, I didn't see that coming.

He continued, "I have studied your brief, but I find Ms. Duarte's argument more persuasive."

"I wasn't aware that Ms. Duarte had filed a response." I glared at Jordyn who smiled and responded.

"It was filed under seal, and because of the sensitive nature of what we disclosed, we decided to seek the court's guidance about providing counsel with our argument."

"And how did you seek the court's guidance? Not by *ex parte* communication, I hope."

"Certainly not," she bristled. "We filed a motion asking for guidance, also under seal. We are dealing with highly sensitive matters that touch on national security. I would think that you would appreciate my clients' position."

I wasn't happy. "Who decides what touches on national security? Your clients?"

"Enough, counsel. You will behave with decorum in my court. My decision on a jury trial is final. I will rule on Ms. Duarte's motion for guidance in due course. I will not allow you, Mr. Patterson, to accuse this court of *ex parte* communications. All communications with this court are made in open court or by written motion."

It would fall on deaf ears to explain to the Judge that when you file a motion under seal and don't provide opposing counsel a copy of your motion, you are in fact engaging in *ex parte* communications. Besides, I had bigger fish to fry.

"I apologize, Your Honor. I spoke out of school, but I'm somewhat frustrated by counsel's reliance on the phrase 'national security.' That said, I am obligated to advise the court that I will appeal your order denying my request for a jury trial and will seek a stay of all proceedings until the DC Court of Appeals has an opportunity to decide the matter."

I waited for a reaction from the judge and Duarte. Naturally, Moorman spoke first. He was all smiles.

"I appreciate the heads up, Mr. Patterson. But I hear someone threatening to file an appeal almost every day. Do what you must, but if you've checked, you know I have a pretty good record on appeal."

I fudged. "I have, and I'd say it's better than pretty good. Nonetheless, and with all due respect, Your Honor, your order significantly affects how we proceed from this point forward. My client and I feel strongly about a jury and the merits of our motion."

Jordyn was in a bind. An appeal would slow down her freight train, for how long no one could know. Moreover, the DC Court of Appeals was a totally different animal. They might feel differently than Moorman about gag orders and "national security." They might rule against her motion that all filings be made under seal, and that meant the press would surely appear on the scene, raising questions her clients would rather avoid.

She did what any good lawyer does when faced with a dilemma.

"Your Honor, I wonder if I might have fifteen minutes with co-counsel."

"Certainly, counsel. The court will be in recess for, let's say thirty minutes."

He gave the sounding block a good thwack with his gavel and left for chambers.

While Jordyn and twenty other lawyers huddled, (it looked more like a rugby scrum than a huddle), Duke and I formed a two-man huddle of our own.

"The appeal was quick thinking, Jack," he said. "Wonder what she's up to now? No telling what she'll do next, that's for sure. I guess my days at your table are over. No lawyer wants someone looking over his shoulder."

"I don't know about that. Let's meet at Barker's after court. I have a few ideas, and if things happen as quickly as I expect, I'll need all the help I can get."

I couldn't believe I had taken his bait, but I did have some thoughts about a role Duke could play. He was a wild card, but for now he was part of my hand.

I noticed Stanford walking over to our table, huddle over.

"Got a second, Jack?"

I had no idea why he was even here, especially sitting at plaintiff's table. The federal government had no role in the civil litigation. Why would he so blatantly take the plaintiffs' side?

"Sure," I responded, waving at the empty courtroom. "What's up?"

"Maybe there's a compromise to be had here. What if I arranged for you to have limited access to your client. In exchange, you won't appeal the judge's denial of your request for a jury. You could raise the issue after the trial, after the verdict has been rendered."

I couldn't believe my ears. The government was conspiring with business to get me to drop my appeal, and in exchange they were holding hostage access to my client. What had the world come to? I could feel Maggie's glare and took a deep breath. There are places for losing one's temper, but a courtroom is not one of them.

"I'm sorry, William. Good try, but waiving a jury trial is a show-stopper for me. I'll take the issue all the way to the Supreme Court if I must. Jordyn knows I'm right on this issue, and you should be ashamed of yourself. Go back to Justice and tell a few of the career professionals what you just proposed. Find me even one who thinks you did the right thing."

His face turned beet red with anger, but he, too, held his temper. He turned without a word and walked back to his huddle.

Maggie said, "You'll pay for that, but you were right. I'm surprised you kept your cool." Duke nodded in agreement. I relaxed a bit and gave her a smile.

The huddle finally broke up, and Jordyn told the clerks that she was ready when the court was. A few minutes later, the judge returned and waved in her direction.

She rose and said, "The plaintiffs withdraw their objection to a jury trial, Your Honor."

Moorman's eyebrows rose above the rims of his glasses.

"Does that mean you are asking to the court to withdraw its order, Ms. Duarte? If I my ask, what is the reasoning for your change of heart?"

I looked up, more surprised by Moorman's stern tone than by the plaintiffs' request.

"Your Honor, although without merit, Mr. Patterson's decision to appeal your order and seek a stay of these proceedings creates a real hardship for our clients. His appeal will unnecessarily delay a resolution of this case. My clients feel that although a jury is neither necessary nor warranted in this complex litigation, such a delay creates an increased national security risk."

I was ready to blow my top. Maggie squeezed my knee tightly to keep me quiet. National security, my ass. I waited for the judge to call on me for a response, but apparently, he didn't think my opinion counted for much.

"In that case Ms. Duarte, we will set this case for a jury trial. I will advise counsels of the date soon. I recommend both parties review my standing order regarding jury trials and how I conduct *voir dire*. Please pay attention to the prohibitions aimed at jury consultants who invade the privacy of potential jurors. In case you're thinking of appealing this order, Mr. Patterson, the DC Court of Appeals has already given my standing order its blessing."

I didn't think I deserved that slap, but I had a jury trial. My mouth remained shut, but I was surprised when Moorman said, "If there is nothing further, court is adjourned."

I jumped to my feet, "Your Honor, what about access to my client and a bond hearing?"

Moorman scowled, "I don't enjoy repeating myself. If you want anything from this court, file a motion. But a word of advice, Mr. Patterson. You got your jury trial. If I were you, I'd quit while I was ahead."

With that he retired to chambers.

39

THE COURTROOM EMPTIED QUICKLY, no idle chit chat between counsels. Duke and I agreed to meet at Barker's in an hour. It wasn't worth our time to walk back to the office before I met Duke, and I sure didn't want to run into Hans in the park. Maggie, Brian, and I found a bench in the hall outside the courtroom, and we carried on our business there.

Brian asked, "When do you think he'll set the trial?"

I said, "I still think they'll try for a rush to judgment, push the pedal to the metal, but the judge must convene a jury, ask the jury pool to send in answers to questionnaires, find a date that's good for both parties, etc. Normally, a judge would call both sides into chambers, and we'd go over all the preliminaries before a date was set. That's why I was surprised when he left the courtroom so quickly. Now that opportunity has been lost."

"I suspect he'll wait for marching orders from Jordyn. I'd say we are still a few months away from a trial."

"A few months?" Brian asked. "That's pretty quick."

"It is, let's not let any grass grow under our feet. Start drafting our request for client access and for a bail hearing. Also come up with a first draft of discovery requests—the usual interrogatories asking for potential witnesses, experts, etc. and a request for any documents they will introduce at trial. And just because she made me mad, file a notice to take the deposition of every corporate president she represents. I know that's a big ask, let me know if you need me to hire someone to help.

"Jordyn will use 'national security' to object, and Moorman will agree to whatever she says. But the very thought of my deposing her clients will give her heartburn." I laughed.

"Jack, don't get carried away." Maggie warned.

"Don't worry; I won't. But if the judge delays convening a jury, I just might try to depose a few corporate presidents. A few depositions in Silicon Valley, or even Napa, sound pretty good right now."

Brian had stepped away to take a call. When he returned, still holding the phone, he looked worried.

"That was Martin. About the time you announced your intent to appeal, two men tried to break into the office. Martin had arranged for it to be guarded while we were in court, and his people stopped them, but they eluded apprehension. A different twosome tried to get into your home, but security at the condominium stopped them in time. The police have them in custody." He paused, then added, "How could they have known what happened in court so quickly?"

"Someone must have slipped out of the courtroom when Jordyn asked for the recess," I replied. "This is Hans' doings. It's meant as a message, but I'll be damned if I'm going to back down."

"Well, at least the police have two of the intruders," Maggie said before I could say anything else. "Jack, if you don't mind, I think I'll pass on the meeting at Barker's. I can do more good at the office helping Brian with your motions and checking to make sure nothing was tampered with. Take Clovis with you."

"Okay, but you know Duke will be disappointed," I kidded.

She had gathered her papers and risen. Now she turned to face me. "Aren't you at all concerned? Men trying to break into the office and your home? How can you joke about such things? Your attitude…" She certainly wasn't joking.

"Maggie, Maggie—calm down," I broke in, now standing as well. "Of course, I'm concerned. But am I intimidated? Am I going to roll over and play dead? No! The more they push, the more I'm going to push back. I'm convinced that the only way we'll all be safe, the only way we can return to some form of normalcy, is to win this lawsuit. I'm not sure how I'm going to do it, but my concerns will only disappear when a jury says, "verdict for the defendant, David Ruple."

It was meant to be a pep talk, but she was clearly still shaken. I tried to give her a hug, but she turned to Brian, and I watched as they walked down the long hall. I wondered how much longer she'd be able to handle the stress.

Poor Brian! I'd already loaded him with work, but there was much more to be done. I offered again to hire temporary help, but he said he felt sure he and Maggie could manage everything, especially now that we had more time. I needed research on possible counterclaims we could bring against the companies. I also knew there were unique procedural rules in patent and trademark trials and suggested he contact a lawyer I had worked with a few years ago, Jacob Lee. He was the finest intellectual property attorney I knew. He was a scratch golfer and owed me a favor. I'd kept his dog, Fergus, over a long weekend, a very long weekend, so he could go to the Masters in Augusta.

I gathered my belongings and followed them to the courthouse steps where I found Clovis waiting as well. Maggie had calmed down a bit, and she and Brian soon left for the office. Clovis and I walked to Barker's, but neither of us had much to say. He was on edge because of the break-ins, and I couldn't stop thinking about Hans.

It was a relief to find Gloria and Duke safely seated in the Grill at Barker's. I noticed they were both sipping on their first cocktail of the day, although in Gloria's case, one could never be sure it was her first or fourth. Clovis and I stuck to iced tea, ignoring Duke's gibes. Gloria asked for the special crab salad, while the rest of us indulged in a Barker's cheeseburger.

After we'd been served, I told Duke as much as I was willing about what might happen next. I also gave him some ideas about how he could help when we went to trial if he was willing to participate. Gloria wanted him to be there, if only so he could relate the day's events to her over a cocktail. She simply couldn't bear the thought of sitting in a musty old courtroom all day.

When Gloria excused herself, Duke said, "I appreciate the introduction to Cheryl. She is one fine woman. But don't mention her in front of Gloria. That woman wants all my time."

I tried without total success to stifle a laugh. "My lips are sealed but be careful. I wouldn't cross either one."

Gloria soon returned, and we spent the rest of lunch talking about strategies to get access to David. I wasn't sure how much David wanted to see his mother, but I understood her need to see him.

Clovis excused himself to take a call. When he returned, he was grinning from ear to ear.

"What's so funny?" I asked.

"You wanted a jury trial? Well, you got one. Court convenes Monday at nine a.m. sharp."

40

Trial on Monday, this coming Monday? How could that be?

I soon found out. The judge's clerk told Brian that a trial scheduled at that very time had unexpectedly settled. Moorman had decided to use that jury to hear our case. According to the clerk, who seemed to like Brian, the judge laughed and said, "Well, the plaintiffs want a quick resolution, and Patterson said he could be ready any time. Why waste a jury?" I was suspicious, but it did me no good. In this game, like most, you play the hand you're dealt.

Of equal concern was that all requirements about sharing witness lists, discovery, and expert's credentials had been removed from the court's standing order. We'd be flying blind.

Regardless of whether Moorman had consulted with Jordyn before setting the new date, there was zero chance he'd be open to changing it. I now had one weekend to prepare for a jury trial, with no discovery. Over fifty years ago, lawyers used to try cases without discovery, but not anymore. Lawyers are rarely surprised at trial these days. Pre-trial discovery unearths all there is to know about the opponent's case. We were about to venture back into the Wild West, when trials were full of twists and turns, not to mention six-shooters.

I called Brian and told him to rally the troops at the farmhouse. I wasn't about to risk anyone listening in on my strategy, even if I didn't have one yet. I reminded Brian to bring the judge's "updated" standing order on jury trials. I also asked him to try to get a list of the jurors, where they lived, and their background.

Despite the judge's admonition about jury consultants, there is nothing nefarious about getting basic information about each juror, such as age, sex, and occupation. I felt sure Jordyn and her cohorts knew all there was to know about the potential jurors. If Hans knew all my credit card numbers and spending habits, I bet Jordyn's clients could easily find out what type of toothpaste the jurors used. I told Brian to find out who the lawyers were on the case that had settled. Maybe they would share information on the jury panel.

I'm old fashioned, but it bothers me that we have no privacy anymore. A person might browse through a website looking for a new sweatshirt. The next thing he knows, he's inundated with emails from sweatshirt makers, and when he reads the daily news online, the website is full of ads for sweatshirts.

I got off my silent soap box and asked Clovis if he had any news; I'd seen him speaking quietly into his headset as he drove. He told me we were being followed—nothing that seemed dangerous, just one car a few lengths back.

"Do you want me to lose them," he asked.

"Nah, I'm not up for high-speed chases right now, and we'll be well-protected at the farmhouse. I'm trying to think through all we need to accomplish between now and Monday. Now that I think about it, we should have swung by my place. I'm going to need some clothes for the weekend, and my court suit on Monday. I wear a special suit for jury trials. It's a little threadbare, and not too expensive. A lawyer can turn off a jury when he wears an expensive suit and a fancy watch."

"I think I may have heard you mention that once or twice," he replied, struggling to keep a straight face. "Don't worry, Maggie is way ahead of you. She and Brian went by your place to pack a suitcase on their way out of town. And be forewarned: Stella told her to pack your gym clothes, too. She wants to put you through your paces."

Stella runs a high-performance gym in Little Rock. When we'd all stayed at the farmhouse a few years ago, Stella held morning workout sessions. I enjoyed watching. The very thought of a workout with Stella gives me cold shivers.

We pulled in the driveway just a few minutes ahead of Maggie and Brian. While they all unpacked and compared notes, I sat down in the den with Stella and Rita.

"Sorry, Jack, but no luck yet. We have no idea what David's software does." Stella shook her head in frustration.

"What about the box?" I asked. "Find anything interesting there?"

Rita answered, "I can't find any method, any organization to the material at all. Just lots of jumbled notes with his scribblings, sometimes on both front and back, but nothing to clarify them. I'm still working on it, but so far, nothing."

"Keep trying. We've got a deadline now," I urged, trying to sound confident.

I felt a little overwhelmed, so I took a walk down to the fishing pond. I'm a good lawyer, in fact a very good trial lawyer, but right now I felt like a fish out of water. I would face a hostile judge, who would rule against any objection I raised. I assumed Jordyn knew everything there was to know about every juror, while my decision to strike or accept a juror would be based on appearance and whether they would look me in the eye. I would have to cross-examine experts who knew David's software backwards and forwards, while I knew absolutely nothing about it. And I was sure Jordyn would throw in a few traps. For all I knew, she'd already interviewed my client! After wallowing in a self-imposed pity party for a few minutes, I literally shook myself off like Jacob Lee's dog, Fergus, had on my new carpet and strode up the hill to the house.

I found them all waiting in the great room. I gave them each additional research to do, experts to contact or motions or briefs to prepare. I warned Mike and Martin not to let their guard down. Hans and his hitmen were surely waiting somewhere.

My first job was to look carefully at the judge's standing order concerning selection of the jury. As he had emphasized, the judge was not a fan of using *voir dire* to pre-try one's case. The judge would ask the questions of the potential jurors, and he would entertain suggestions, but no questioning by counsel was permitted.

He restricted the number of strikes allowed, and his order cautioned against contacting potential jurors. The order contained an unusual provision that restricted post-trial contact with jurors, but I didn't see how that could become an issue. All in all, it seemed that a jury should be in place by the end of the day. I asked Maggie to find out if we knew an attorney who had tried a case in front of Judge Moorman, someone who could be a good resource as to how he conducted a trial.

I spent the rest of the afternoon making notes about potential themes to use with the jury. I don't usually write my opening or closing arguments before a trial. It doesn't make sense to box myself into a specific concept or strategy, especially in a case where I had no idea what the evidence might offer. Instead, I thought about how I might simplify my arguments to make them more understandable to a layperson. Many professionals don't like their cases decided by juries because surely only degreed professionals can understand complicated legal issues. They have an argument, but experience has taught me that in most cases juries get it right, sometimes better than a panel of professionals. Common sense often rules over expertise.

I had to return a call from Royce, who was irritated by the quick trial date and the closed courtroom. He had hoped to monitor the proceedings. He calmed down once I explained the situation. Sadly, I had to decline his very serious offer to call the judge personally. I would have given a lot to listen in on that conversation.

I asked him to explain the circumstances to Thibodeaux and to double check on David's security. His call reminded me to ask Rita about court clothes for David. Whether through actual spite or simple laziness, court officials routinely make the accused appear in front of a jury in an orange jumpsuit and shackles. "Oh, sorry—his other clothes were delivered too late" was a common justification. So much for the presumption of innocence.

Rita said that David had one suit that he wore in front of their special clients. Curious, I asked what made a client "special." She answered with perfect brevity, "They pay." Brian volunteered to make sure David was properly dressed and well-groomed on Monday morning. I thanked them both, happy to be able to check at least one thing off my worry list. Security and transportation for my team was another detail that concerned me, but Mike assured me they'd gone over the arrangements twice. Clovis grimaced, and I forced myself to quit worrying. My team had prepared for trial before and knew their respective duties.

I spent almost all of Saturday focused on the unique procedural rules involved in a patent case. Jacob Lee was incredibly generous with his time and advice, and I 'hit the law books' hard. I use the phrase out of habit, but of course but most legal research these days is accomplished via the Internet. Maggie asked if I was worried that Hans might be monitoring my research.

"I certainly hope he is. The ins and outs of when to object to certain evidence is exactly what I want them to think I'm focusing on." I told her, as we strolled to the pond that afternoon.

"Okay then, what exactly are you worried about?"

"I have a complex trial beginning on Monday. I don't know either the intent or potential use of David's software or how the opposition will explain their position that the software rightly belongs to them. I feel sure that Jordyn has more than a couple of surprises in her bag of tricks, and to top it off I've never tried a patent case. I know I could be ready in a year, but instead I have one weekend."

"Well, you did ask for this," she reminded me.

"You're right, I did, and I still believe a quick trial works for us, but I've never felt so ill-prepared. Flying by the seat of my pants hardly describes it."

On Sunday afternoon I called everyone into the great room. They watched in silence as I dealt out the first of two sets of index cards I'd prepared.

"I hope to be able to give this first set of cards to David. I've written on each one a question I want him to answer. Hopefully, he can answer them during the breaks."

They each looked at their cards while I dealt out the second set. "The second set of cards, which you'll notice are blank, is for you. Please take as much time as you need to write down anything you'd like to ask me or him. When you all have finished, we'll discuss your questions.

Mike asked, "You sure you want me to participate? I don't know anything about the case itself." He looked thoroughly confused.

"Absolutely. You are just like every prospective juror. You don't know anything about the case yet. What would you want to know if you were in their shoes?"

"I'd like to know how long I would be sitting here."

The others smiled and nodded. "Exactly, and that tells me not to drag out questioning. But do try to think what you might want to ask David as well."

"I have a question," Maggie piped up.

"Can it wait?" I asked.

"No, it cannot. What are we having for dinner?" she asked.

"For those who participate in my little card game, Clovis has a surprise." I tempted them.

It took about thirty minutes before they had all handed their cards back to me. We had a lively discussion, which was as good as pretrial preparation as I could imagine. They came up with good questions for David that I incorporated into mine. They also peppered me with questions about my opening argument and how to cross examine the patent experts. We finished with a logistics discussion. Stella and Rita wouldn't be allowed in the courtroom. We had to find a way for them to communicate with us, and us with them. Since I had little expertise in software language, I anticipated that Jordyn's expert might be communicating in Greek. Simply put, I needed Rita and Stella to act as translators.

When we had finished, Clovis covered the large dining table with newspapers and disappeared. To everyone's delight he reappeared a few minutes later bearing an enormous tray of Atlantic blue crabs and corn on the cob, both hot off the grill. He passed around wooden mallets and crab forks and we all dug in eagerly. To quench our thirst, he offered a variety of beers from Wicked Weed Brewery in Asheville. I contributed a few bottles of nice chardonnay as well as an excellent New Zealand sauvignon blanc.

It was the perfect ending to our weekend of hard work. We were able to forget about the trial, even Hans for a while, and enjoy each other's company. Tomorrow would be a different matter. I hoped we'd all live to tell the tale.

41

I LIKE TO GET TO THE COURTROOM EARLY, soak in the atmosphere, and watch as the gallery fills with spectators, potential jurors wander in, and court clerks busily prepare their workspace. A good friend once gave me a great coffee table book containing pictures and the history of various old court rooms. It's in a bookshelf now, but I spent many hours enjoying both the pictures and the narratives.

Judge Moorman's courtroom was less interesting. The furniture was sparse and had been made by Prison Industries, which is a large inmate-training program operated by the Bureau of Prisons. The furniture is study and practical, but I haven't seen any pieces featured in coffee table books. Sadly, the room boasted no spittoons or ceiling fans.

It wasn't long before Jordyn's army of lawyers and paralegals swooped in and began unpacking their briefcases and setting up their laptops. Potential jurors and lawyers for the computer companies filled the gallery. Duke hadn't yet arrived when the clerk summoned Jordyn, Stanford, and me to chambers to meet with the judge.

The judge's chambers contained a large desk behind which the judge sat, as well as a smaller one for his clerk. The walls held a few family pictures, but there were no bookshelves. Jordyn, Stanford, and I sat in chairs across from him.

He frowned and got straight to his point. "I hope all of you have read my standing order. I will conduct *voir dire*. Do either of you have any questions you'd like me to ask?"

Jordyn handed the Judge three pages of questions. He sighed and turned to me.

"I have no questions to submit, Your Honor. I'm quite sure you'll do an excellent job without my help."

Jordyn was flustered. I knew she was ready to object to any questions I might normally ask, but now I had stolen her first clap of thunder.

She asked, "What do you mean you don't have any questions to suggest? You must have worked with a jury consultant!"

The judge looked as though he were ready to eat me alive.

"No. I haven't even spoken with a jury consultant. I don't even have a list of the potential jurors. Do you?" I asked Jordyn. "The judge's clerk told Brian it wasn't available."

I turned back to Moorman before she could answer. "Your Honor, I decided that I wouldn't spend the little time I have worrying about jurors. Your order is clear. You and you alone conduct *voir dire*, and we are not to have any contact with the jury pool either directly or through a consultant. Your order directs us to send or give to you, in writing, any questions we'd like to have addressed. Well, I simply don't have any suggestions for you. *Voir dire* is your provenance, not mine."

I knew Jordyn must have used a jury consultant who probably knew all there was to know about every potential juror. I had seen the thick notebook Jordyn's team brought into the courtroom labeled "Jury."

Jordyn wasn't satisfied, "Your Honor, I fear Mr. Patterson is playing tricks with your standing rule regarding *voir dire*."

I was, but not in the way Jordyn feared. I responded, "Your Honor, why does Ms. Duarte keep accusing me of tricks? I am simply doing my level best to follow the rules you set forth."

The judge answered her. "Mr. Patterson must act in the manner he thinks most beneficial to his client. I can't make him give suggestions. If there's nothing further, let's get this show on the road."

"One more thing, Your Honor?" It was time for me to throw my first bomb.

"Go ahead," he sighed.

"I assume that at the beginning of the trial you plan to introduce both counsels to the jury. Is that correct?"

"That's correct," he replied, straightening his tie. "And...?"

"Well, may I enquire how you plan to introduce Mr. Stanford? If you tell the jury that Mr. Stanford is a deputy assistant attorney general with the Department of Justice, the jury may get the impression that the U.S. government has taken sides in this case."

Of course, that was exactly the impression Jordyn wanted to create, but I wasn't going to let her get away with it, at least not if I could help it.

"Mr. Stanford, do you have anything to say regarding this issue?" he asked. "I hadn't thought of it before now, but I understand Mr. Patterson's point."

Stanford hesitated, but finally responded. "I believe the court is aware of the pending criminal matter involving the same software and the same defendant. I suppose that in a strange way I'm in the same position as Mr. Madigan. The government has an interest in who owns this software."

"Do you plan to offer any evidence or question any witness?" the judge asked.

"No, Your Honor," he answered.

The judge seemed satisfied, "How about this—I won't introduce Mr. Stanford to the jury as an official with the government. As far as the jury will know, he is a lawyer helping Ms. Duarte. I will treat Mr. Madigan much the same way. Does that satisfy you, Mr. Patterson?"

"Yes, it does. Thank you, Your Honor." I answered.

From my point of view, it would have been better if Moorman had thrown Stanford out of the court entirely, but beggars can't be choosers, and I had thought of a possible way to use him to our benefit. Besides, no matter how much I might object, the jury would know Stanford was on Jordyn's side. Since he always stood right next to her, even the dullest juror couldn't miss the implication.

When we walked back into court, I was pleased to see my client sitting at our table in a coat and tie. Duke was there as well, wearing a leather jacket but regular tie and slacks. I wondered if Moorman would notice the pattern on his tie—little cowboys on horseback attempting to lasso little bulls. His cowboy boots must have cost him a fortune. Maggie had already passed David our cards, and he was busily at work scribbling answers.

As soon as I sat down, he asked, "How is Rita? Why isn't she here?"

"She's okay. She asked me to give you this. I pulled her letter out of my coat pocket. I had suggested she write him a note assuring him she was safe with us, telling him what she was working on, and explaining why she wasn't in the courtroom.

David read through it while we waited on the judge.

He whispered, "Tell her I love her, will you?" I nodded and gave his arm a squeeze just before the judge strode into the courtroom and we all rose once again.

Moorman was not in the mood to dawdle. "Madame Clerk, call the first fourteen jurors."

The names were drawn, and the first twelve were seated in the jury box along with two alternates. The judge asked a laundry list of basic questions about whether the jurors knew the lawyers, David, or the computer companies. Nobody knew me, David, Duke, or Jordyn. A few had heard of the plaintiffs, but nobody knew anyone who worked for the companies. I am always surprised when jurors fail to recognize the parties or lawyers in a case. We think we know a lot of people, but we really don't. Nor do they know us.

I was also surprised when the judge said, "Ladies and gentlemen, I doubt this case will last more than a couple of days. Do any of you have a reason why you can't serve for that length of time?" No one raised their hand.

A judge would usually have asked both of us before the trial how long we thought the case could last, but Moorman hadn't. He had probably asked Jordyn during one of their *ex parte* meetings they both so vigorously denied. It would be interesting to see how Jordyn intended to prove her case in such a short time. I wasn't about to slow the train down.

Next came the judge's explanation about challenges. Either party could challenge a juror for cause, meaning there needed to be a reason valid to the judge for excusing the juror. Each side was also given three preemptory challenges, meaning no reason was needed to throw someone off the jury panel. This is how jury consultants make their money and when lawyers do a little dance with their opponents, each trying to outmaneuver the other. In essence, if you can get your opponent to strike someone you don't want, you get an extra challenge. In a normal situation, with a normal judge, both parties get as many as six to eight preemptory challenges, but Moorman clearly thought jury selection was a waste of time.

He asked, "Do either of you want to challenge anyone for cause?"

Jordyn said, "No, your honor."

"Mr. Patterson?" he asked.

"No challenges, your honor." I said with a broad smile. "This jury looks good to me."

He frowned but continued. "I usually conduct all questioning of the prospective panel. Furthermore, after I've finished my questioning, I always ask the lawyers for both sides to give me any questions they think are important. Ms. Duarte gave me a few suggestions this morning, and Mr. Patterson had no questions and no objections. Given the agreement, I see no harm in letting Ms. Duarte ask her own questions.

I had seconds to decide whether to object. The judge and Jordyn had obviously devised this arrangement beforehand, so I said nothing. Jordyn didn't bother to look surprised as she walked to the lectern. She did give me a sugary smile that implied "Poor Jack, you are out of your league."

Duke, on the other hand, spoke right up, his questions directed at me, but for all to hear.

"You going to let them get away with this? She's about to try her entire case during *voir dire* without you getting a similar opportunity. The judge said he would be the only one asking questions."

I shrugged, but Moorman almost came out of his robes.

"Mr. Madigan. Another outburst and you will find yourself in contempt and thrown out of this courtroom for the remainder of the trial. I allowed you to sit at counsel's table and to consult with Mr. Patterson, but you are to remain quiet, do you understand?"

Duke mumbled something and sat down.

Duke had accomplished two things I couldn't: he'd let the jury know something wasn't right, and he'd gotten under Jordyn and the judge's skin. I hated to admit we might work well together.

As expected, Jordyn used individual *voir dire* to tell the jury all about her case and what a villain David must be with questions such as:

"Ladies and gentlemen, my clients were forced to bring this lawsuit when the defendant attempted to claim our intellectual property was his by filing for patent and copyright protection for the software he stole. Have any of you been victims of theft?" Next—

"The defendant's grandfather is the head of a Louisiana crime family. Would that information alone prevent you from rendering a fair and impartial verdict for my clients?" and finally—

"Do any of you have friends or relatives currently in the DC jail who may have run across the defendant, David Ruple?"

That one brought me to my feet, but before I could object the Judge interrupted.

"Ms. Duarte, you came too close to the line with that one. Ladies and gentlemen of the jury, please disregard that question."

Fat lot of good that did. All his little scold had accomplished was to make the jury wonder why David was in jail and emphasize that he was.

Jordyn wasn't through.

"My apologies, Your Honor." She turned to the jury and continued.

Ladies and Gentlemen, Mr. William Stanford is sitting at my table. He is with the Department of Justice which has a keen interest in this case. Do any of you know him or anyone else who works at Justice?"

Back on my feet, I raised my voice, "May we approach, Your Honor."

At the bench I whispered, "Your Honor, in chambers you agreed not to identify Mr. Stanford in your *voir dire*. Now Jordyn has done just that."

"Ms. Duarte?" he asked.

"Mr. Patterson objected to your identifying Mr. Stanford. I submitted this question in my list of suggestions, and Mr. Patterson didn't object. I felt it was fair ground. Besides I didn't tell the jury whose side William is on."

"If there's any doubt whose side he's on, it's on your right." I responded angrily, looking directly at Stanford, who was indeed standing by her right side. "Your Honor, I must call for a mistrial."

The judge banged his gavel, this time striking his desk rather than the sounding block. "Mistrial denied. I will instruct the jury to disregard the question if that's what you want."

"Thanks, Your Honor, but no thank you." Such an instruction would only emphasize the involvement of the Justice Department.

"Ms. Duarte, are you almost finished? I want to keep this case moving."

Jordyn promised to speed up her questions, but she continued in the same measured tone, asking questions that implied that my client had stolen her clients' software, that my client was in jail and a member of a notorious crime family; and that the U.S. government wanted her to win. Well, not in so many words, but she came close.

Duke let slip one more outburst, loud enough for all to hear, this time directed at me.

"Are you actually trying to lose this case?"

Jordyn's brows went sky high as she looked to the judge, who said nothing. No one else did either, so she resumed her questioning.

When she had finished, the judge said, "Ladies and gentlemen, we have come to that stage in a trial where the lawyers give me what are called preemptory challenges to the jury panel. We'll take a short break. The marshal will escort you to the jury room. Court will resume in fifteen minutes."

After the jury filed out of the courtroom, the judge asked for our challenges. Jordan handed her challenges to the judge. I looked at the judge and said I had no challenges. This mild response seemed to enrage her.

"Your honor, Mr. Patterson is making a mockery of this trial. He has no suggestions for *voir dire*, now he has no challenges. He refuses to participate but has asked you to grant a mistrial."

The judge sighed and responded, "He will not get a mistrial. Each of you has fifteen minutes for opening argument. I will cut you off if you go longer."

Duarte feigned objection.

"Judge, I can't possibly limit my opening argument to fifteen minutes. This is a complex case."

It was time for me to irritate her a little more.

"It's not that complicated, Your Honor. She can have most of my time. I won't need but a minute."

My generous offer finally got to him.

"I oversee the procedures in this trial, not either of you. Ms. Duarte, you will have fifteen minutes. Mr. Patterson, either participate or get out of the way.

"Thank you, Your Honor. I will. I notice that all three members of the jury Ms. Duarte struck by way of her preemptory challenges are African Americans. I object to the clearly discriminatory use of her challenges."

It's not unusual for attorneys representing corporate clients to go to great lengths to eliminate minorities from a jury panel. They're usually a little more subtle than Jordyn, but with only three challenges she had little choice but to be obvious. I knew my objection would be fruitless, but from the look she gave me I knew it had served its purpose.

"Objection denied. Marshal, please bring in the jury panel."

When the panel returned, the judge struck the three jurors Duarte wanted off the panel. It was hard not to laugh when the new jurors walked in—one was African American, and one appeared to be from India or Pakistan. He asked all three a few basic questions, and then swore in the jury to hear our case. I didn't dare to even glance in Jordyn's direction.

"Ms. Duarte, you may begin."

42

As JORDYN GOT TO HER FEET, a man I knew well opened the door at the rear of the room and took a seat near the back. Solomon Banks had been my boss at the Justice Department and was now a professor of antitrust law at Georgetown Law School. Stanford leaned over to whisper something to Jordyn.

Jordyn immediately asked to approach the bench and almost before I could join her, said, "Your Honor, a person has just entered the courtroom who is not associated with any of the law firms involved in this case. I thought he might be a member of the press, but my colleague, Mr. Stanford, recognizes him as a former employee of DOJ. As this case involves vital national security issues, could you find a way to excuse him without disclosing the nature of this case? I suspect this is another one of Mr. Patterson's ploys."

I smiled and turned to the judge, "Your Honor, I do know the gentleman to whom she refers. He is Solomon Banks, former Assistant Attorney General for the antitrust division. You'll have to ask either him or Mr. Stanford why he's here. I have no idea."

"You're lying," Duarte hissed. "You were seen talking to him at the law school the other day. Your honor, I believe Mr. Patterson should be sanctioned for violating your gag order."

Jordyn had just confirmed that I had been followed.

"Your honor, I did not mention any part of this case, or even that I might have any interest in it, when I met with my old boss the other day. Instead of allowing Ms. Duarte to make wild accusations, perhaps you could call him to the bench and ask him yourself."

Jordyn continued to fume, seemingly unaware that her "colleague" Stanford was tugging at her sleeve.

The judge called Solomon to the bench.

"Sir, this trial is closed to the public. Please identify yourself and tell the court what interest you may have in this case."

"Of course, Your Honor. My name is Solomon Banks, and I teach antitrust law at Georgetown. I met the Attorney General for lunch the other day, and we talked about old times. Jack's name, I mean Mr. Patterson's, came up, and I told him we saw each other from time to time. He told me that Jack and one of his best young trial lawyers would be going at it and suggested I might want to sit in. I didn't have a class today so I thought I might watch today's proceedings. I didn't know the courtroom was closed. The AG didn't mention it."

Jordyn couldn't help herself. "Patterson told you what the case was about, didn't he? Your Honor, I'm sure Mr. Patterson has violated your gag order."

Before the judge could say a word, Solomon addressed her in the stern tone that made many a law student cringe. "Young lady, the last time I saw Jack he told me he was planning to retire. He didn't mention this case or any other for that matter. I've never known Jack to speak out of school. If you doubt my reason for coming here today, I'd be happy to get the Attorney General on the phone. He told me about the case at lunch." Solomon pulled his iPhone out of his pocket.

Stanford came to Jordyn's rescue, "Your Honor, the Attorney General told me only this morning that Mr. Banks might drop by. I apologize. I forgot to mention it to Jordyn, I mean Ms. Duarte. Mr. Banks is here as a representative of the Department of Justice, and at our next recess I will explain to him our national security concerns. I'm quite sure he will abide by the court's gag order."

The last thing Jordyn wanted was an antitrust expert sitting in on this trial. She didn't apologize or even respond, but she did manage to get her temper under control. She returned to her table without a word, and I followed suit. I hoped she would forget her opening statement, but she didn't. Within a few moments and despite her protestations about time limits, she gave a very well-prepared fifteen-minute opening.

"The plaintiffs were forced to bring this case against Mr. Ruple to prevent his theft of software designed, developed, and owned by my clients. The evidence will show…"

Her opening was a work of art, leaving the strong impression that my client was a gangster who had stolen her clients' software. She intended to prove their case through testimony from an expert witness who would say that David's software was an identical replica of what her clients had spent years in developing.

When she finished, she gave me a smug smile and sat down. Her train was back on track.

I rose from my chair and spoke to the jury, "Ladies and gentlemen, at the close of this case the judge will instruct you that anything said by the lawyers is not evidence, and that you should base your case solely on the evidence. Accordingly, I will not waste your time with an opening statement, because what I might say, or what Ms. Duarte just said, is not evidence."

I emphasized the last three words, but as I got back to my table I turned back to the jury and said, "She just told you that the defendant stole her clients' software. In case you're wondering, let me assure you that not a word of her accusation is true."

Before I could find my chair, Jordyn was out of hers. "Objection, Your Honor. What he just said might be his opinion, but it's certainly not evidence."

I responded before Moorman had a chance to react, "She's right. What I said isn't evidence. But for the record, all that stuff she said wasn't evidence either, it was pure hogwash."

Some of the jurors were laughing, but the judge wasn't.

"Mr. Patterson, I find your conduct inappropriate. I have a good mind to hold you in contempt."

Before he did, I responded in earshot of the jury. "Why, Your Honor? I could have wasted the jury's time as well as yours with fifteen minutes of explaining why Ms. Duarte will not be able to prove her case. I thought the word 'hogwash' would get my point across in much less time. I mean no disrespect to counsel, but she will not be able to make her case. Would you like me to explain why? I have the time."

The last thing Jordyn wanted at that moment was for me to demonstrate the deficiencies of her case. She gave Moorman a slight head shake, and he told her to call her first witness. I had upset her momentum, the jury was still giggling, and I had made my point.

"The plaintiffs call Dr. Arthur E. Thomas," she announced.

Dr. Thomas had earned a PhD in software engineering from Stanford as well as a list of other credentials as long as his arm. It would have been fruitless for me to question his qualifications or expertise. He wore wire rim glasses, spoke in an educated tone, and sported a well-trimmed beard. He projected the very epitome of a learned college professor.

Jordyn greeted her expert warmly, thanking him for his appearance and verifying his academic credentials. She then verified that he had reviewed the plaintiff's software and David's application for trademark protection. Finally, she came to the crux of his testimony. "Dr. Thomas, in your opinion is the software claimed by Mr. Ruple the same as the one developed by the plaintiffs."

"I'd say it is identical," he said and then took the next hour to compare the software's x's and o's in minute detail, pointing out the similarities on a big screen.

When he finally turned off his laser pointer, Jordyn asked, "Dr. Thomas, in your expert opinion did Mr. Ruple steal his software design from my clients?"

He answered, "Most certainly. The coding is virtually identical, and in my opinion one person alone could not have been able to design this program."

43

AFTER JORDYN CONCLUDED HER EXAMINATION and again thanked Thomas
for his expert opinion, the judge called a recess for lunch. Not only
did the break give the jurors much needed time to eat, but it also
gave them time to talk among themselves about Dr. Thomas's testimony. Despite the judge's admonition not to talk about the case
among themselves, we all knew they would. They always did.

As soon as Moorman rose, the marshal quickly took David's arm
to lead him back to his cell. He also swept up the cards David was
working on, the ones I'd asked him to respond to. I watched calmly
as they disappeared through the side door of the courtroom. I had
no doubt that my questions and his answers were now in the hands
of both Jordyn and Stanford.

I quickly objected, emphasizing again that I had been denied
normal access to my client. My objection was quickly overruled—again.

Fortunately, I had seen this larceny coming, and while Jordyn
was fawning over Thomas as his testimony ended, I'd switched the
cards David had answered for new ones. The new ones asked far
more interesting questions, such as "who won the NCAA National
Basketball Championship in 1994?" and "who beat undefeated
Georgia in the 1969 Sugar Bowl?"

Both Brian and Duke had noticed the switch, and we enjoyed
a quick laugh when I returned to our table. We'd had our fun, but
we hadn't yet been able to slow down the opponents' train. The
proceedings were moving faster than I could have expected. Jordyn
was confident again, and with Moorman's help the trial could be

over this afternoon. I had planned to reserve cross-examination of Thomas until I presented our defense, but with a little unforeseen help from David I decided on a different strategy.

David had slipped one note into Brian's hand before he was taken away. It said:

Ask Him If Their Software Works!!!

I stared at his words—surely it worked. I needed to find out why David was so insistent. But the Marshall didn't bring him back to the courtroom until the judge and jury had returned from their lunch break. I had no time alone with him at all. I was also wary of the adage that a lawyer should never ask a question when he doesn't know the answer. I certainly didn't know whether the software worked or not. I didn't even know what it was supposed to do.

"Begin your examination, Mr. Patterson," Judge Moorman directed.

I had decided to begin by making Jordyn and her co-counsel nervous.

"Dr. Thomas, may I call you Art?" I began.

If I continued to address him as Doctor, I would reinforce his credentials.

"I'd prefer you called me Arthur," he replied with a smile.

"Objection, Your Honor. I believe Mr. Patterson should address the witness as Doctor or Doctor Thomas." Jordyn interrupted.

Before the judge ruled, I responded. "Your Honor, if Ms. Duarte interrupts me after every question, we're going to be here all afternoon and tomorrow, too. I didn't interrupt her during direct even once."

The judge didn't want to slow this case down.

"Ms. Duarte, the witness said he wants to be called Arthur. You did a good job of establishing his credentials. Let's move on. And please try to hold your objections to a minimum. Go ahead, Mr. Patterson."

"So... Arthur," I began with a smile. "You testified this morning that you examined the plaintiffs' software line by line and then compared it to my client's software line by line. Is that correct?"

"Yes, that is correct," he answered.

"There are twenty plaintiffs in this case. Please tell the court which plaintiff developed the software."

Jordyn was on her feet, but the judge stopped her. "It's a reasonable question."

Arthur looked confused.

"Do I need to repeat the question?" I asked, again with a smile.

He hesitated, but finally answered, "My understanding is that it was developed as part of a collaboration."

"A collaboration? Oh, I see. You mean to say that twenty software engineers from twenty different companies all met in one room and developed this software? Is that right?"

Thomas looked uncomfortable, as did every lawyer for the companies. I turned and directed the barest hint of a smile toward Solomon, who was now sitting in the front row of the gallery.

"I have no information regarding how many engineers were involved. I was hired to compare the two software programs and to be an expert witness."

"Who hired you?"

"Ms. Duarte's law firm," he answered.

"Then I'm sure Ms. Duarte prepared you for this next question, Arthur. How much are you being paid by Ms. Duarte?"

I don't usually bother to ask about expert witness fees. But in this case, I wanted the jury to know that Arthur's testimony had been bought and paid for, especially since I couldn't produce my own expert.

Arthur relaxed a bit. "My fee is seven hundred dollars an hour for my review, and six thousand dollars a day for depositions and trial testimony."

"I'm sure you're worth it." I mumbled loud enough for the jury to hear me.

"When did this collaboration of engineers who developed the software in question occur?" I was venturing into uncharted waters.

"I believe the coding was complete in May of 2023, but I feel sure they've done some tweaking on it since then," he answered.

"Did they file for trademark protection for their software like my client did?"

"No, they didn't. But that's not relevant." He had regained his confidence.

I knew the answer to my next question.

"And why not?" I asked.

"When it comes to software, it's first to invent, not first to file. The plaintiffs finished in May; Mr. Ruple didn't file for protection until June of 2023. As I testified earlier, it's clear he copied the plaintiffs' work."

I was convinced the plaintiffs had copied David's work, but without discovery I couldn't argue with their assertion that they had invented the software in May.

"Arthur—how do you know my client didn't invent his software earlier than May?"

Arthur gave me a kind smile. "Because no individual could have developed this software on his own. It is identical to the plaintiffs' invention. Ergo, he had to have copied theirs."

"Unless the plaintiffs stole his work and copied his design? Right, Arthur?"

Jordyn couldn't stand it any longer.

"Asked and answered, your honor. Dr. Thomas has said more than once that Mr. Ruple is incapable of developing this complex a product on his own. Besides, the dating is clear. My clients finished their work in May. The defendant copied it and tried to patent it in June. Does Mr. Patterson have any proof that his client invented this software before May?"

Moorman was clearly bored. "Let's move on, Mr. Patterson."

"Yes, Your Honor. Arthur, how did my client steal the plaintiffs' software?"

"Wh...what do you mean?" he stammered.

"I mean, Ms. Duarte has loudly and repeatedly alleged that my client stole her clients' software. You have testified he copied it. But there is no public filing by the plaintiffs for trademark protection. Did my client find such dangerous software on the Internet?"

He looked puzzled, as did the jury, but managed to come up with a response.

"No, Mr. Paterson, it is not on the Internet. Maybe he obtained it by hacking into their computers."

"Oh, come on Arthur. It's okay to admit you don't know."

"He had to have hacked into one of their systems," he repeated stubbornly.

"You would have this jury believe that the biggest computer companies in the world don't have protection from a lone hacker. Arthur, did any of the twenty plaintiffs or anyone at the companies they represent tell you how David Ruple got a copy of their software? Or even how it could have happened?"

"No."

"So, you really don't have any idea how my client could have stolen the software, or whether he did. Your response that he must have hacked his way into one, or even all twenty, of these very sophisticated computer systems was nothing but pure conjecture on your part."

"Was that a question?" he asked, looking toward Jordyn. "Do I need to answer?" Jordyn looked dumfounded.

I had made my point. The problem was that I had no proof that David had developed the software other than his own testimony. To allow him to testify would in essence waive his fifth amendment rights, and I couldn't take that risk. At least I had the jury wondering how my client "stole" the plaintiff's product. I girded myself for the next set of questions I had for Arthur. Jordyn hadn't asked, and I had to.

"Arthur, I'm curious about one point and a bit surprised that Ms. Duarte didn't ask you in her direct. The prosecution has emphasized repeatedly how complex and special this software is. Can you tell me what it does?"

44

JORDYN AND STANFORD WERE BOTH ON THEIR FEET demanding a conference in chambers.

I asked within earshot of the jury, "Why all the secrecy, judge? All I asked was what it does."

Judge Moorman ignored me and told the jury we would take a ten-minute break.

We waited in silence until the jurors had dutifully followed the marshal out of the room. Without introduction or permission, Jordyn turned quickly to Moorman. "Your honor, the nature and function of my client's software is critical to our nation's security. We can't have our trade secrets exposed just to satisfy Mr. Patterson's curiosity."

I was ready for her objection. "Then drop your damn lawsuit, Jordyn."

My language caught everyone off guard, and I continued before anyone could react.

"The prosecution has withheld access to my client, filed motions and briefs without letting me see them, and now they don't want me to ask their witness what this software does, all in the name of "national security." If their software is so special, so hush-hush, why sue my client?

"They opened their own can of worms by filing this lawsuit and getting their paid expert to testify that my client couldn't have developed this software on his own. Well, he did. And the only way the jury will understand why he did, is for them to understand what it does."

Moorman sighed and began rubbing his face with both hands,

as if he could make the issue disappear. Jordyn's objection had put him in a box. He knew I was right.

He finally spoke. "Mr. Patterson, I understand your concern, but I don't see how I can let you follow this line of questioning."

I pulled out my ace card. "Your Honor, if you rule in her favor, you will give me no choice but to take this matter to the DC Circuit, where I will seek a stay. I don't want to; I'd rather proceed with the trial. But what this software does is critical to my client's defense."

Neither Jordyn or Stanford wanted either the subject matter or their shenanigans brought before the DC Circuit. Nor did the judge.

"What if I instruct the jury, and I will make it very clear, that they may not speak to or in any way communicate with anyone about what they are about to learn until I instruct them at the end of the trial," Moorman proposed.

Since neither Jordyn nor Stanford were willing to argue, they had no course but to agree. The judge asked the marshal to bring the jury back into the courtroom, and I resumed my cross-examination.

"Arthur, you have stated that both parties' software is essentially the same. What does it do?"

Dr. Thomas responded, "Well, it's complicated, but I'll try to explain."

He spent a great deal of time giving a very detailed explanation of the messaging and code, using very technical language. After fifteen minutes not a soul in the courtroom, other than he and David, had any idea what the software did.

I wasn't about to give up. "Arthur, I'm sure the jury appreciates your detailed technical explanation, but for those of us who aren't software engineers, can you explain what it does in layman's terms?"

"I'm not sure I can," he answered.

"Oh, come on, Arthur. Don't make me pull teeth. We're all waiting with bated breath. What is the software's purpose? What can it do?"

Arthur was caught between a rock and a hard place. He looked to Jordyn, whose face gave him no encouragement. He delayed a little too long.

Judge Moorman leaned over his desk and glared at him. "Dr.

Thomas, Ms. Duarte cannot answer the question for you. You have presented yourself as an expert in the field of software development. Answer Mr. Patterson's question.

Thomas swallowed hard and replied, "Yes, Your Honor,"

He turned to face me. "Essentially, it creates an application, what you would call an 'app,' for your phone, iPad, or computer that makes it difficult for someone who didn't create a particular record to be able to access it."

I was puzzled. "Can you give me an example?"

"Well, let's say you have a driver's license. You could pull up the app, check a box, and no one could access your driver's license, or the information on it, through the internet except the issuing authority."

"Wow," I said softly. "Are you saying that if I had a criminal record, no one could access that record except the court where I was convicted? That is, if I had the app and if I checked the right boxes?"

"Exactly," he answered, sounding more confident.

"Are the records destroyed?" I was now fascinated.

"No, but no one can access them or even know they exist except the affected party and the person or entity who created the record."

"Wow!" This time my excitement was evident. "You mean when I go on the internet to buy shoes, no one needs to know except Nike? No more ads for shoes every time I open my phone?"

"If you check the right boxes in the application, that's correct," he smiled, happy to agree.

"Sounds complicated. But aren't there already products that allow a user to block people from accessing one's private information?"

Warming to the subject, he smiled again. "There are, but none are so simple to use, or so broad in scope. This software is as complex and creative as anything I've ever seen. Yet a child could easily understand how to use it."

"Hmmm. It sounds to me that if the public at large had access to this app, it could change the way both the plaintiffs, law enforcement, and foreign intelligence organizations do business. Is that correct?"

Jordyn looked miserable, but Thomas was now in his element. "Yes, sir! And we're not talking about just our judicial system. Our entire economy is built on access to information. This software would restore privacy to anyone who can afford to buy the app. It's a real game changer."

I finally knew why everyone wanted David's software. Internet companies make their living by knowing what we want and selling our buying habits. If I visit even one site looking for walking shoes, within seconds every site I frequent contains ads for shoes. If I buy a set of wine glasses for a friend's birthday, I am instantly inundated with ads for glasses, wine, cocktail napkins—anything to do with entertainment, on every site I open. You can purchase ad blockers, but they're complicated to use, and most can be easily bypassed.

The government had a bigger problem. If an individual had access to this software, no one would know whether he had a criminal record or not. That person could go to another state, apply for a job, register to vote, and apply for a driver's license without anyone suspecting a thing. After paying a fine or serving his sentence, his slate would be effectively wiped clean. I couldn't imagine how it might affect intelligence gathering, both home and overseas.

And this example revealed just the tip of the iceberg. Our government and economy depend on information. David's software cut off the flow. Anyone could be as private as he or she wanted to be—well, almost. No wonder everyone was in such a tizzy. Individual privacy doesn't exist anymore, but with David's application it might come close.

I still hadn't developed a defense to Jordyn's lawsuit, but at least I knew what I was up against.

I had another line of questions for Dr. Thomas but decided to wait until I called him back to the stand. I passed the witness to the prosecution.

Jordyn's redirect was a regurgitation of her basic themes. Her clients' software was developed before David's and was identical to theirs, thus it must have been copied. She emphasized repeatedly that David was not capable of developing such complex software. She then put on a series of witnesses who bolstered her case that the design was completed in May.

None of them could tell me how David was able to steal their

invention, so my cross-examination was brief. I pointed out that
twenty companies had purposely ignored antitrust laws to develop
their invention. Unfortunately, I didn't make any headway with my
antitrust inquiries, except with Solomon. After all, none of these
companies were on trial today.

I was tired and depressed when David handed me a note asking
why I hadn't asked if the plaintiffs' software worked. I assured him
again that I would when the time was right.

Jordyn rested her case at a few minutes after five that evening.
The judge released the jury for the night, admonishing them not
to discuss the case with anyone, not even their spouses. Before he
banged his gavel to conclude the day, he called both Jordyn and
me to the bench.

"Mr. Patterson, I want to give this case to the jury by early afternoon tomorrow. We'll begin tomorrow morning at nine o'clock sharp.
I hope you won't try to drag this case out."

Great, I thought. Moorman had already decided the case and
was ready to send David to the lock-up for good. I knew it would
do no good to respond to his provocation, so I kept my tone even.
"Your Honor. I'll be ready. But I'd like to make sure of one thing
before we're dismissed.

"Okay," he sighed, "Go ahead; what is it now?"

"I feel sure Ms. Duarte has asked Dr. Thomas to be present in
the courtroom to hear my witnesses. But in case she hasn't, I want to
make it clear that I haven't released the witness. He is to be available
if I want to call him during my case in chief."

Jordyn was surprised. "What else can he say?"

I didn't bite, remaining silent. I wanted her to spend the night
preparing Arthur to respond to whatever I could possibly ask—at
seven hundred dollars an hour.

Judge Moorman seemed equally puzzled but agreed. "Ms.
Duarte, please have Dr. Thomas available. I don't want to give Mr.
Patterson any reason to ask for a delay. I expect both of you to be
prepared to give your closing arguments tomorrow. I mean for this
case to go to the jury sooner rather than later."

He brought his gavel down with unexpected force, and we were suddenly free to go. The marshal appeared immediately, and I had no chance to speak to David again.

Moorman couldn't be criticized for dragging his feet. The upshot was that I had less than twenty-four hours to come up with a defense. Nothing like a little pressure.

I was more than ready to leave but didn't see Duke anywhere. Maggie and Brian had gathered our belongings and were waiting at our table. Brian told me that Duke had left quickly, almost before the judge had dismissed us. I shook my head and asked Maggie to find him. I needed to speak with him before tomorrow.

45

WE DIDN'T DRIVE BACK TO THE FARMHOUSE IMMEDIATELY. Maggie had reached Duke and arranged for us to meet both him and Gloria at Barker's again. There was a possibility I might have to call Gloria to the stand. It would be a risky move, and I needed to get some idea of what she might say. Surprise testimony from your own witness is seldom a good thing. We met at Barker's downstairs grill again. They seemed to like the ambience, especially since they were eating and drinking on my dollar.

I asked Gloria if she knew anything about David's cousin, taking care not to disclose anything we had learned about his software during the trial.

She was on her second martini by now and more than willing to elaborate. "Oh, I bet he was trying to help his cousin Richard. Richie's a good boy, but he got in with a bad crowd when he was a teenager. He got caught selling more than just a little weed and was sent to Angola. He's out now, trying to turn his life around. You know, get a real job, be a good citizen and stay out of my father's business. He's got a nice girlfriend who's encouraging him, but it isn't easy. Having a record is a huge obstacle. His mother told me he'd asked David for help, but I don't know what David could have done. I haven't seen the boy in years. I should have visited him in prison, but I didn't. Couldn't face seeing him in a place like that."

Everything Gloria had just told us would be considered hearsay and inadmissible, but at least she was willing to talk. I tried another way.

"What kind of witness do you think Richard would make?" I asked.

Gloria shook her head. "Like I said, Richie's a good boy at heart, but he does have a temper. A guard gave him a shove when he was at Angola, and he lost his cool, knocked the guard out cold. His temper got him an extra six months in solitary. From what Duke's told me about Duarte, she would eat him alive."

Scratch Richard as a witness.

"Gloria, could you recognize David's handwriting?"

She laughed. "Do I look like a mother who checks her son's homework?"

Very funny. I waited in silence until she responded.

"Look, David and I talk, but we don't write. Anyway, who writes? It's all email now. The last time I saw his handwriting was probably when he sent me a Mother's Day card years ago."

I'd run into a dead end.

Duke asked how he could help, and I gave him a few ideas about how to get under Jordyn's skin. I left Barker's feeling totally frustrated.

Brian said he wanted to clean up some work at the office, so Clovis drove Maggie and me back to the farmhouse. We rode in silence for some time. I had almost dozed off when I realized Maggie was speaking to me.

"Okay, Jack. Don't tell me you're trying to sleep. What's the matter?"

You're usually full of yourself after the first day of a trial. You want to talk about what happened and what you expect to happen the next day. By the way, I thought you were brilliant today." she said with a smile.

I couldn't find a return smile, but I found I did want to talk after all.

"Thanks, Maggie. I appreciate your confidence, but we're in a Catch-22 situation. The only way I can prove that David invented the software is to call him to the stand. But if I do, I waive his fifth amendment rights. He can say how and why he created the software, but he possibly faces a lifetime of criminal charges if he does. We still don't know what the government is accusing him of doing, but if I

let him take the stand, I am sure Duarte and Stanford will find a way
for him to put himself in jeopardy. Gloria told me why he wanted to
help his cousin, and now I have a good idea when he first had the
idea that led to the software and his application. I've got to find a
way to prove it without putting him on the stand.

"I have the perfect defense to the criminal charges, but the
moment he testifies, it's game over and he lives out his life in jail.
If I had even fifteen minutes alone with him, I'm sure he would say
that between keeping his software and a life in prison, he'd give up
his software in a heartbeat."

"That's not a hard choice," Maggie commented.

"No, it's not. If I put him on the stand, I make the wrong choice
for him. I've thought about seeking *habeas*, trying to get Moorman
to delay the trial so I can think through this with David. But my gut
tells me I have one chance to win both cases, and a delay will blow
it. Besides, Moorman isn't about to grant a delay. He doesn't care
a tinker's damn about David. He's made a deal with the devil and
just wants this case to be over, preferably with his own skin intact."

Maggie responded, "Jack, I trust your trial instincts more than
anyone I know. This case and these issues are tough. You'll find a
way to win; of that I am certain."

An oddly hoarse voice from the front seat commented "Ditto."
All three of us laughed, and I did my best to change the conversation
to a more agreeable topic. But I couldn't help thinking about David,
alone in a jail cell wearing an orange jumpsuit.

We finally pulled into the driveway to the farmhouse, and I
asked Clovis to find Royce and ask him to send me certified copies
of Richard Ruple's court papers. Everyone else was waiting for us in
the great room. I explained to Stella and Rita what we now thought
David's software was supposed to do. Armed with new information,
they returned to searching David's box. Brian was hard at work
drafting proposed jury instructions. Maggie and I settled down on
the sofa with a glass of cabernet to work through a possible closing
argument.

David's note kept swirling in and out of my mind. Surely he
knows whether his own software works.

*****

We'd gone through the fourth iteration of my proposed closing argument, when Rita suddenly ran into the room, clutching several small pieces of paper in her hand. She was out of breath, not from exertion, but from the excitement of her find.

"Look! I found it! I found David's first scribblings about a software that limits access. I told you he used to sit at ball games and doodle. Well, this baseball scorecard is just that."

She handed me a scorecard from a Phillies/Nats game last year. I must admit that my first thought was how could the Nats have won that game? The Phillies' best pitcher… but the game faded from my brain when I noticed that beneath the smudges of ketchup and mustard someone had scribbled what every gamer would recognize as computer programming code. The scorecard was dated October 1, 2022. The Nats were awful last year, but on that day, they beat the Phillies 13-4. Garcia went three for five with five RBIs. I was at that game and remembered it well.

Stella followed Rita into the room, grinning from ear to ear. I raised the card and asked, "Is this the code we've been looking for?"

"It is. It's the beginnings of the formula for the software that you described in court today. David must have come home that night and continued to work on it. We found more of his coding in the bottom of the box. Once we found the score card, we knew what we were looking for."

"No doubt it's his handwriting?"

"None. I've compared it to other samples. It's his."

But how could I get these documents into evidence? I could ask David, but again that was a non-starter for the same reason as before. We could put Rita on the stand but given her relationship with David that was not without risk. Another approach came to mind, and I whirled it around for a while. It was iffy, but it was all I had.

We split up into two teams. One prepared Rita to testify that she found the scorecard in David's box, and that it was his handwriting. The second team worked on my idea. It was worth a try.

After two hours, I reassembled the two teams and ordered everyone to bed. Tomorrow would be a long day.

On the way to our rooms, I asked Maggie, "How did Rita do?"

"She's scared, she's in love, and Jordyn will eat her alive. She knows coding, but she's fragile when it comes to David. I wouldn't risk it, but it's your call."

I responded, "Problem is, she may be all we've got."

46

I TOSSED AND TURNED ALL NIGHT, going over and over my examination of witnesses and closing argument in my mind. I had no doubt that whoever testified, whatever happened, Moorman would submit this case to jury tomorrow. I've tried several high-profile cases, defended people accused of murder, but this situation was unique, a tightrope. One wrong step and my young client could fall into a life spent in federal prison.

I must have enjoyed a few hours of sleep because the next morning I woke full of energy and determination. We all had an early breakfast and were soon on our way to DC. Both Clovis and Big Mike kept a careful watch for Hans or anyone else who looked suspicious. We made it without incident and were soon going through security at the entrance of the E. Barrett Prettyman Federal Courthouse.

Neither Rita nor Stella would be allowed in the courtroom unless I called her to the stand. Big Mike would sit with them, and Martin's men were disbursed throughout the courthouse just in case Hans appeared. They would be unarmed but hopefully so would Hans.

When I entered the courtroom, I was greeted with a surprise. Solomon had brought a guest. I knew who she was and walked over to greet them both.

"Jack, let me introduce Virginia Pruitt. She's the new Assistant Attorney General for the antitrust division," Solomon said with a grin.

"I'm delighted to meet you," I said, extending my hand.

"It's nice to meet you as well," she responded, taking my hand with a smile. "I had dinner with Solomon last night. He mentioned he'd been observing an interesting trial and that I might want to join him today. He wouldn't tell me what it was about, but since I've never seen the famous Jack Patterson try a case, I thought I might come. I called William Stanford last night to tell him I was thinking about coming, and he all but begged me not to. His reluctance made up my mind. I hope you won't disappoint me."

I bet Stanford didn't want her here. I also bet the fur had flown when William told Jordyn. Virginia Pruitt was one of the administration's more controversial appointments. A former Harvard law professor, she was known as a firebrand when it came to enforcement of antitrust laws. She had been confirmed by a small majority of the Senate, and rumor had it that she was already shaking up the entire antitrust department at Justice.

When Jordyn and her entourage entered the courtroom, she stared directly at Virginia and Solomon, who had taken seats near the rear of the room. If looks could kill, Ms. Pruitt would already be in her grave. Once again, David was the last person to enter before the judge banged his gavel.

"Mr. Patterson, please call your first witness," Moorman announced.

"The defense calls William Stanford to the stand."

Panic set in immediately. Everyone in the courtroom, including the jury, heard Jordyn say, "What the hell?" She rose to address the judge.

"Objection! Your Honor, attempting to call Mr. Stanford for the defense is totally inappropriate. We were given no notice he would try to pull off such a blatant attack on counsel. The only information Mr. Stanford could have that is relevant to this case is classified and protected by the attorney-client privilege and the work-product privilege." Visibly confident, she turned her smile on the jury.

"Not quite everything," I interrupted, addressing the judge. "Your Honor, I have no intention of asking Mr. Stanford about privileged information. Ms. Duarte told the jury that Mr. Stanford works for the government and, moreover, that he believes my client is a crook. His testimony is vital to my case."

"Do you mean to elicit from Mr. Stanford the fact that your client has been indicted? Are you sure you want to do that?" Moorman asked, clearly puzzled.

"Yes, and I have a few other questions for him as well," I responded.

Stanford himself spoke up, earning a glare from Moorman. "May I remind the court that Mr. Ruple's indictment is sealed because of national security."

"Your Honor, I haven't even been allowed to see the indictment. I promise not to ask Mr. Stanford about its details." I'd seen the judge's glare as had everyone else.

Jordyn stared directly at the judge, who looked at his desk, refusing any eye contact with her. She'd asked for a quick trial with no witness lists or opportunity for discovery. He thought for a few seconds and did the right thing.

"Objection denied. Take the witness chair, Mr. Stanford."

I waited patiently while William was duly sworn in, hoping that maybe now I'd get the truth.

"Mr. Stanford, are you the lead counsel in the criminal case against my client, David Ruple?"

Squirming a bit in his chair Stanford said, "I am."

"I won't ask you for any details of that case or what is in the indictment, but am I right in supposing that the software in question in this case is a part of your case against my client?"

"You are," Stanford wasn't going to volunteer anything.

"And am I right that the U.S. government takes the position that David Ruple designed the software in question, not the twenty plaintiffs here today?"

William looked in vain to the judge for help.

"Answer the question, Mr. Stanford," the judge instructed.

"You are," he answered with a look of disgust.

I paused to let his answer sink in. The government's indictment of David as the creator of the offending software was clearly inconsistent with Jordyn's claim that her clients were responsible for its design.

"In fact, my client has been sitting in DC's jail because you believe the software in question is his creation."

Jordyn rose again. "Your honor, Mr. Patterson assured the court he would not get into the details of the indictment."

Moorman surprised me. "Mr. Patterson, can you rephrase your question?"

"Thank you, Your Honor. I believe I can."

"Mr. Stanford, please don't tell me what's in the indictment, but my client remains in jail because you ordered his arrest. Is that right?"

"Yes, that is correct."

"And you ordered his arrest because you believe my client is the author of the software in question. Am I correct?"

Jordyn objected. "What Mr. Stanford believes or doesn't is not a matter of fact. He is not an expert in software development." She was right, but she sure was throwing Stanford under the bus.

Judge Moorman sustained her objection.

"Let me ask another way," I smiled at William. "Did you tell me that you believed David Ruple designed the software."

Jordyn jumped up, but before she could object, I said, "Your Honor, I'm not asking him what he believes, I'm asking him what he said. I am not asking for the truth of what was asserted, just that he said it."

The judge nodded, "Go ahead, Mr. Patterson."

"Mr. Stanford, did you tell me that you believed my client designed the software which is at the heart of the plaintiffs' claim?"

"I did, but...." he stopped abruptly.

"But, what?" I asked.

"Nothing," he mumbled.

"But what, Mr. Stanford? I don't really care, nor do I want to know, who's pulling your strings, who's been directing your behavior. My client has been indicted and locked away since he filed for trademark protection because both you and the U.S. government believe he designed it and must be stopped from developing it at all costs. Yet since the beginning of this trial you have sat with Ms. Duarte and the plaintiffs, helping her pursue her clients' claim that they created the software. Can you explain your statements or your actions, because for the life of me I can't."

Jordyn shrieked, "Objection."

I gave her a smile and said, "I withdraw the question, Your Honor."

47

I'D MADE MY POINT. I looked at Solomon. He was smiling, and Virginia Pruitt looked shocked. I didn't object to Jordyn's request for a recess. In fact, I looked forward to her cross-examination of William.

The judge didn't give her much time. After a ten-minute break he brought the jury back in. "Your witness, Ms. Duarte."

She approached the witness stand and smiled. "Mr. Stanford, what you might have said or what you might believe is not binding on this jury, is it?"

"Certainly not."

"And if this jury finds for the plaintiffs, you will accept the verdict, correct?" she inquired.

"Absolutely."

"Pass the witness." She sat down quickly.

"Any re-cross?" the judge asked.

"Just a few, your honor." I stepped to the podium and asked, "Absolutely, huh, Mr. Stanford? I take it then the criminal charges against my client will be dropped if the plaintiffs win today?"

"Well, not exactly. It won't be up to me. There are other factors in play that I'm not at liberty to discuss," he hedged.

The government wasn't about to let David out of jail any time soon. They didn't want his programming skills loose and unfettered. They were afraid of what he might create.

"Mr. Stanford, if you will accept 'absolutely' a verdict for the plaintiffs that says they created the software first and that my client copied their design, shouldn't you let him go immediately and indict all twenty of the plaintiffs that same day?"

"Objection, calls for speculation." Jordyn sounded tired.

I responded, "It does, your honor, and I withdraw it. But it's certainly something to think about."

Not wanting to lose my momentum I said, "Defendant calls Dr. Thomas to return to the witness stand."

No objections. I felt sure Jordyn had spent most of the night preparing the good Dr. Thomas for my questions.

The judge reminded him that he was still under oath, and I began.

"Arthur, I'm sure you spent a good deal of time preparing for your testimony in this trial. Did you review Mr. Ruple's application before the patent and trademark office?"

He seemed a little taken aback. "I did. In fact, it was his application that I used to compare with the plaintiffs' work."

"That's right," I said with a smile. "You even put it up on a screen to better show the jury how they were similar. Correct?"

"Not just similar," he corrected me. "They are identical." He was obviously proud of his expertise.

"Okay—let's look at Mr. Ruple's application again." Maggie was Johnny on the spot. David's application and the relevant software immediately appeared on a big screen in front of the jury.

"I see that much of the information isn't typed. It's in Mr. Ruple's handwriting."

"That's correct. I believe Mr. Ruple was in a hurry and filled out his application partially by hand." His tone was arrogant.

"And this is the document you used to arrive at your conclusions?" I asked.

"That's correct. I compared this document to the plaintiffs' invention and determined they were the same."

"You didn't use drafts or other preliminary documents from the plaintiffs to reach your conclusions?"

"No, my testimony was based solely on a review of both Mr. Ruple's application, and the software developed by the plaintiffs."

"Thank you. Let's keep this document on the screen and compare it to another."

The scorecard, complete with mustard stains, popped up next to the application. Brian gave copies of the scorecard and David's yellow pad to the judge and Jordyn.

Jordyn was livid. "What is this? Are you trying to authenticate this document through this witness? He's never seen it before."

I answered, "I was going to ask him that very question, so thank you for pointing that out."

Before she could respond, I quickly turned to speak to the judge. "Your honor, you instructed me to speed up my examination. I have a witness who is willing to authenticate this document was found in my client's files and is in his handwriting. If Ms. Duarte wants to question its authenticity, I can produce a witness this afternoon who will validate the handwriting."

The handwriting on both documents was identical and clearly David's. Moreover, the jury had been looking at it for several minutes now. Jordyn didn't know who my witness was, but she risked alienating the judge and the jury if she slowed down the proceeding for such an obvious matter. She opted to sit down.

I continued, "Arthur, can you please compare the programming language on the scorecard and his yellow pad to the language in his application for a trademark?"

Arthur needed time to come up with the explanation.

"Well, this is a multi-page document. It would take time to do a line-by-line comparison." He might as well have said, "drop back and punt."

"I'm not asking for a line-by-line comparison." I was asking the obvious. The handwriting was identical, and the coding was the same. The judge and jury could see the same thing I saw. "Ballpark, Arthur. Do they look identical?"

"Well, I don't know about identical," he fudged.

"Identical is your word, Dr. Thomas. How about you show the jury where the coding is different?"

I waited for his answer, wondering idly why witnesses usually look to either their lawyer or a spouse for help, as if they could somehow silently communicate a believable response.

He must have "heard" my musings. He shot Jordyn a silent plea for help, sighed and conceded. "Without time or the tools for a thorough examination, I can't identify any differences."

So much for the fun part.

"Arthur, what is the date on the scorecard?"

This question brought Jordyn back on her feet. "Objection. Dr. Thomas has never seen this document before today. Counsel would have him testify that both documents were created on the scorecard's date. For all we know, Ruple grabbed a piece of paper after he stole my clients' product."

I responded, "As I said, we can have someone authenticate this document if necessary. My question to this witness was not intended to determine the date of the application document. I just wanted to know if he could read the date on the program. As you can see, Mr. Ruple must have been enjoying a hot dog at the time."

That brought a good laugh from the jury. Even Moorman smiled. Jordyn wasn't amused, but she did sit down.

"Once again Arthur, if you can, please tell us the date on the scorecard."

"October 1, 2022."

"Oddly enough, I was at that game. You know, it's neither here nor there, but I can't understand why anyone puts ketchup on a hot dog. Give me mustard, just mustard, nothing else. Do you remember who the Nats played that night?"

Arthur was irritated, "No, I don't. I don't go to baseball games."

"Oh, that's a shame, Arthur—you're missing out on a lot. Does the scorecard mention who they were playing?"

The answer was in big letters on the screen. Arthur responded, "The Philadelphia Phillies."

"That's right, and the Nats won, 13-4," I said as I turned to walk back to our table. I knew the judge wouldn't let me continue.

Before I sat down, David mouthed, "Ask him if it works!"

I whispered back, "Are you sure?"

"Ask him."

"What the hell," I thought. After all it was his software.

I turned back to the podium.

"Dr. Thomas, in the course of your preparation for your testimony did you consult with plaintiffs' software engineers?"

"I did." He was clearly relieved to return to his comfort zone.

"Did they show you the application it creates?"

"They did."

"Now this might be a foolish question, but since I don't know much about computers past email and Word, did it, well, did it work?"

I'd finally hit a nerve. No one could miss the panic on Dr. Thomas's face.

"Dr. Thomas, please answer my question. Does the software work?"

48

THERE COMES A MOMENT IN ALMOST EVERY TRIAL. It can be a confession from a witness, a statement by counsel, or a judge's ruling, but when it occurs, the course of the trial changes dramatically. The look on Arthur's face when I asked him if the software worked was that moment. The jury, the judge, and even Jordyn were visibly stunned, and I had a different case altogether.

At first Arthur tried evasion. "I explained before that the software needed tweaking."

"I'm not talking about tweaking. You gave us examples of what it was supposed to do. Does it do what it's supposed to do?"

He stumbled again. "Well, it's complicated."

"My question is not complicated. Does it work, or not?"

Arthur looked at Jordyn again, but she was as interested in the answer as the rest of us.

The judge intervened. "Answer the question, Dr. Thomas."

With a deep sigh, he gave in. "As it now exists, the software doesn't perform the functions it was designed to do."

"You mean it doesn't work." I didn't want there to be any doubt.

"No, it doesn't work," he snapped.

"Do you know why? What exactly is the problem?" It really didn't matter, but I knew the jury was interested.

"It's missing something, some lines of code or something."

"Are the software engineers for all twenty plaintiffs working on a solution?"

Arthur smiled. "Night and day."

"Any success?" I asked.

"Not as far as I know."

Jordyn didn't know where I was going, but she realized her case was headed downhill in a hurry.

"Objection. Relevance, your honor. Counsel is getting way off field here."

"Sustained, move it along Mr. Patterson. You've made your point."

I had made my point. I didn't know the answer to my next question.

"Dr. Thomas, you testified earlier that my client's software is virtually identical to the plaintiff's. Does my client's work?"

"No. The plaintiffs' engineers replicated his software. His is missing something as well."

"Software engineers for twenty different companies can't fix either one?" I asked.

"I'm sure it's only a matter of time."

"Maybe they should ask my client how to fix it. Thank you for your testimony, Dr. Thomas."

I asked Moorman for a ten-minute break and sat down. I wanted Arthur's testimony to sink in with the jury, but more importantly I needed time to think. Should I call David or Rita to the stand? Once again, the marshal hurried David away almost before the judge's gavel struck. I had no chance to ask him why the software didn't work.

Moorman was nothing if not punctual. He brought his gavel down exactly ten minutes later. Jordyn's cross examination of Arthur was decidedly brief. What could she ask? Nevertheless, she had him point out that he wasn't vouching for the authenticity of the scorecard, nor was he a specialist in repairing software. Arthur looked immensely relieved when she finally dismissed him.

Judge Moorman wasted no time before calling both Jordyn and me to the bench. "How many more witnesses do you have, Mr. Patterson? I'm trying to gauge when we should take a lunch break today. I want to instruct the jury and give them the case this afternoon if possible."

"At this point, the defense rests," I answered.

Jordyn couldn't believe it. "What? You're not calling Ruple to the stand? You're not going to authenticate the doodling on the scorecard? You must be nuts."

Duke had joined me at the bench. For once, the judge didn't take offense at his presence. He turned to me and said, "You are nuts. She'll eat you alive. All the jury will remember is Jordyn telling the jury that David must have stolen the software. Otherwise, he would testify."

"If she does that, we get a mistrial," I responded.

Jordyn got huffy. "And just what makes you think that?"

I answered, "The case of Liles vs. Crockett decided by the Honorable Judge Moorman."

The judge smiled. Jordyn groused. "I'm not familiar with that case."

I was more than happy to recap the case for her.

"In that case, a civil case by the way, the plaintiff tried to make a big deal about the defendant not testifying. Judge Moorman ruled that since the defendant was under indictment in an unrelated case, the plaintiff's attorney couldn't mention his failure to testify in his closing argument. It would violate his fifth amendment rights. The plaintiff took it up to the DC Circuit, and Judge Moorman was upheld. Do I need to file a motion to keep Ms. Duarte from mentioning it during her closing?"

"You did your homework, Mr. Patterson," the judge said with a smile.

"Thank you, Your Honor. You do have an excellent record on appeal."

Jordyn tried to interrupt, but Moorman waved her away. "Okay, let's get this show on the road. Submit your proposed jury instructions, and I'll look them over during our lunch break. Do you have any more witnesses, Ms. Duarte? No? Then how long do you think you need for closing arguments?"

Things were moving way too fast for Jordyn.

"Judge, I had no idea Mr. Patterson would rest. I need a little time."

"You'll have plenty of time during lunch break, Ms. Duarte. I intend to give this case to the jury after lunch. How much time do you need for closing?"

She was obviously flustered but recovered quickly.

"At least two hours, your honor," she stated firmly.

"I'll give you thirty minutes. And you, Mr. Patterson."

"Thirty minutes will be plenty, Your Honor, However I do have several motions. I've learned that in patent and trademark cases, procedural motions must be made or waived."

"Grab a sandwich during the break and come back to chambers. I'll deny everyone's motions and go over the jury instructions."

At least he was honest.

We returned to our tables, and he addressed the jury, "We're going to take an early lunch break. When we return, you'll hear closing arguments from both counsels. Then I'll give you this case to decide. Again, don't talk about this case with anyone, including each other, until I've given you instructions. We'll be in recess until one p.m."

49

MY STOMACH WAS TOO NERVOUS TO EAT ANYTHING, even a sandwich. Moorman was true to his word. He denied every motion Jordyn or I made. He knew a jury's verdict was hard to overturn on appeal, while granting motions was a sure way for a judge to get reversed. I had a few minutes to myself after chambers, and I spent every one of them second-guessing my own decisions, primarily not calling David to the stand and not asking Rita to authenticate the scorecard.

The only bit of humor during the break came when Duke suggested he and Jordyn go out for drinks after the verdict. He told her she was "one fine looking filly," to which Jordyn turned crimson and told Duke where he could go. I thought he was lucky to get off so lightly. Duke didn't bat an eye.

Jordyn was obnoxious and as cold as ice most of the time, but she was masterful in front of the jury. She pointed out that Dr. Thomas had said the two softwares were identical and that David alone could not have created such software. It was too complex for one person to design, and I had failed to call an expert on my own to rebut his testimony. She said that my baseball scorecard could just as easily been created after the fact, and no one had established its authenticity.

She carefully avoided referencing David's failure to testify, but she used his criminal indictment to label him a criminal and liar for filing for intellectual protection claiming the software was his idea. Finally, she tried to turn the software's failure to work against David. Its failure to work proved that it could only have been developed by a team of software engineers.

Now it was my turn.

"Ladies and gentlemen of the jury, the judge has instructed you not to set aside your common sense and beliefs in rendering your verdict. I ask the same. Ms. Duarte would have you believe that my client, acting alone, was able to hack into the research being done on a collaborative basis by twenty of the largest computer companies in this country, without their knowledge, and that they only discovered the hacking and theft when Mr. Ruple filed for intellectual property protection. Do you believe that?

"She doesn't deny that the handwriting on the baseball scorecard and my client's application for a patent are the same, but she would have you believe he created the scorecard after the fact. Do you really believe those mustard and ketchup stains weren't acquired at a ballpark? Do you believe that my client saved that scorecard, stains and all, way back in October to create a duplicate of a software that Ms. Duarte claims didn't even exist until the following May?

"She would have you believe that the U.S. government and the Department of Justice didn't do their homework before they indicted my client. She wants you to believe that the Department of Justice and her very own co-counsel are completely wrong in believing my client designed the software in question. David sits in jail without a computer or access to his lawyer because our government believes he is a national security risk—not the clients she would have you believe invented the software.

"Let me ask you this. If her clients designed the software in question, why doesn't it work? Software engineers for twenty-some companies are working night and day trying to come up with "what is missing"—the specific words used by their expert. If they designed it, shouldn't they know what's missing? Do you really believe that the twenty largest computer companies in the United States, who compete daily, all got together to design a software that would put them out of business? Such a scenario is surely ludicrous.

"These companies are at each other's throats every single day, but Ms. Duarte would have you believe that these companies joined hands around the campfire to create the one invention which would shut them all down. If that's the case, where is the document that memorializes this 'collaboration?' Again, that's not my word, but that of their expert. The lack of documentary proof that this collaboration exists speaks loudly don't you think?

"Let me ask you one final question. If the software doesn't work, what are we talking about? Why have the plaintiffs wasted both your and the court's time. My client's doodles on a scorecard are nothing more than an idea, apparently. One of you may think of a way to cure cancer, or harness artificial intelligence, or a way to create energy out of sand, but those are only ideas unless and until they work. Until they are designed, built, tested, and work they are only ideas, possibilities—not intellectual property.

"This case is not about who designed what. I believe we have pretty much established that both the original idea and design of this software are my client's and his alone. This case is about an idea that would force the plaintiffs to do business in an entirely different manner. An idea that is more than just frightening to them. It is unacceptable to them because they could no longer share your personal information among each other. If you want to buy a pair of shoes on the internet, that fact would remain between you and the shoe company. If David's software were to work and become available, you would have a means of protecting your privacy to whatever extent you think is best. That outcome won't happen if the plaintiffs get their way today.

"Ms. Duarte asks you to let her clients continue to prey on your privacy. Her clients want you to give them my client's idea, an idea unique to David which only he can bring to completion, which they will quietly lock away, along with David, unknown to almost anyone and never to see the light of day. Ask yourself which makes more sense—her twenty clients conspired among themselves to design a product that puts them out of business. Or did my client have a brilliant idea that could protect your privacy?

"Her clients will stop at nothing to keep David's idea from becoming known to the public at large. 'Stopping at nothing' includes claiming they designed the software and conspiring with the Justice Department to have my client locked away in the name of national security. Ask yourself this: if her clients designed the software, why hasn't Ms. Duarte called even one of the many engineers working 'night and day' to fix its missing code to testify in this trial. Surely, she should be able to produce at least one of them who could show you his notes, his scribbles, samples of his programming efforts, or a draft of the software. You've seen my client's mustard-stained scorecard, his hand-written notes, and his handwritten filing with the patent office. Where is a single scribble from the engineers who work for those companies?

"The judge has instructed you that it is not my client's obligation to prove that he designed the software. It is rather the plaintiffs' burden, by a preponderance of the evidence to prove that they did. But not one of the plaintiffs has given any corroborating evidence; they've only given their word and asked you to believe them. Ask yourself—what sort of software is so complicated that Dr. Thomas refers to it as brilliant, that exists without one single note or draft? Ms. Duarte has made a big deal about authenticating the scorecard. But the question you should ask is 'where is your proof, Ms. Duarte? Where is your scorecard?'

"If her clients own the software, why haven't they produced the team or even a single person who can say 'Look what we did! This was my idea!' If you had been that person or part of that team, wouldn't you have wanted some credit? Maybe even a raise? Where is the person who says these are my notes? Where is the person who says she knows what's missing?"

Judge Moorman spoke up, "Your time is about up, Mr. Patterson."

"Thank you, Your Honor. Ladies and gentlemen, it would be easy to say this case is only about who designed a piece of software. But to use Mr. Madigan's comparison, it's really a David and Goliath story. It's about corporate America trying to stifle the idea of a single person. My client's idea upsets their apple cart. It's not good for their business. Its success would require them to change, to think differently about how their business model affects individual citizens, how it affects you.

"Progress begins with an idea. Don't let the plaintiffs halt progress."

50

THE JURY WENT BACK TO DELIBERATE, and after I literally begged, Stanford and the judge allowed David and Rita to sit together at our table while we waited for a verdict.

I was chatting about nothing with Solomon and Virginia Pruitt when the marshal burst into the courtroom and boomed, "Your Honor, the jury has reached a verdict." You could have heard a pin drop. The jury had only been out twenty-seven minutes.

The judge didn't seem surprised. I was. And I grew even more worried when not one of the jurors would look me in the eye as they walked in and resumed their seats in the jury box—a longstanding sign of bad news. For a moment, I thought of Hans, but immediately banished the thought that he might have gotten to the jury.

When they were all seated the judge asked, "Madam Foreman, has the jury reached a verdict, and has it been signed as instructed?"

"Yes, Your Honor."

"Please hand the verdict to the clerk," he instructed. The clerk accepted it from the foreman and immediately handed it to the judge.

Judge Moorman's eyebrows raised as he read the piece of paper. "Oh, shit," I thought.

He handed the verdict back to the clerk and she read it.

"We the jury find for the defendant. We also have one question. Are we allowed to assess damages against the plaintiffs?"

So much for longstanding signs. You could have knocked me over with a feather.

*****

I had cautioned David not to react one way or the other to the verdict, but it was hard not to when Duke let out a loud cowboy "yahoo!" The judge banged his gavel again, glaring at Duke, who couldn't help a sheepish grin.

Moorman ignored him and addressed the foreman. "I take it that since the verdict was signed only by you the verdict is unanimous?" She confirmed his supposition.

"Ladies and gentlemen, thank you for your service. You ask about damages, but that is not part of your charge. May I remind you not to talk about this case to anyone. You are excused."

He watched the marshal escort the jury out, gathered his robes and left in a rush, without a word to anyone or even a backward glance. Moorman had clearly been in cahoots with Jordyn at first, yet in the long run several of his rulings had benefited our side. Sometimes the evidence can turn even the most hostile judge. I wondered what... but there was no time for wondering.

Brief pandemonium set in. My side hugged and smiled; Duke even did a little dance. Jordyn's team quietly packed up. I went over to her table and shook everyone's hands. It's what lawyers do, no matter what the outcome. It also gave me the opportunity to remind Stanford that David was still locked up. He said he wished he could set him free, but that he had to let the Attorney General know what had happened first. He promised he'd call as soon as he could.

I congratulated David. He was grateful but understandably apprehensive. "What happens next?"

I answered, "Next? Next is getting you released from jail and the charges officially dropped. It's time for you to get your life back."

"They can have the software for all I care," he said. "As Dr. Thomas said, 'it doesn't work.'"

"I'm curious. How did you know it wouldn't work?"

"Because I left out an entire page of language from my application. They'll never figure out what's missing. My favorite college professor taught us to always leave out a page of code when you file for patent protection. That way no one can copy your invention. I'm sure glad I took his advice!"

Brian took Rita's arm and guided her through a side door of the courtroom. The marshal led David away, hopefully for the last time. Maggie handed me my briefcase, and we walked out of the building into sunshine so bright it was almost blinding. But not so blinding that I didn't notice Hans standing at the foot of the steps. I turned quickly to shield Maggie and was about to shove her forcibly into the crowd of departing lawyers, when I heard a voice call out, "Jack, stop! It's okay. I've got him." A woman's smiling face peeked out from behind Hans who looked totally disgusted. Two burly DC policemen held his arms tightly, and Lisa Eckenrod still had her Glock 43 jammed into the small of his back.

"You owe me skybox tickets to a Commanders' game," she said with a big grin.

Hans had been waiting for us to leave the courthouse, but as I later learned, Lisa had been within shouting distance ever since I'd suggested she couldn't protect me without detection. It dawned on me that she had been the woman who looked familiar to me at Nany O'Brien's and the restaurant in New Orleans. Remind me not to underestimate her again.

William Stanford turned out to be a man of his word, at least on this issue. He called me bright and early the next morning.

"Jack, can you meet me in the Attorney General's conference room this afternoon? I'll make sure your client is there as well. Say around two o'clock and you will be free to consult with David as much as you'd like."

Maggie and I arrived at the Justice Department a few minutes before two and were escorted upstairs to the AG's conference room. Virginia Pruitt was chatting with a few of the plaintiffs' lawyers. William and Jordyn stood aside from the others, still a team. We joined David at the large table. He appeared to be somewhat in awe of his surroundings. Who could blame him? After all, Robert Kennedy had used the room as his office when he was the Attorney General, and his picture still hung over the enormous fireplace at the far end of the room. I was happy to see David in street clothes, no cuffs or shackles.

When everyone had taken a chair, Virginia tapped her water

glass with a pen and began. "The attorney general asked me to chair this meeting. First, welcome back to your old haunt, Mr. Patterson. Ms. Matthews, it's nice to meet you. Mr. Ruple, it's very nice to see you in street clothes." That generated a few quiet snickers, which she ignored. "There's no sense rehashing how this matter came to such a sorry climax. But be clear, changes will be made, and those responsible for this debacle will be held to account." She turned to look directly at William and Jordyn, who were staring at the carpet. I could almost feel sorry for him. He had obviously been acting on orders from above. Jordyn was a different matter. She only cared about winning.

"Mr. Patterson, I understand a person whose name is Hans has threatened you and your family as well as members of your legal team. The DC police have turned him over to the FBI who are interviewing him. As it turns out, Hans is very cooperative. You may have noticed that some of the plaintiffs are not represented here today. Hans has already provided information sufficient to prevent them or their attorneys from attending. Let me assure you, justice will be served. Is that satisfactory?"

I liked the way this meeting was going. "It is, thank you. And I'm glad you've been given the lead."

She smiled and looked at David. "Mr. Ruple, on behalf of the Department of Justice and the United States government I apologize for the way this matter was handled. Words cannot express my disappointment in certain individuals, corporate entities, and representatives of our government. Such flagrant disregard for both the truth and individual rights will not be tolerated, at least not on my watch. As of this moment, you are free to go, but I hope you will choose to stay. We have one remaining issue to deal with, which I hope we can resolve today."

"Yes, ma'am," David replied. "I never intended to create such a problem. The least I can do is try to help straighten out the mess."

I wanted to give him a bear hug.

"Okay," she continued, all business now. "If I may be direct, law enforcement needs access to the information your software restricts. And the computer companies need time to find ways to operate without relying on the information your application may be able to restrict. Mr. Patterson was correct when he told the jury that your software could put the plaintiffs out of business and our nation's economy into a nosedive. I suspect that if I gave you access to any decent computer, you could restore whatever's missing in your software, and all hell would break loose."

David had been put through the proverbial wringer over the last few weeks. He was exhausted, and I knew he was ready to abandon his creation, just walk away. I had hoped to suggest a potential solution, but Virginia was addressing the problem to him.

He gave me a sideways glance and said, "Why don't you ask my lawyer? It seems to me that he's done a pretty good job so far." Hmm, maybe not so exhausted after all, I thought, choking back a laugh.

Virginia looked to me. "Any thoughts, Mr. Patterson?"

I asked for a minute to organize my thoughts. Since I'd been awake thinking about the issue for most of the night, it didn't take long.

"I'm not an expert in valuing software, but perhaps the following would be agreeable to all parties. David agrees to sell the missing language and the software to the government and the plaintiffs for a certain sum. Plaintiffs and the government agree that the software will not become part of the public domain for an agreed upon period of time. The specified time frame will be long enough for the companies to alter their business models, but soon enough to satisfy the antitrust division at Justice. In addition, David agrees not to publish or disclose the existence of his software to anyone else without the consent of both the software companies and DOJ. The companies agree to work with David regarding DOJ's concern about access to government records. Finally, plaintiffs will come to some resolution with Ms. Pruitt about her antitrust concerns. She hasn't mentioned these concerns, but they are clearly the elephants in the room."

Virginia looked at Jordyn, who still represented the companies involved in the debacle. "What do you say, Ms. Duarte?"

Virginia came to sit with us while Jordyn took a few minutes to consult with her co-counsel. After several minutes of whispers and headshaking she said, "I simply don't have the authority to agree to such a broad and unstructured deal."

I wondered if she would ever learn to quit while she was ahead.

Virginia responded quickly. "Here's another idea, Ms. Duarte. Suppose I give Mr. Ruple a computer right now. He can provide the missing computer language to DOJ, we'll make a separate deal with him along the lines Mr. Patterson suggests, and I will open an antitrust investigation into the companies you represent. You know, the more I think about it, I like that idea better than Mr. Patterson's."

"No, no. That wouldn't work at all," Jordyn quickly objected. "Let me think. How much are we talking about for the software?"

"I can't say for sure. I would need to talk to experts like Jacob Lee, but I'd say between ten and twenty million," I replied.

"That's blackmail," she all but shouted. Nope, I shook my head, she would never learn.

"Temper, Ms. Duarte," I admonished, malice intended. "Call it what you like, but I'd call it a pittance considering what your collective companies make in a year. If I were you, I'd be trying to hire Mr. Ruple to help you come up with a fix, but that idea can wait for another day. We can either agree to work out a price or work with Justice without you. Your choice."

I was winging it, and it felt good.

Jordyn asked for more time to consult. She returned looking defeated. "We agree to the deal in principle, but the devil is in the details."

Virginia quickly quashed any plans Jordyn might have to drag out the fine print.

"I intend to personally supervise the development of this agreement and will go over every line of the final document. I expect to see a rough draft of an agreement on my desk within the week. Mr. Patterson, I suggest you consult with Mr. Lee. I believe your hasty estimation of the monetary worth of your client's work is low. I would pay more than twenty million for the government's portion of the settlement alone."

No one had anything more to add, she turned to David with a smile.

"Mr. Ruple. You are free to go."

51

DAVID RODE BACK TO THE FARMHOUSE WITH ME, where he and Rita spent the rest of the night together. Over breakfast the next morning, he told me he would agree to whatever I suggested regarding the software. When all the kinks had been ironed out and the 'deal was done,' he and Rita wanted to take some time off. Neither of them had ever been out of the country and thought Costa Rica might be a good place to relax. Rita added that her best friend Missy and her long-time boyfriend had been several times and loved it. He asked me to be generous with his mother, repay his grandfather whatever he had spent, and insisted I pay myself what anyone would consider a most generous fee. I was given his complete power of attorney.

Several days later, I flew to New Orleans on Walter's jet to meet with Thibodeaux, Gloria and Duke in tow. Tom had invited Gloria to New Orleans for a heart to heart before she and Duke left for Vegas, ostensibly to recover from the "stress of the trial." They certainly made a strange couple. I couldn't help but wonder how long they'd last when her share of David's money ran out.

My suspicions about Royce had been off base. I'd thought he might be the mole in Tom's organization, but the mole turned out to be the head of another of the New Orleans' families. I decided not to ask what happened to him.

Over drinks at the hotel, I did ask Gloria to tell me about Royce. She poked at her olives for a few seconds before replying. "He can be a real jerk. In fact, he's a jerk most of the time, but his loyalty to my father is without question. Father had a secretary for years named Kathy Peters, who had a child—Royce. There were plenty of rumors about my father and Kathy, but no one in the family ever dared to raise the subject with him. Frankly, I don't believe Royce is any relation. He doesn't look anything like a Thibodeaux.

"Anyway, Kathy died when Royce was about—oh, I'd say nine or ten. My father paid for Royce's education, including law school at SMU. That's where he learned to play scratch golf and turned into a real snot. After he graduated, Dad brought him into the business, and over the years he's earned his bones. He tends to speak out of turn, except when Dad gives him 'The Look.' Since he was a kid, he's always thought everyone was out to get him, to take his place with Dad. And who knows? He's probably right. I mean, he's such an easy target."

She took a healthy sip of her martini and looked me straight in the eye, "Loyalty means a lot to my father; Royce may be a jerk, but he is loyal."

*****

I took a cab to the French Quarter where I was to have lunch with Royce and Thibodeaux at Antoine's. As we turned onto Bourbon Street, we were stopped by a small parade. There's always some sort of parade in New Orleans; they just seem to pop up out of nowhere. I asked the cabbie to let me out as close to Antoine's as he could. I would walk the rest of the way.

I had almost reached the restaurant when someone from the watching crowd put his arm around my shoulder. When I turned in surprise, I saw the knife and heard a familiar voice say, "Oh, Jack—don't you ever learn? Let's get out of this crowd. And remember—one false move and you're dead."

I had no doubt that he meant what he said. Yelling would do no good; the noise in the quarter was deafening. As we walked, I wondered how Hans had again escaped the clutches of the FBI and why no one had warned me. He directed me through several side streets and into a deserted alley between two buildings.

"Turn around!" he ordered.

I was now face to face with my nemesis.

"Thought you'd won, didn't you? Too bad you won't have time to enjoy the feeling. It's the end of the line, Jack. I told you before I should have killed you in the swamp, but this alley will have to do. Smells much the same, and the rats who'll soon be gnawing at your flesh. They make a nice substitute for gators."

I tensed as he shifted the knife for the plunge, but the noise of a person charging up the alley distracted us both.

"Drop the knife, Hans."

Hans's speed surprised me. He turned and threw himself at the new voice. His attack would have thrown most anyone off their guard, but she reached for the arm rushing toward her, twisted it down and flipped him in the air. He landed flat on his back, her stiletto heel squarely on top of his throat.

"One false move, and you're dead," she mimicked, as she reached down to jerk the knife from his hand. I had no doubt she meant what she said.

She had managed to shove me against one of the buildings. "Good God!" I gasped, trying to get my voice under control. "Lisa! How did you know? How did he get here? And how…" I stopped and took a deep breath, noticing her purple spiked hair and piercings. She fit in perfectly with the residents of the quarter.

She smiled and spoke, "Credit Maggie. She said Hans didn't seem the type to finger his employer or cooperate with the FBI, and he'd been released by the FBI once before. She placed a call to an old friend of yours at Justice—Peggy Fortson.

"Turns out the FBI had released him again, under the guise that he was a cooperating witness. Peggy took over, and now the Attorney General has asked her to lead an internal investigation of the FBI. You've been under surveillance for days. We figured Hans might try something in New Orleans, but the parade separated you from your protection in a split second."

She glanced toward Hans who had begun to lift one hand and increased the pressure on his neck with her heel. "I told you to stay still. Don't tempt me."

"What do we do with Hans if we can't trust the FBI?"

"I thought we might hand him over to your friend Thibodeaux?"

Hans's eyes went wide, and he begged, "Nooo!"

"You deserve it," she snapped as she twisted her heel against his throat.

"Peggy has already put together a special unit of agents who are working directly for her. She knows every single one and told Maggie they don't take kindly to fact that one group of bad apples has managed to severely compromise the reputation of the entire FBI. At least she hopes it's just one group."

"Your protection will be here any second, and so will Clovis. He's here on Maggie's orders. He'll escort you to lunch and stick to you like glue as long as you're here. Maggie and Peggy are worried that a few of Hans's buddies might be in town as backup. I bet they won't hang around long if they are. Not once they hear we have Hans, and Thibodeaux knows what they tried to do."

Clovis arrived with a group of agents who quickly relieved Lisa of her charge. He kidded, "What do you think of Lisa's new look? Stella gave her a few tips." I laughed, and we resumed my walk to Antoine's.

Tom and Royce were waiting when we arrived. Per David's wishes, I gave them a full report. Tom asked me to tell David that he should consider the fees he paid to be a gift. I told him I doubted he would accept, but that I'd bring it up. Tom also told me a little more about the traitor. He told me I had been right when I'd suggested he should look for an insider whose money problems could make him vulnerable to the kind of money that a computer company could use to entice him. Again, I chose not to ask about the traitor's fate.

Thibodeaux offered to put me on retainer, but I declined. I explained that I had decided to close my law office for good. I would resolve David's matter with Jordyn's clients and take the position of in-house counsel to Red Shaw and the Lobos.

They both appeared doubtful and asked me to keep an open mind about the future. Royce added they could give me as much, or as little, work as I wanted. I didn't want to offend either of them, but I'd had enough of working for the "family."

At the end of our meeting, Royce invited me to join him for dinner at a "club" where he was a member. He intimated that his

club not only served excellent food but also provided "adult entertainment." Royce may be loyal to Thibodeaux, but he's still a jerk.

I declined his invitation. I told him that I appreciated the offer,
but I'd been invited to spend a weekend in Lafayette with a noted
environmental scientist who had arranged for me to attend my first
crawfish boil. She'd also told me not to count on spending the entire
evening eating crawfish. I was happy to hear she hadn't forgotten
our unfinished business.

ACKNOWLEDGMENTS

My wife Suzy read, reread, edited, and contributed to every draft of *The Light of Day*, as she has for each of my books. More important is what she has brought to my life every day over these last fifty-three years. I won't try to describe the many ways she has supported me, but I will tell you that her pancakes, sausage, and eggs over-easy for breakfast are a source of delight almost every weekend.

My children, their spouses, and my nine grandchildren have each in their own way contributed directly to my efforts to tell a good story. My sister Terry is my biggest fan, and her keen perception of human nature and innate common sense continue to amaze me.

My deepest thanks and appreciation go to the professionals at Beaufort Books. Eric Kampmann believed in me and Jack Patterson from day one, and he never gave up on me during my period of "Covid Blues." Editorial Director Megan Trank has been a true and dear friend, a constant source of support and assistance. Emma St. John is surely a marketing whiz.

She was willing to jump in on short notice to guide "the horse into the barn." Thanks to Martin Short once again for his brilliant cover design and Rio Santisteban for his editing skills. Alexa Schmidt carried the ball across the goal line, and I look forward to many more touchdowns in our future.

My entire family is forever grateful to George and his family, without whose generosity none of my novels would be a reality.